A VERY SPECIAL LOVE

Janice Sims
Courtni Wright
Kayla Perrin

ARABESQUE
BET
BOOKS

BET Publications, LLC
www.msbet.com
www.arabesquebooks.com

ARABESQUE BOOKS are published by

BET Publications, LLC
c/o BET BOOKS
One BET Plaza
1900 W Place NE
Washington, D.C. 20018-1211

First Printing: May, 2000
10 9 8 7 6 5 4 3 2

Printed in the United States of America

Mother's Day is a special time of the year. This is the day we honor the most important women in our lives. In A VERY SPECIAL LOVE, Arabesque favorites, Janice Sims, Courtni Wright and Kayla Perrin pay honor to some very special women, each in her own unique way. We hope you will enjoy these stories, and as we know, only a mother can offer A VERY SPECIAL LOVE.

BOOK YOUR PLACE ON OUR WEBSITE AND MAKE THE ARABESQUE ROMANCE CONNECTION!

We've created a customized website just for our very special Arabesque readers, where you can get the inside scoop on everything that's going on with Arabesque romance novels.

When you come online, you'll have the exciting opportunity to:

- View covers of upcoming books

- Learn about our future publishing schedule (listed by publication month and author)

- Find out when your favorite authors will be visiting a city near you

- Search for and order backlist books

- Check out author bios and background information

- Send e-mail to your favorite authors

- Join us in weekly chats with authors, readers and other guests

- Get writing guidelines

- AND MUCH MORE!

Visit our website at
http://www.arabesquebooks.com

CONTENTS

THE KEYS TO MY HEART

Janice Sims

Is it the way that you move or the
curve of your hips
that causes expressions of love to fall
from my lips?

Or is it some indefinable ENTITY that
speaks to my spirit,
uplifts, frees and makes commitment so desirable
a thing that I no longer fear it?

Who gave you permission to capture my soul
and make me hunger for you whenever we're apart?
Was it the angels in Heaven or the Big Guy Himself?
Was *He* the one who gave you the key to my heart?

—The Book of Counted Joys

Every Morning

A little after three A.M., Kiana Everett awoke with a start, her brow damp with perspiration. As her eyes became accustomed to the dark, she sought the face of her four-year-old niece, Courtney, sleeping beside her. She exhaled air between full lips, relieved she hadn't awakened Courtney when she'd come out of the nightmare. Feeling dry-mouthed, anxious and disoriented, she headed to the kitchen for something to drink. She breathed slowly, inhaling and exhaling deeply. Sometimes the exercise helped her to calm down.

Would the grisly images ever be exorcized? Why hadn't she waited for Eddie to get there before identifying Dionne's and Kevin's bodies? Because if she hadn't seen them with her own eyes, no one would've been able to convince her Dionne was gone. Her sister. Gone at thirty-four. Her life and that of her husband of six years, Kevin, ended by a drunk driver who'd run, head-on, into them. Kiana knew she was wrong for thinking it, but the only consolation was that the driver had died in the crash, too. Patrick Beardsley was his name. She knew Beardsley had family who were probably mourning him as well. But where were they when he was behind the wheel of a two-ton SUV, driving in the wrong lane of I-75, ten miles outside of Gainesville, after imbibing so much booze, the coroner later said, that it was amazing he'd been able to turn the key in the ignition let alone drive a vehicle onto a busy interstate.

In the kitchen Kiana switched on the light, and as it illuminated the dim corners of the cheerily decorated room which was painted in pale yellow and white, she felt herself calming down.

Going to the refrigerator, she opened the door and reached in to get a caffeine-free Diet Coke. She didn't need the caffeine at this hour. She briefly placed the ice-cold can on her forehead, thinking the coolness would help dispel the anger inside of her that was reaching the boiling point. Beardsley was dead, so she blamed his family for not preventing him from driving drunk. She had to blame somebody. It was all so senseless. Two young, talented, much-loved people—gone because of one fool's lack of sound judgment.

Kevin Merrick had been a family physician on the staff of Shands, which was affiliated with the University of Florida. It was one of the largest teaching hospitals in the state. That's where he'd met Dionne, who was an R.N. Together they'd established the Health Center in Damascus, Florida, Dionne's hometown. They were making a home for themselves in Damascus. Now all their dreams had gone up in smoke. Destroyed the split second Beardsley pointed his SUV in their direction.

The October breezes coming through the cracked kitchen window felt cold on Kiana's sweat-moistened skin. She went and shut the window and listlessly leaned against the counter after doing so.

In a moment of pure selfishness, she lamented her own situation. Until the recent tragedy she had been hoping that Carter Henderson, head football coach at nearby Damascus Springs High School, would propose marriage soon. But after she told him she was going to rear Courtney now that Dionne and Kevin were gone, Carter had backed off. Kiana had been amazed by his reaction. She firmly believed that if he loved her he'd welcome Courtney with open arms. Carter had been intimidated by the idea of becoming a father so soon after marriage. For a long time, he'd thought of Kiana as an unattainable prize. He just wanted to relish the victory for a while. He needed time to consider becoming a father. Kiana wouldn't accept that explanation. Now she wondered if she'd been too hard on him and if her actions had been too precipitous. *Everything* was happening fast. Carter was right to ask for time to think. Still, a small part of her wondered if he would react to future crises the way he'd reacted to this one: by pulling away from her. She'd never known her own father or brother to run from a problem. It had changed her opinion of Carter. Just as, she supposed, he'd begun to see her in a different light. How could he love her if he couldn't weather this storm alongside her?

Thinking a bit of late-night TV might help put her back to sleep, she pushed away from the counter. However, when her bare feet hit the plush carpeting of the living room floor, the phone rang. Turning, she hurried back to the kitchen. She'd never bothered having an extension put in the living room.

She snatched up the phone in the middle of the third ring.

"Hello!" she answered a bit breathlessly, her tone urgent. Phone calls in the middle of the night rarely boded well.

"Is it true?" a deep male voice full of anguish and disbelief asked. "Tell me it isn't true."

Frowning, Kiana looked down at the cordless phone grasped tightly in her hand as if it could give her a clue as to who this *nut* was, calling her after three o'clock on a Sunday morning with a stupefying question. *Is it true?* Is *what* true?

Wearing an impatient grimace, Kiana spoke into the receiver. "Listen, whoever you are, it's a quarter past three. Why don't you go sleep it off . . ."

"This is . . . Kevin . . ."

Kiana's heart thudded in her chest. He *did* sound like her brother-in-law. The same deep baritone, New England accent, and unique cadences. But it couldn't be Kevin because they'd buried Kevin more than three weeks ago, beside Dionne, in the family plot in the cemetery behind St. John A.M.E. Church.

The caller's speech was slurred. No doubt he'd been drinking. So perhaps he hadn't said *This is Kevin.* She'd probably missed a word or two in the translation.

"If this is your idea of some kind of sick joke . . ." Kiana said harshly, her tone warning. "I swear I'll . . ."

"I'm Kevin's brother, Gabriel," the caller cried suddenly in a desperate bid to be understood.

Kiana's sigh came out sounding like a weary groan. "Why didn't you just *say* so in the beginning? Gabriel? . . . Yeah. I've been trying to get hold of you for weeks now. Where've you *been?* I was beginning to think you'd never phone!"

"I know. I just got back from a four-week trip to East Africa. There was no way I could be reached. I'm sorry. But is it true, these messages on my machine . . . Are they really dead?" He sounded as if the weight of the world were pressing on him. But underneath the burdensome resignation of doom was a glimmer of hope.

Kiana walked up and down the tiled floor wishing she could tell him, *No, it isn't true. It's all a cruel joke. They're fine. I don't know who started these malicious rumors but it's all a lie. Dionne and Kevin are safely in bed*

*at this moment. They just built a new home, you know.
Courtney has a playhouse in the backyard.*

"Are you still there?" he asked, his voice low and
tired.

"Gabriel, I'm very sorry but, yes, Kevin's gone.
Dionne too . . ." Her voice caught and she thrust a
fist to her mouth, hoping to muffle a sob. She held
the receiver away from her.

"Oh, God, no!" he cried. Then she heard him
erupt in an angry tirade as he cursed the Fates, his
voice rife with pain and grief. Kiana was silent
throughout the outburst. She knew the feeling. Her
anger had been the only thing that had kept her going these past few weeks.

"I'm sorry," he said after awhile. He sniffed. "I
can't believe my baby brother is dead."

Again, Kiana empathized. Tears rolled down her
cheeks into her mouth as she continued now. "It happened on September twenty-sixth. They were coming
from Orlando on I-75 north of Gainesville. A drunk
driver ran, head-on, into them. Dionne was driving.
She tried to swerve, the Highway Patrol report stated,
but wasn't able to in time. We . . . We waited a week
before burying them. We tried our best to get you
here. I phoned every friend and relative in Kevin's
address book."

Gabriel's breathing became labored. Kiana knew
he was trying to hold back tears. "I can't talk now,"
he announced hoarsely with barely contained bitterness. However he continued to do so. "I can't understand this universe. Kevin . . ." A sob escaped. "Kevin
was the best human being I knew. Totally devoted to
helping others. Totally devoted to Dionne and Courtney. You know, he didn't have much of a family before he married Dionne." He sniffed again. "I'll wait
if you want to go wash your face," Kiana offered
knowingly. What she meant was: *Go blow your nose.* But

she didn't know Gabriel Merrick so she didn't want to say something as personal as that to a stranger.

"All right," Gabriel said.

Kiana heard him place the receiver on a hard surface. Then, even though she listened intently for background noises, she heard nothing else until he picked up the receiver again a couple of minutes later.

"How's Courtney?" He paused before going on. "Did she see them like that?"

Kiana tilted her head up, tears still flowing. She'd wondered about that, too. The moment she'd arrived at the hospital and the doctor had told her that Courtney had survived the crash because she'd been buckled into the back seat, her mind had taken her there. *Had* Courtney been unconscious following the accident or had she awakened to see the bloody bodies of her parents in the front seat?

A highway patrolman, Officer Derek Reed, a young, good-looking black guy with sympathy in his dark eyes had been at the hospital that night. He'd assured Kiana that Courtney had been unconscious until they'd delivered her to the hospital. He'd ridden with her in the ambulance to North Florida Regional Hospital. He had a three-year-old daughter and when he saw Courtney he couldn't bear to let her out of his sight until he knew she'd be all right. At that point it was already too late to do anything for her parents.

Kiana told Gabriel Merrick the entire story. When she'd finished, he said, "I'm glad. She shouldn't have to grow up with that being the last image she had of her parents."

"She'd be so happy to see you," Kiana said, hoping to turn the conversation in a less macabre direction.

"I'll be there as soon as I can drive down," Gabriel told her, his voice clearer now.

"Oh, you're driving? Don't you live in Connecticut?"

"Bridgeport. Yes."

"Won't that take several days?"

"I have two months left on my sabbatical so I have time to spare. Plus I need a day or so to clear my head before I get there. Then I can spend some time getting to know Courtney again. I'm afraid I've been an absent uncle. Now that I'm going to be a full-time parent, I should give us both a chance to get used to the notion."

Kiana stopped pacing the floor when what he was saying registered. Perhaps she hadn't heard him correctly. "I'm afraid you've lost me," she spoke into the receiver. Her deep, husky, southern-accented voice got quieter. "What did you mean by becoming a 'full-time parent?' "

"You *were* expecting me to come collect Courtney, weren't you?" He sounded incredulous and a bit put upon. First he hears for sure that his brother is dead, and now he's going to get flak from Dionne's sister about a decision Kevin and Dionne made years ago?

"When I came in tonight I went through my mail. There was a letter from Kevin's attorney explaining what had happened and that I'm now Courtney's legal guardian. It appears that Kevin and Dionne had it put in their wills years ago. This isn't news to you, is it?"

Kiana had begun pacing again while she listened to him. "They just didn't get the opportunity to change their wills. Kevin loved Damascus. He wanted Courtney to grow up here. They told me that if anything should happen to them, they wanted *me* to raise Courtney right here where her mother grew up." She knew she shouldn't have tagged on such a proprietary statement, but Gabriel Merrick had gotten her hackles up. He wasn't the only one who'd suffered a loss. Courtney was all of Dionne the Everetts had left. He was going to have to produce those so-called legal papers he spoke of and have the law serve them to her before she'd hand Courtney over to him.

She heard him sigh. "Ms. Everett, I didn't phone you at three A.M. in order to get into an argument with you. I was under the impression you already knew about the arrangement and you were just caring for Courtney until I could come for her."

"I understand English," Kiana said, irritated. "You already said that. All right. *You* have legal papers saying you're Coco's guardian. *I* have Coco. Possession is nine tenths of the law."

Gabriel laughed harshly. "Maybe in your part of the country."

"Meaning?"

"Meaning we don't handle things quite that way in Connecticut, Ms. Everett."

"Call me Kiana. You're Kevin's brother. That makes you family."

"More southern mores?"

"I don't know you, *Gabriel*, so I'm going to give you the benefit of the doubt and assume your comments weren't intended to be prejudiced. All I meant was, the way I was brought up, when two people get married, as Kevin and Dionne did, the two families merge. So *you're* family. Now what that means is, you and I can agree to disagree but we must eventually come to an understanding. Come on down to Damascus. You're welcome here. I'll reserve a room for you at the inn. There's only one but it's clean and run by wonderful folks—"

"Kiana . . ." Gabriel impatiently interrupted her.

"Yes?" Kiana asked, her voice soft and ever so polite.

"You sound as if you're going to try to persuade me to leave Courtney in your care. I don't want you to get your hopes up, because Courtney's all I have left. Our parents died years ago. We have no other brothers or sisters. Courtney's it. I'm *not* going to give her up to you. Let's be clear on that. Don't even entertain the thought of this turning out in your favor."

"Gabriel, we're both upset," Kiana returned reasonably. "We can't work this out over the phone. Just come to Damascus. By the way, how long can you stay?"

"I beg your pardon?" Wariness colored his tone.

She decided to put it in words he'd understand. "How long will you give me to prepare Coco for being uprooted? A week? Two weeks? Three? You mentioned a sabbatical earlier in our conversation. Why not give it a month? A month before you take her back to Bridgeport. She's already been through a lot. This has been her home ever since she was born. She has her aunts, her grandparents right in town. An uncle and aunt nearby with two small children around her age. Cousins she adores. Be reasonable."

There was nothing but silence as Gabriel considered her proposition. Then he said, "A month. I'll stay in Damascus for a month. But within that length of time, we have to agree that you can't give me any opposition. I'm not coming to engage in open warfare. As you pointed out, our niece has been through enough already. She doesn't need to witness us battling over who gets to raise her."

"It's a deal," Kiana readily agreed. "A month should be long enough. Call me when you get to Gainesville and I'll come get you and show you the way to Damascus."

Gabriel chuckled. "I have a doctorate in English. Don't you think I can read a map?"

Kiana was not the least bit put off by his show of ego. "Well, if you decide you need me, just call the house. I'll leave a message on the machine telling you where you can reach me. I'm the supervisor of the nursing staff at a local care facility. I also work part-time at the Health Center here in Damascus."

"You work two jobs? Can you do that and raise Courtney, too?"

Kiana laughed softly. "Gabriel, when I'm at my full-time job, Courtney is being well taken care of by the good women of St. John A.M.E. Church. Her grandmother volunteers there in their Head Start program in the mornings. In the afternoon, Courtney goes home with her grandmother. I pick Courtney up at my parents' home when I get off from work. From seven to nine, two nights a week, I volunteer at the Health Center. While I work, Courtney enjoys the company of the other children in the Center's playroom. Between patients, I check on her to make sure she's all right. We've only been on this schedule for three weeks, but it's working out just fine."

Kiana yawned. She covered the receiver with her palm.

"I heard that," Gabriel said. "I've kept you up long enough. I'll go. I'm sorry for calling you in the middle of the night, but I had to know."

"Don't apologize," Kiana said sincerely. "I'm sorry for your loss, Gabriel. We all loved Kevin. He made Dionne happy and for that I'll always be grateful to him. Besides that, he was a kind, thoughtful and generous human being. Some of the folks in Damascus are suspicious of strangers, but Kevin won their trust in no time."

Kiana could hear the smile in Gabriel's voice when he said, "He was always able to charm just about anybody. When we were growing up he never got punished for anything. He talked our parents out of whatever form of punishment they had in mind for him."

"Didn't that irk you?" Kiana asked, smiling too.

Gabriel chuckled. "We were far enough apart in age so that we weren't competitive in that sense. He was just my annoying little brother whose shenanigans were vaguely amusing."

"How much older *are* you than Kevin?"

"Only four years, but sometimes I feel much older."

That makes him thirty-eight or nine, Kiana calculated, trying to get a mental image to go with that deep, well-modulated voice.

"I'm thirty-eight," Gabriel said, a note of laughter in his voice. "Now. How old are you? And don't claim that lame excuse women hide behind when trying to be evasive."

"The women in my family have never seen any reason to lie about their ages," Kiana informed him smugly. "I'll have you know that my grandmother is seventy-seven and looks twenty years younger."

Laughing, Gabriel reminded her, "You still haven't answered the question."

"I'm thirty-two. My mother had a penchant for giving birth every two years. My brother Edward came first. He's thirty-six. Dionne was next. She was thirty-four. Then I came along. Finally, Kerry brought up the rear. She's thirty."

Gabriel sighed. "Three siblings. I envy you, Ana."

He'd said it indolently. *Ah-Nah.* A slip of the tongue? Or was it meant to incite something between them? Because it had. At the mention of the innocent appellation a warmth slowly suffused Kiana, beginning in the pit of her stomach and spreading to the rest of her body until she felt a distinct tingle in her pleasure points.

She cleared her throat. It was late. She was tired. She chalked it up to longing. When she needed Carter's strong arms around her providing support and reassurance, he'd left her alone. Now this man, a man she'd never seen before, was giving her comfort via telephone from more than a thousand miles away. Besides, it was only her imagination. He hadn't intended for his tone to be so seductive. It had been a misinterpretation on her part because her own emotions were still so raw.

Recovering, she said, "I meant what I said earlier, Gabriel. You're to consider us family."

"You don't realize what that offer means to a man who finds himself practically alone in this world, Ana." There it was again. This time there could be no mistaking the intonation nor the deliberate choice of the name. He'd meant it.

The house was so silent, all Kiana could hear was the ticking of the grandfather clock in the foyer. Why was she standing there trying to figure out this man's reasoning behind calling her Ana? Maybe he gave everyone he met a nickname. Perhaps he had a bad memory and shortening peoples' names helped him remember them better.

"Describe yourself to me, Ana."

Kiana laughed softly. "And you need this information because . . ."

"So I can imagine the face that goes with the voice. Tell me. Are you tall or short? Or somewhere in between? Do you wear your hair long or in a bob? Are you thin or stout?"

"Do you have a thinness fetish?"

"No. As a matter of fact I like *healthy* women."

"Healthy as in they can jog five miles without stopping, or as in they have a little meat on their bones?"

"Which one are you?"

"I'm both."

Gabriel laughed delightedly. "Who would've guessed I'd be laughing after that horrible news? Life is a bit perverse, don't you think?"

"After the happenings of the last few weeks I would

have to say I agree with you," Kiana told him frankly. "Something is definitely wrong with the universe when two people like . . ." She choked up. She was not yet past the point where the thought of Dionne and Kevin ceased to wring emotions from her. Maybe in a few more months—or years. But not this morning.

"It's all right, Ana. You don't have to talk," she heard Gabriel say. "I'm going to go now. I'll see you in a few days. Don't worry, I'll recognize you when I see you. You'll be the fine sister with meat on her bones out for her daily five-mile jog. Good-bye for now."

Kiana heard a dial tone and she walked over and hung the receiver back on its base. Wiping tears from the corners of her eyes, she sniffed. What a strange conversation they'd had. Initially she'd been the one to offer comfort. Then they'd nearly gotten into an altercation. And finally he'd been the one to utter consoling words to *her*. Gabriel Merrick. Kevin's brother. Age: thirty-eight.

Did he resemble Kevin, who'd been tall and good-looking? Or was he a short, chubby bookworm of a college professor who wore horn-rimmed glasses and a tattered wool blazer with suede patches on the elbows?

She turned and began walking toward the bedroom. She'd felt sleepiness hit her in the face somewhere in the midst of her last rumination about Gabriel.

In the bed, as she pulled the covers up to her chin and settled down between the cool, fresh, flowery-scented sheets, her eyes briefly focused on Courtney's peaceful face. Yes, all was well for the time being. Sleep claimed her shortly after that thought.

In Bridgeport, after hanging up the phone, Gabriel swiftly strode to the rear of the house, through the kitchen, where he opened the back door to allow an impatient Max, his two-year-old golden-coated Labrador retriever, inside. He squatted and met Max's eyes. "Hey, Bud. Sorry about putting you out there like that, but I had to speak with that particular lady without interruption and you know how you like to bark to get my attention whenever I'm on the phone." He rubbed Max's chin and Max rewarded him with a soft whine of pleasure. Rising, Gabriel locked the door and went over to the pantry to get Max a Milk Bone treat. Max padded after him, recognizing at once why his master was going into the pantry. He jumped up onto his hind legs and caught the hard, liver-flavored treat between his teeth, barely missing Gabriel's fingers.

Gabriel shook his head. "You wouldn't bite the hand of the one who feeds you, would you?"

He turned away, leaving Max gnawing happily on his reward. If he was going to get on the road in the morning, he should throw a few things into a bag.

He was a man with few pretensions, hence he led a simple life. His house was modest, a small Cape Cod on a corner lot surrounded by maples. He'd chosen it because of the yard. The previous owners had landscaped it to look like a Japanese garden complete with marble stepping-stones and deciduous dwarf trees. It was an oasis for the eye and the soul. Even in winter, when snow was on the ground, Gabriel could look out his back window and enjoy the sight of the garden.

In the bedroom, he switched on the light and went into the closet where he'd placed his large suitcase, which he hadn't fully unpacked yet. No time. Once he'd gotten in a few hours before, the first thing he did was read his mail. And there it was, the letter from Kevin's attorney Nathan Guilford. The words had initially appeared incomprehensible to his mind. Here this attorney was telling him in flawless legalese that his only brother was dead, along with his sister-in-law. And his niece was now his legal obligation. It was tough to wrap his mind around that after an interminable flight from Kenya with a six-hour layover in London. After that, he'd gone to his bedroom where he kept the answering machine and the red light on it was blinking like a beacon. *Press me,* it seemed to command.

He did. Her mellifluous voice instantly made him wish that what she had to say would make the nightmare of the letter vanish. He reached for a lifeline. She'd calmly said, "I'm Kiana Everett, Dionne's sister. This is important. As soon as you get in you need to phone me. My number is 904-555-2368." She had repeated that message, or a close rendition of it, five times. Gabriel listened to every one of them. And then, because he saw no way to avoid doing so, he'd dialed her number. As he stood there, knowing full well why she'd phoned him even though she had not given him an inkling as to why she needed to speak with him, he *still* found himself wishing she'd tell him something different.

After asking her if it was true and realizing she finally understood who he was, it was the anguish in her voice when she answered his question that was his undoing. He instinctively knew this woman wouldn't lie to him. Kevin was indeed gone forever.

Now he stood in the middle of his closet, a tall, well-built man of thirty-eight dressed only in a pair of worn Levi's and oblivious to the chill in the October air of the house in which he'd neglected to turn the furnace on earlier. After picking up Max from his best friend Daniel's house, all he'd wanted to do was go home and relax. Maybe get a bite to eat and turn in. He was drained. Tomorrow was Sunday, he and Dan had a standing appointment to do some sculling on the lake. They'd both been competitive rowers on their college teams. They still practiced the sport because it kept them in good shape and gave them the opportunity to talk. Dan was his one true friend. He'd been looking forward to Sunday because he was curious as to what Lourdes had been up to while he was in Africa. Dan would fill him in on all the goings on at tiny Baylor College where they were both professors. Learning if Lourdes Beaumont *Ledoux*—he had to keep in mind that she was a married woman now—had missed him while he was gone was suddenly of little importance to him. There was a little girl in Florida who needed him.

"Auntie!" Courtney's shrill voice rose to a pitch like an opera singer's at the end of an aria, drawing the last note out for all it was worth. "Grandma phoned. Get up! She says if we don't hurry, we're gonna be late for Sunday school." She shook the bed to emphasize her point. "Come on. I made breakfast."

Kiana moaned as she reluctantly opened her eyes. Her brain was still a bit fuzzy from lack of sleep. Did Courtney say she'd made breakfast? She sniffed the air. Good. Nothing was burning. The house was safe. She leaned into the pillow, her eyes slowly closing. "I'll tell you what, Coco. *You* go to church with your grandma this morning, okay? I think I'll just sleep a little longer."

Courtney shook the bed more violently and bent down close to Kiana's ear. "Grandma says if you don't go to church, you're gonna bust hell *wide* open!"

Kiana sat up in bed. Laughing, she grabbed Courtney and pulled her into bed with her, kissing her plump cheeks and hugging her tightly. "Your grandma has a way with words."

Courtney wiggled out of Kiana's embrace, and once her feet hit the floor she took off running, her favorite mode of self-propulsion. "The day's half over," she tossed over her shoulder. Another sage saying she'd gotten from her grandmother. "Better get a move on!"

Sighing, Kiana swung her legs from the bed, stood and stretched lazily. In her opinion Sundays were meant for sleeping late. But she'd rarely been afforded the opportunity. Since she was a child, her mother, Evelyn, had been making sure that when Sunday morning rolled around her bottom would be warming a pew in St. John A.M.E. Church. The only member of the family who'd been able to escape Evelyn Everett's mandate was her husband, Edward. Buddy to anyone who'd known him for more than two minutes, Buddy gave notice to anyone who'd listen that if God wanted him on Sunday, He knew where to find him: sprawled in his easy chair with a can of beer in one hand and the remote in the other, watching the game. It didn't matter what kind of game. Football in fall. Baseball in spring. Just so it was men on the screen engaged in a contest of wills.

As the principal breadwinner in the family, Buddy felt it was his God-given right to drink beer and belch on Sunday. And when the good Lord called him home, he'd go with the remote clutched in his hand.

Still dressed in her p.j.'s, Kiana trudged into the kitchen. Sunlight streaming in through open curtains stung her eyes. She squinted at Courtney who was sitting at the table eating cereal. A large box of frosted flakes, a jug of lowfat milk, a clean cereal bowl and a spoon sat on the table. That was how Courtney "made" breakfast. Kiana sat down and poured frosted flakes and milk into her bowl. She smiled at Courtney. "Thanks for preparing this scrumptious feast for me this morning, Miss Merrick."

Courtney crinkled her nose in distaste. Her dark

brown eyes sparkled with pent-up laughter. "Auntie, you forgot to plait your hair last night."

Kiana's hand went to her thick, black, shoulder-length hair. It had come loose during the night. No wonder. After getting off the phone with Gabriel Merrick she'd dreamed a faceless man was pursuing her through the darkened streets of Damascus. Undoubtedly she'd tossed and turned in her sleep.

She smiled at Courtney. "Guess what? Your uncle Gabriel phoned while you were sleeping last night. He's coming to see you."

Courtney gave a high-pitched scream of delight. "Uncle Gabe is coming?" She jumped up from her chair, ran around the table and threw her arms around Kiana's neck.

Kiana hadn't seen her this excited since the accident and was happy to see the animated expression on Courtney's dark brown face. Kiana rocked her in her arms a moment before setting her back on the floor. "I take it you really like your uncle Gabe."

"He's funny," Courtney said. "He can talk like a duck."

Composed now, she went and sat down. With her hand poised on her cereal spoon, she said seriously, "I don't know what a duck would sound like if it could talk, but Uncle Gabe would probably come close."

Kiana sat nodding and eating her cereal. She remembered Gabriel had mentioned he had a doctorate in linguistics. Perhaps he did imitations of voices for the amusement of his adoring niece. She told herself not to form advance opinions of him, to wait until she met him. But it was difficult not trying to build a personality around that wonderful voice she'd heard the previous night. And, too, she wondered why he'd aroused her interest. She'd been nearly engaged to Carter three weeks ago. He hadn't asked her, but he'd been hinting about the possibility for months prior to their spat. She had *felt* the proposal was coming. What did the fact that Gabriel Merrick's voice had made her warm last night say about her level of devotion to Carter? Could she have misgivings about Carter being the right man for her?

She had to admit that Carter's past history of being a player gave her pause. Would he be capable of being faithful to one woman? She couldn't ignore that since their disagreement there had been rumors about him and Pamela Hodges. Pamela made it no secret that she had the hots for Carter. They were both teachers at Damascus Springs High School, Carter in physical education, Pamela in social studies. Kiana's best friend, Veronica, the girls' physical education instructor, frequently reported that Pamela threw herself at Carter every chance she got. Kiana repeatedly shrugged it off. It wasn't in her makeup to be distrusting. The way she looked at it, if you didn't have faith in your partner you didn't have anything.

However now that she and Carter had argued, would he see that as an out? Was it really over between them?

". . . And he has this dog named Max who can balance a rubber ball on his nose . . ."

Coming back to the present, Kiana realized Courtney had been regaling her with tales of her uncle Gabe the whole time she'd been daydreaming about her situation with Carter.

She smiled at Courtney. "Max, huh? Is he a big dog or a little dog?"

"A medium-size dog," Courtney replied knowledgeably. "With big brown eyes. I hope he brings Max."

After the service, the congregation of St. John A.M.E Church gathered outside on the grounds and caught up on each other's lives. The weather was perfect for standing outside: sixty-five degrees with a clear blue sky overhead and a slight breeze.

Kiana stood on the lawn in a group with her mother, Evelyn; her sister, Kerry; June Darton, the minister's wife; and Bess Calhoun, Kerry's best friend. All the ladies wore conservative dresses or skirt suits. Courtney was off playing with the other children. All three Everett women glanced in her direction every now and then to make sure she was still in their eyesight.

"You and Carter haven't worked things out yet?" June Darton asked Kiana, a concerned expression on her attractive face. She ran a manicured hand over her steel-gray curls. "That isn't good. You need to talk. Maybe you and Carter should get some counseling."

Kiana quickly pondered the notion of counseling with their minister. She'd always respected Benjamin Darton. However she didn't believe Carter would go for it. He was an extremely private person. There were many facets to his personality *she* still wasn't privy to. She couldn't see him opening up to Reverend Darton.

"It can't hurt to talk to him about it," Evelyn put in. She was tall and stately. Her hair was short, mahogany with silver streaks. Both her daughters were tall as well. Kiana, five eight, and Kerry, five ten. They'd both excelled at sports in high school and college. Kerry had gone to college on a basketball scholarship. Kiana had played softball on the University of Florida women's team. However, she'd attended nursing school there on an academic scholarship.

"He's here today," Kerry offered, looking at her sister with an amused gleam in her dark brown eyes. Kiana smiled faintly. Kerry always accused Kiana of avoiding confrontations. Instead of meeting a problem head-on, Kiana would skate around it, hoping it would subside on its own and she wouldn't have to directly deal with it. Kerry was more aggressive when dealing with problems. With people, too. Nobody messed with Kerry Everett and got off scot-free. It was her take-charge attitude that had gotten her elected chief of police, the first woman and the first black to become police chief in the history of the small Florida town. That and the fact that she'd graduated in the top ten percent of her class at the police academy. Before the academy she'd been a decorated Marine. Law enforcement was in her blood.

"I'll see if he's willing," Kiana said finally after being stared at by all four women for the past few minutes.

Kerry shot her a skeptical look. Kiana ignored her. "Kevin's brother phoned last night," she said, changing the subject to a topic she knew would get them all off her case.

Love Blues

"Man, you're slapping those oars in the water like the Devil himself is in behind you," Daniel shouted as he struggled to keep pace with Gabriel. Gabriel was the lead man in the shell that morning. He was putting so much into his rowing that his seat was sliding fore and aft with such rapidity that Daniel imagined sparks would soon be coming from the rollers. The air was brisk but Gabriel's shirt beneath his jacket was plastered to his chest. "I would've canceled but I figured a little exercise would go a long way in helping me to get my head straight before taking off for Florida."

With this preamble, Daniel knew something was seriously wrong. Gabriel was not one to admit mental distress, no matter what was going on in his life. When Lourdes had gone to Paris last year on her own, already engaged to Gabriel, and had an affair with Guy Ledoux *and* brought him back to the States flashing a wedding ring on her finger, Gabriel had shown little emotion. He certainly hadn't admitted to needing time to get his head together.

Daniel couldn't imagine his wife, Deborah, doing something like that or *his* not going downright ballistic. On Deborah *and* the other man. Whatever emotions Gabriel had felt, he'd kept them to himself, saying only that Lourdes would eventually regret her actions and come running back to him. But it would be too late for a reconciliation because he'd seen her true colors and would never again be able to trust her. Today Lourdes and Guy Ledoux, she an instructor at Baylor College and he a celebrated artist, had become a source of amusement for the two friends. They joked about Lourdes's obsession with being on the society page of the local paper, but they were sympathetic when they heard Guy had been unfaithful to her.

"You want to talk about it?" Daniel asked after another spray of water hit him in the face. He lifted his oars from the water. Gabriel immediately felt the cessation of effort from his partner. He raised his oars also and the shell coasted. Sighing, he turned his face to the sky. "Kevin and Dionne were killed in a car accident while I was in Kenya. I found out about it when I got back to the house last night."

Daniel was momentarily stunned to silence.

They just drifted on the lake for a couple of minutes with the breezes cooling their sweat-moistened skin. Both men were still, as the shell could tip over with any exaggerated movement.

"Oh, God!" Daniel said quietly, his tone reverent and sorrowful. *"Both* of them? What about Courtney? Is she all right? Why didn't you call us last night? You shouldn't have been alone."

Gabriel's answer to that was to begin rowing again.

Daniel joined him and they headed back to shore.

"There was nothing anybody could do for me last night, man. The only thing that could make it better would be if it were untrue. And that isn't going to happen." Once Gabriel started talking, Daniel knew from years of experience not to interrupt him. "Courtney's physically fine. Her aunt told me she had some cuts and bruises but they've healed. It'll take a long time for her heart to heal, though." He put the oars in the water again. Daniel followed suit. "I've been named her legal guardian and I don't know if I can handle the job."

They rowed a while before Daniel said, "Sure you can."

Laughing, Gabriel said, "You know me, Daniel. I've spent a lifetime avoiding entanglements. That I even got engaged to Lourdes was a miracle. That she left me for a man who could express his emotions was inevitable. What do I have to give a little girl? She needs to be nurtured."

"You're not devoid of emotions, Gabriel, you're just stopped up. You haven't yet been compelled to express what's inside you. You loved your parents. You loved Kevin. You might not have shown it often enough but they knew how you felt about them."

"That's just the thing. *Family's* always willing to overlook your shortcomings. Courtney is only four. She won't be able to discern that I love her unless I can demonstrate it. I mean, all the times I've seen her, I was able to entertain her, make her laugh. But I'm going to have to do better than that when she's living with me. My bag of tricks will eventually be exhausted."

Daniel reached up and briefly squeezed Gabriel's shoulder. Allowing his hand to fall, he said, "You'll just have to do what the rest of us mere mortals do, my friend. Wing it!"

Gabriel chuckled softly. "How are you and Deborah surviving two teenagers?"

Daniel rowed with a steady rhythm. He shook his head. "By the skin of our teeth! Haven't you noticed the shell-shocked expressions on our weary faces?"

"Abuno disceomnes?" Gabriel asked.

Daniel strained his brain to recall the Latin he'd learned at his Catholic high school. "From one learn all?"

"Exactly," Gabriel said. "You're telling me not to worry, that Courtney will teach me everything I need to know about how to raise her."

Daniel laughed. "Hey, I'm better at this wise older friend thing than I realized."

Gabriel laughed, too. "I just hope I don't get any trouble from Dionne's family when I go to collect her. She's staying with Dionne's sister. I have a feeling Ana . . . no . . . *Kiana* Everett is a woman who usually gets what she wants."

"You could tell that from one conversation?"

"Just the sound of her voice made me want to give in to her."

"You know what they say about the South and the women down there," Daniel intimated.

"No, I don't," Gabriel replied, expecting another one of Daniel's ribald jokes.

"The weather isn't the only thing that makes you want to come out of your clothes. Deborah's from South Carolina. I tell you, there's something about her accent that makes me quiver whenever she calls me big daddy."

Chuckling, Gabriel said, "That was a bit more than I ever needed to know about you and Deborah."

"Auntie, can I . . ."

"May I," Kiana gently corrected Courtney in mid-whine. She knew what Courtney was going to ask before it was out of her niece's mouth. Practically every Sunday after church, Courtney wanted to go to her grandparents' home and help her grandmother whip up one of her Sunday cakes. Courtney liked having first dibs on the uncooked batter.

Kiana bent to place a kiss on Courtney's cheek. "Don't eat too much batter. You might get a stomachache. I'll be around about six or seven to pick you up."

Courtney beamed at Kiana and ran across the churchyard to the parking area down the grassy slope, where Evelyn was waiting for her by her late-model, champagne-colored Chevrolet Impala.

With a wistful expression on her face, Kiana watched her go. She turned and began walking in the opposite direction back to the church. A few minutes before, she'd seen Carter following Reverend Darton down the steps of the basement where there was a recreational room set up. Athletic equipment which was used in the various youth athletic programs the church sponsored was stored there. Reverend Darton probably wanted Carter's opinion on something and had asked him to take a look at their supplies.

Kiana felt knots of tension in her stomach as she descended the steps. Her arrival wouldn't be a surprise. The sound of her footfalls reverberated in the expansive space beneath the hundred-plus-year-old edifice.

When she was nearly at the foot of the stairs, she bent her head and peered into the dim room. "Hello! Reverend Darton, Carter?"

"It's just me," Carter's voice said from deep inside the room.

Kiana stepped down and stood a moment as her eyes adjusted to the lack of light. She heard Carter coming toward her. Then she heard a light switch being thrown and suddenly the room was illuminated.

"Ben left by the side door," Carter explained as he walked toward her with a baseball mitt on his right hand. He made a fist and pounded it into the mitt, testing its sturdiness. Looking into Kiana's eyes, he said, "I've missed you, Kiki."

Sighing, Kiana closed the space between them as Carter tossed the mitt onto a nearby table.

Once in his arms, Kiana turned her face up to his. Carter smiled warmly. Dimples appeared in both his golden-brown cheeks. Kiana reached up to trace a finger along his square jaw. "Carter, I've missed you, too. I was wrong to expect you to immediately accept my decision. I didn't give you time to think. *I* wasn't thinking straight myself. We'd just lost Dee and Kevin and I was angry, so angry!"

Carter's strong hands massaged her back. She felt the muscles in his arms and chest working as he held her firmly against him. Kissing her forehead, he said, "You belong in my arms."

Carter ran his hand up her back to her neck and into the thick, wavy hair that fell to her shoulders. The heavy, silky tendrils threaded between his fingers. He bent his head to kiss her and Kiana turned her face just as his mouth would have descended upon hers, and his lips brushed her cheek instead.

"Carter, we're on church grounds."

"There's no one here," Carter said in her ear. "God understands how I feel about you. How much I've missed holding you." He lowered his gaze to look deeply into her eyes. "Marry me."

Kiana's lips parted in unspoken astonishment. Carter took advantage of her surprise and his mouth fell on hers in a hungry kiss.

The feel of his insistent mouth on hers, the male scent of him, and his hard-muscled body all worked together to turn Kiana's knees to jelly. The kiss deepened and soon they were pressing their bodies closer, kissing all the exposed skin on each other's faces and necks that had been left uncovered by their conservative attire.

Tears of relief sprang to Kiana's eyes. Carter loved her. She knew it now. She'd been afraid that the argument had put an insurmountable wall between them. When they parted she smiled slowly. "What happened?" Her eyes searched his. "Why did you decide that now's the time to take this step?"

Carter wiped her tears away with his fingertips. "I'm no good without you." He kissed her fingers. "I need you in my life. It's that simple. I know you were hurting when you said you didn't think I'd ever grow up. That I'd never be able to bring myself to give up my so-called freedom. But we all make mistakes. And if I'm not willing to forgive and forget, then I'm not good enough for you."

Kiana took all he said in and marveled at the amount of emotional growth he'd undergone in the past three weeks. Perhaps the time they'd spent apart had been for the best after all.

Then in dulcet tones a feminine voice called from the top of the stairs, "Carter!"

Kiana hadn't been the only woman to see Carter descending the basement steps.

Kiana didn't move a muscle. But Carter abruptly let go of her and put some space between them. She studied the expression on his good-looking face. Panic? He nervously cleared his throat. "Down here," he said with forced enthusiasm.

Pamela Hodges's pump-shod feet were frozen in place when she saw that Carter wasn't alone. To her credit, the look of surprise that crossed her features was fleeting.

She smiled as she moved farther into the room. At five seven, she was nearly as tall as Kiana. She had on a forest green dress that displayed her curvaceous figure, and its hem fell two inches above her knees, revealing long, shapely legs.

"Oh, hello, Kiana. How *are* you? I hope you're holding up well," she said sympathetically.

For the life of her, Kiana couldn't muster up a

smile. "Pamela. Yes, we're all holding up well, thank you."

"I'm glad. If there's anything I can do to help just let me know." She moved forward and placed a hand on Kiana's arm. "As you know, I lost my mother two years ago, so I know what you're going through." She let her hand fall to her side.

Her dark, almond-shaped eyes looked directly into Kiana's. It was then that her expression changed from sympathy to triumph. And Kiana *knew*. Pamela felt she'd bested her in some way.

Never friends but acquaintances who'd always managed to be civil to one another in social settings, she and Pamela had rarely held a conversation of longer than five minutes. So why was she giving Kiana this blatantly belligerent signal? Unless . . .

Kiana turned her gaze on Carter again. She willed him to meet her eyes. He glanced at the floor, at the wall ahead of him. Finally he looked at Pamela and said, "Kiana and I were discussing something important, if you don't mind."

His tone told Kiana more than she wanted to know at that moment. It wasn't friendly nor askance. He wasn't asking Pamela to leave, he was *telling* her to. He was irritated by her intrusion.

Pamela stared at him for a split second, then apparently chose not to take umbrage. She turned on her three-inch heels and hastily retook the stairs.

Once she was safely at the top, she called, "Things are not always as they seem, Kiana!"

Kiana took a deep breath, slowly released it and turned her eyes on Carter. "Care to explain what all of *that* was about?"

Carter chose to profess ignorance of what she was alluding to. "All of what?" His eyes were on his wing tips when he said it.

Kiana recognized the cornered note in his tone

immediately. But she wasn't going to base her argument on something she couldn't prove. And did it really matter what he said, when the guilt had been written all over his face?

"Did you sleep with her?" she asked softly.

To the point and to the jugular.

Carter closed his eyes and sighed. Opening them again, he looked heavenward. "Kiana, you're not going to jump to conclusions because of the way Pamela spoke to me when she thought I was down here alone, are you? You know how she's always flirting with me. She flirts with anything in pants!"

"I'm not asking you this because of how she behaved. I'm asking you because of the way *you* behaved, Carter. Just answer the question. Yes or no?"

Carter was silent.

Kiana continued to seek his gaze, but he wouldn't look directly into her eyes.

"How can you ask me something like that, Kiana? Aren't you the one who has always espoused the view that without trust you have nothing?"

"So you didn't do it?"

"Just by asking that question, you've proven that you don't love me, Kiana. That you would believe anything Pamela Hodges would say is amazing to me since you know she's been hitting on me for years."

"Well, did she finally hit the right spot?"

Their eyes briefly met and Carter sighed heavily.

Shaking her head in exasperation, Kiana went to leave. Carter's hand shot out, grasping her arm and holding on tightly. "Kiki, okay. Something happened. But it was nothing. Believe me. Nothing at all."

With his admission, Kiana's legs suddenly felt weak. But she had to know all of it. She slowly turned to face him. Her eyes looked straight into his. "Nothing? Nothing at all? Exactly what does 'nothing at all' mean to you, Carter? Does it mean you only kissed?

Or maybe you fondled each other? Or perhaps it means she pleasured you and you just lay there and let her? Or does it mean you had sex but you used condoms, therefore it was nothing at all? Please explain."

Carter's face screwed up in a frown. He chewed his bottom lip. He appeared to be straining in the hopes that she'd let him off the hook and drop it. "I don't want to hurt you any more than I already have. Don't ask me to be specific. Why do you need to know what happened? It happened. Isn't that enough? I was upset. You had told me that you had no faith in my ability to accept responsibility, and I was hurting. She was there. That's all. She was conveniently there when I needed someone to talk to. And I was weak. I used her as much as she used me. I wanted *you*. But she was there." *That's why she gave me that smug look,* Kiana thought. *Because she'd had my man.*

"I'm not going to be specific," Carter flatly refused. He held her gaze. "You'll either forgive me or you won't, Kiana. And judging by your upbringing and the way you've always conducted yourself, I'm willing to wager the answer is you won't. So why should I embarrass myself by describing to you, in detail, the most spiritually degrading night of my life? I regretted doing it the moment it was over. It's you I love, Kiana. I truly love you, and I've done this thing that I can't take back. I wish I *could*. But it's a fact now. Something I'll have to live with."

"So that's why you were willing to forgive me?" She couldn't believe how thrilled she had been a few minutes before when he'd asked her to marry him. *Marry him?* Why would he ask her after what he'd done? In some desperate attempt to make it up to her? Did he actually wish to purge himself by doing what he considered the right thing? And if Pamela hadn't shown up, would he have ever admitted to the act? Probably not.

"Thank you, Lord, for watching out for me!" she cried.

Carter stared at her, confused.

Kiana backed away from him. "Good-bye, Carter. I love you, too. And I might have been able to go on from here, but at some point down the road I would've begun to have doubts. That you could make love to another woman and justify it because we'd argued . . . That makes no sense! Married couples argue. Would you find comfort with someone else every time we had a fight? No. I might love you but I'm not stupid. I know when to cut my losses. And that time is right now."

She turned her back to him. Catching her off guard, Carter grabbed her and angrily jerked her around to face him. He looked at her through slits. "Don't go all high and mighty on me, Kiana Everett. You're partly the cause of this whole mess. You were cold to me. You made me feel like I wasn't good enough. *Strong* enough. What is it with you? You expect so much from a man. I'm not a saint. I'm made of flesh and bone. So I didn't live up to your expectations. Have I suddenly become something you can wipe off your shoe and keep walking? You owe me more than that!"

Kiana wrenched her arm free of his hold. Glaring at him, she asked, "Look the other way, Carter? Have you conveniently forgotten about the time in Miami? I forgave *that*. Once was enough for me. You swore you'd never cheat on me again. It was early in our relationship. Before we'd made a commitment to one another. So I convinced myself I had no right to expect you to be faithful to me. This time it's different. We've been dating nearly three years and there was an understanding between us. We were trying to build something together. Give me one reason why I should look the other way this time."

Carter walked around her, looking at her from all angles while Kiana stood with her arms akimbo awaiting his reply.

He stopped in front of her and quietly said, "You should forgive me because it's what God would want you to do."

His eyes were pleading with her. Kiana stared into them a long while, but in the end she couldn't bring herself to bend. Time and time again she'd heard stories of women, some relatives, some friends, some she knew only by name, who had forgiven their spouses over and over again, losing a bit of their self-respect each time they chose to turn a blind eye to their partners' cheating ways.

Did she really need a man in her life so badly that she'd sacrifice anything to have him? After the incident in Miami, in which Carter had gotten intoxicated while at a buddy's bachelor party and taken the featured exotic dancer to a nearby hotel afterward, Kiana had forgiven him, but she hadn't forgotten. In fact she had never told her mother or sister about it because she knew what their reactions would've been. *And you're still dating him? Kick that cheating dog to the curb!*

Now she cocked her head to the side and said, "I don't believe God would hold it against me if I got out of this one-sided relationship while the getting's good." She backed away from him. "And I hope you'll someday find it in your heart to forgive *me* for pushing you into Pamela's arms, Carter. I believe God would want you to do that."

She turned and ran up the stairs, not even pausing to get one last look at Carter over her shoulder.

Once outside, she saw that most of the parishioners had gone home. The parking area was empty except for a few vehicles. She spotted Kerry leaning languidly on Kiana's battered beige and brown Jeep Wagoneer and let out a disappointed sigh. Why wasn't Kerry on patrol or something? She'd probably stuck around to give her yet another lecture on how best to live her life.

Kerry met her halfway. "I saw you follow Carter into the basement. How'd it go? Will I be wearing one of those frilly pastel numbers to your wedding in June?"

For some reason the image of Kerry in a frothy, ultra-feminine frock struck Kiana as hilarious. She burst into hysterical laughter. She laughed until tears rolled down her cheeks.

Kerry laughed too at first but when Kiana didn't stop after a few minutes, she became concerned. Pulling Kiana around to peer down into her face, she sternly asked, "What's the matter with you? Nothing's *that* funny."

Kerry shook Kiana. "What happened?" She looked in the direction of the basement steps. "He's gone. He left while you were falling to pieces. Level with me, Kiki."

Kiana tried to breathe deeply and found that mucus was clogging her passages. She reached into her shoulder bag, extracted a couple of crumpled tissues and blew her nose. Turning her reddened eyes on Kerry, she finally said, "There won't be any wedding, sis. I just broke up with Carter."

Kerry drew herself to her full five feet ten inches before cutting a contemplative glance in the direction Carter had driven off in a few minutes earlier. She returned her gaze to Kiana's face. "Why?"

"Because he slept with Pamela Hodges."

"What?!" Kerry shouted.

Grabbing Kiana by the arm, she pulled her not toward Kiana's Wagoneer but toward the unmarked car that she, as chief of police, used in the performance of her job. A large white SUV, it had enough horsepower underneath its hood to catch Carter before he crossed the county line, which was where he'd better be headed if he knew what was good for him.

Kiana stopped walking and smiled up at her younger sister. "Kerry, I don't exactly know what you're thinking, but forget it! We're not going to confront Carter. I've already done that.

"I'm going to stop by Moore's Inn and make a reservation for Gabriel Merrick, and then I'm going home," she said resolutely. Her tears had stopped flowing. She blew her nose again, and she sounded less like Donald Duck when she added, "I know you love me and if I gave you permission, you'd beat Carter within an inch of his miserable life, but where would that get us? *You* thrown in jail and out of a career. *Me* visiting you up at the facility for women in Ocala for the next twenty years. No way! Finding out about Carter and Pamela isn't going to break me."

She laughed shortly as she turned back toward her Wagoneer. "Break me? Not hardly! Finding out what he's really made of is liberating. I'm free, Kerry. Free to tell every man who comes near me to keep walking because I don't want anything to do with them!"

Following her, Kerry humphed. "So now *every* man is to be avoided because Carter bruised your heart? Let's go give *him* a few bruises and you'll instantly feel better . . ."

Kiana looked into Kerry's large, thickly-fringed, whiskey-colored eyes. She adored her baby sister. But being in the Marine Corps had convinced her that every problem could be solved with her physical prowess. Some things were best left alone. This was one of them.

"Kerry, I'm thirty-two years old, fairly attractive and I've never been married. Now some folks might say that's a pity because by the time a woman reaches my age she should have met the man of her dreams and had a couple of children. But I look at it this way. I'm not married yet because God hasn't sent me the right man. He'll do that in His own time. Today, He helped me escape a relationship that would have been bad for me in the end. I truly believe that."

Kerry was slowly coming down from the adrenaline rush she'd experienced when she'd imagined chasing Carter down and dropping him with an expertly dealt karate chop to the side of the neck.

She managed a weak smile for her sister's benefit. "You're really okay with this?"

Kiana hugged her and when she let go she tilted her head up and rewarded Kerry with a confident smile. "This time your big sister has adeptly and assertively handled the problem. Carter's out of my life and I know I made the right decision."

Kerry continued walking Kiana to her car. "You know what, girl? This could be just the thing you need. No more Carter. I'm between men. You and I ought to go on the prowl one night. Leave Coco with Mama and Daddy. See what's happening in Jacksonville or West Palm Beach . . ."

"Are males so scarce around here we have to go out of town?" Kiana asked skeptically.

"Spoken like a woman who's been out of circulation for the past three years," Kerry replied, rolling her eyes.

At the Wagoneer, Kiana opened the door and slid behind the wheel. Looking up at Kerry, she said, "Why are we having this conversation? Didn't I just tell you I don't want to *see* another male? Forget about it. I'm going to get fat and happy. I'm going home to pig out on Häagen Dazs and peanut M&M's. I'll let out the waist in my fat jeans. You know, the ones you keep in the back of the closet for those times you're 'retaining' water?"

Laughing, Kerry said, "You should have taken me up on *my* idea. You actually *burn* calories in the process of beating up somebody."

Kiana turned the key in the ignition. The old, reliable Jeep growled a bit but didn't let her down. She put it in gear. "If I've said this once, I've said it a thousand times," she called to Kerry as she pulled away. "You're not in the Marine Corps any longer. You've got to put a choke hold on those macho tendencies."

"Semper Fidelis!" Kerry yelled the Marine Corps motto as Kiana hit the accelerator. *Always faithful.*

City Boy

Wednesday afternoon Kiana took her normal route home from her job as supervisor of nurses at Green Meadows Assisted Care Facility in Gainesville. When she was less than five miles from the turn off, up ahead she saw that a motorist had pulled his car onto the soft shoulder of Highway 441 and had raised the hood of the late-model sport utility vehicle.

Used to offering aid to anyone in need, Kiana followed her first instinct and parked the Wagoneer behind the SUV. She got out to see if she could help. The late afternoon breezes felt cool on her bare arms. She'd showered and changed from her nurse's uniform and into street clothes before leaving Green Meadows. Now she was simply attired in jeans, a short-sleeved sweater set in aquamarine and a pair of white Nikes. Her hair was drawn back in a ponytail.

"Hello!" she called to the man bent over the hood in intense concentration. As she rounded the SUV she was greeted by excited barking. Kiana raised a hand to shade her eyes from the glare of the sun as she peered inside the SUV. The dog had calmed down and was shaking his tail happily. "Hey there!" She tapped on the window in a playful manner before continuing around to the front of the SUV. The man bent over the hood still hadn't acknowledged her hello. Kiana stood a few feet away from him studying his form before saying anything else. Men. Her mother often said that when men were engaged in a task, especially a thing like car repairs, everything else receded into the background for them. This fellow certainly bore out that claim.

She'd been several feet away from him when she'd spoken. Maybe he hadn't heard her. "Excuse me?" she tried again. Nothing.

From the looks of him he was a well-to-do tourist. The SUV was the top of the line. He wore a beautiful brown suede jacket and expensive, pleated, camel-colored slacks that were tailored to fit his tall, lean body just right. On his feet were brown leather loafers. His neat brown dreadlocks were the only non-conservative feature on him.

Kiana loudly cleared her throat, stepped right up to the car and said, "If you don't need my help, just say so and I'll be on my merry way!"

The man straightened up and stared at her. "Where'd *you* come from?"

Laughing, Kiana said, "I parked behind you three minutes ago and said hello to you."

She peered at the motor a few moments. "Mmm. Broken hose, huh?"

The man raised a brow in surprise. "You diagnosed that after taking one look under the hood?"

Kiana reached down and tapped the still-warm hose with a manicured fingernail. "Yeah, it's a goner all right. Better not drive it when the water hose is busted. You could wind up cracking the engine." She turned her gaze on him and smiled, liking what she saw.

He had dark brown skin the color of sun-dried tobacco. A five o'clock shadow marred his otherwise clean-shaven, square-jawed face. His features were angular but with no sharp lines, although his cheekbones were well-defined. His nose was long and prominent. His eyes large, wide-spaced and dark, almost black. His mouth was full-lipped and generous. An altogether masculine face. When he smiled, dimples appeared in his cheeks, and when his lips drew back from strong, white teeth, his eyes mirrored his pleasure.

"You'll have to come with me," Kiana said suddenly.

His eyes lit up. "Are all women around here so friendly?"

He didn't question her offer however. He closed the hood and followed her around the car to the driver's side door where he stopped and opened it.

A golden-brown Labrador retriever gingerly leaped from the front seat and immediately went to Kiana, who held out her hand for him to sniff.

"Max," the man said as he locked the car doors with a push of a button, "meet . . ." He looked at her. "I don't know your name."

Kiana smiled as she patted Max's head. She appeared cool and collected when she answered, "Everyone calls me Kiki." Inside, however, she was doing mental somersaults. Max. Courtney had said her Uncle Gabe's dog's name was Max.

"Hello, Max," she said, still stroking his furry head.

Max responded by licking her hand.

Kiana raised her eyes to Gabriel's. "You didn't tell me your name."

He held out a big hand. "It's Gabriel."

She took it and firmly shook it. "Are you doing the tourist bit, Gabriel?"

She began walking toward the Wagoneer. Max ran ahead while she and Gabriel took their time.

"Not really. I'm on my way to Damascus. Family business."

"I see."

At the Wagoneer, Kiana leaned in and unlocked

the passenger-side door and the back door directly behind the driver's side door.

She held the door open for Max to hop inside. He was apparently used to getting in and out of cars and had no trouble climbing onto the back seat where he promptly lay down.

Gabriel went around, got in and closed the door. He was fastening his seat belt by the time Kiana put the key in the ignition. When the engine came to life, the cassette player automatically switched on. Kiana had been listening to Etta James's *At Last* before she stopped to lend a hand.

Thinking that Etta might not be to Gabriel Merrick's liking, she reached over to turn off the player. Gabriel's hand covered hers. "Please don't. I love Etta James."

Kiana had to remove her hand from beneath his, as he didn't seem in any hurry to break the contact.

Their eyes met.

She looked away first because she had to put the car in gear and pull back onto the road. After checking behind her, she put her foot on the accelerator and they were on their way.

"I take it you live around here," Gabriel said casually.

He didn't feel at all relaxed.

He hadn't felt relaxed from the moment he'd looked up into this woman's big, cinnamon-hued eyes. She wasn't wearing makeup. That was one of the first things he'd noticed about her. No lipstick. Not even eyeliner. Yet her cocoa skin glowed. Her lips were reddish brown. Luscious lips that reminded him of ripe plums. He wondered if they'd taste as sweet.

His eyes rested on her hands as she gripped the steering wheel. Short, manicured nails. Clear nail polish. The skin on her hands looked soft and supple.

Apparently she took good care of them. He hadn't spied a ring. Good.

"So is this the first long trip you've taken her on?"

He had to concentrate on her question.

"Oh, you mean the car. Yeah. How did you know?"

"Just a guess. Where're you from?"

"Bridgeport, Connecticut. Although my brother and I grew up in New Haven."

Kiana felt a twinge of guilt at the mention of Kevin. Why play games? Gabriel might not appreciate being led on, and might accuse her of trying to trick him into something when he found out she'd known who he was all along and had chosen not to reveal herself.

She reached over and turned the volume down on the cassette player. "Gabriel, I have to tell you something and I hope you won't be upset . . ."

Gabriel smiled at her. "You're a highway robber and you're taking me someplace to hit me over the head and steal my wallet?"

Kiana laughed. "No. If I *were* a robber, I would've hit you over the head the moment I realized you hadn't even noticed I'd walked up. Are all professors so focused? Because you didn't even know I was there . . ."

"I knew you were there, Ana."

Kiana's heartbeat sped up and she gripped the steering wheel even tighter. "What gave me away?"

"For one thing, you and Dionne have the same grade of hair: thick, wavy and blue-black. She wore hers down her back like you do yours. And your voice, Ana. I pay attention to voices and language. You have a distinctive voice. Rather gritty and sexy, and your accent is lovely."

Kiana had to remind herself to breathe.

She briefly looked into his eyes before returning her attention to the road. "That's not the sort of thing a relative says to another relative."

"I didn't feel very brotherly toward you over the phone, Ana. After seeing you, I *definitely* don't feel brotherly toward you."

Kiana felt warm being this close to him in the confines of the Wagoneer. She had all the windows up because the temperature outside was forty-five degrees. They'd been experiencing a cold snap the last few days. She cracked her window a bit before saying, "I think you should know that I just ended a relationship with a man who cheated on me, and I'm not a woman you want to trifle with. So you can turn off the charm, Gabriel Merrick. It won't work on me. Let's remember your purpose here is to take my niece back home with you and I'm going to fight it tooth and nail!"

With a complacent smile on his face, Gabriel leaned back in his seat and closed his eyes for a moment. "Say something provocative, Ana."

"I know I agreed not to discuss all this in Coco's presence and I won't go back on my word," Kiana said, ignoring his last comment. "But know this, Gabriel. When I want something I never give up until it's mine."

Gabriel looked at her profile. "I'm counting on that, Ana."

Kiana turned the volume up on the cassette player. "Just listen to Etta. You're trying to provoke me and I'm not going to let you."

Gabriel turned it back down. "I'm not trying to provoke you." He smiled. "I'm just telling you that you're the only woman in awhile who has made me sit up and take notice. I don't lie, Ana. Over the years I've found that it causes needless suffering for the liar and the ones he lies to. When I say I'm attracted to you, I'm not trying to confuse you or bend you to my will. Nothing so sinister. I'm a simple man. I'm not one to spout flowery phrases in order to woo a woman. When I say something to you, you can count on it to be how I really feel. And I don't have the time or the inclination to play games. So I'm telling you now, when I want something I don't give up until I get it either."

Kiana was happy to see the Damascus city limits sign up ahead. In two more minutes she'd have this entirely too good-looking, irksome man out of her car.

When she stopped at the one traffic light in town, she decided to play the part of tour guide. It was a safe role to assume.

Pointing to the two-hundred-year-old antebellum era courthouse on the left, she said, "That's our courthouse. The police department and the fire department both have their offices there, along with, of course, the mayor and other city officials."

Gabriel looked around with interest. Damascus was a charming small town complete with a city square, the major businesses along its main street and a bandstand in the park downtown. It was obvious that the citizens were proud of their town because its streets were clean, the lawns were like lush, green carpets and all the storefronts were colorfully painted and appeared as if the owners spent the requisite time doing maintenance on them. It could have been a scene out of *Our Town*.

"Two years ago we elected our first black mayor," Kiana told him with a note of pride. "He got sixty-three percent of the votes. It would have been impossible to get those numbers without white support. Damascus is about sixty percent white and thirty-five percent black."

"Who makes up the other five percent?"

"Mostly Mexican-Americans," Kiana replied.

After a few more minutes of sightseeing, Kiana pulled the Wagoneer into an Amoco service station.

"This is owned and operated by my father." She parked a few feet from the open service bay and turned to Gabriel. "He's usually finishing up with any major repair jobs this time of day. But if he's busy, I'll get the part we need and go back and repair it for you myself."

"You?"

"We've all worked with Daddy at one time or another. I was the only one of his four children who showed any proficiency whatsoever in automotive repair." She opened her door and got out. "Of course if you don't believe me you can ask him yourself. I make it a habit to never work on anyone's car who has doubts about my abilities."

"I believe you," Gabriel told her as he opened his door, stepped down and peered back at Max, who'd gotten to his feet in anticipation of joining his master. "Stay, fella. We'll be back soon and I'll find you a comfortable spot to bed down in tonight."

Max wagged his tail a couple of times and settled onto the seat. He was a patient pooch.

"Daddy!" Kiana called, her voice reverberating off the service bay walls.

She was careful where she stepped in her snow-white Nikes. Oil was nearly impossible to get out of fabric once it had a chance to soak in.

"Hey, Kiki, what is it, baby? Give me a minute or so. I'm tightening a bolt. You know they can be son of a guns if you don't do it right the first time. How was your day?" her dad called from underneath a Ford pickup with hydraulic lifts on it so high the driver would require a stepladder to get behind the wheel of the vehicle.

"It was good, Daddy. Take your time. We'll wait."

"Who do you have with you? My grandbaby? Coco, is that you?"

Kiana smiled at Gabriel. "No, Daddy. It's Kevin's

brother, Gabriel. His Ford Expedition has a busted water hose. I picked him up about five miles outside of town."

"Those big sports utility vehicles can be rough on water hoses. Your first long trip in her, son?"

Gabriel smiled. Like father, like daughter. "Yes sir, it was."

"Thought so," Buddy said. Then he said to Kiana, "Kiki, get what you need. I'll be here a while. You can handle it. Show Gabriel how to do it in case she blows another one on the trip back to . . . Connecticut, isn't it?"

"Yeah, Daddy," Kiana replied. She was smiling at the way Gabriel's eyebrows had shot up in astonishment when her father had told her to do the repairs herself.

She crooked a finger in Gabriel's direction. "This way."

"See you later, Daddy!" she called in parting.

"Okay, Kiki. Tell your mother I'll be home no later than seven. I promised the Clemons boy he could pick up this monster at six-thirty, and you know I'm a man of my word."

Kiana paused, wondering if her father had said all he wanted to say. Figuring he had, she replied, "All right, I'll give her the message. Later, Daddy."

She looked up at Gabriel. "I don't know where my manners are. Are you tired? Hungry?" She didn't wait for a reply. "Of course you are."

She quickly left the service bay, expecting him to follow. "I'll tell you what, after getting the new hose and clamps from the supply room, why don't we go by my parents' house so you can say hello to Coco? Mama usually has dinner prepared by now. You can have a bite to eat and relax a bit before we go do the repairs on the Expedition. It needs time to cool off, anyway. You can't replace the hose if the fluids haven't had a chance to cool. They could spatter all over the place."

Gabriel just smiled as he followed her back to the Wagoneer. He liked the way her hips moved. He liked everything about her frame. She wasn't thin. But she'd told him that over the phone. She had enough weight on her so that when a man held her, he knew he had hold of something good.

She turned to look back at him. "Is that all right with you?"

"I'm yours to do with as you wish."

Kiana cut her eyes heavenward. "That amateur Romeo stuff has got to go!"

Grinning, Gabriel caught up with her as she reached for the handle of the office door. It was around the corner from the service bay on the side of the building near the customer restrooms. He grasped Kiana by the elbow. In a low voice he asked, "If you didn't want me flirting with you, why did you lead me on the other night?"

Kiana raised her eyes to his as they stood there with the glass door open. Luckily, her father's five employees were all occupied elsewhere on the premises. "Lead you on? When did I ever lead you on?"

" 'How much older *are* you than Kevin?' " Gabriel mimicked her words of Sunday morning.

"I was just making conversation!" Kiana hissed, regarding him through narrowed eyelids.

Gabriel chuckled. "Sure you were. You were trying to figure out if I'd be right for you." He leaned in. "Here I am. Am I what you expected?"

Kiana pulled the door open. Gabriel followed her inside and waited while she went into the back room. She returned a couple of minutes later clutching two small boxes in her hands.

Gabriel openly ogled her as she walked past him. Blushing, Kiana went straight for the door and didn't stop walking until she reached the Wagoneer. Max gave her a pitiful whine, as if to say, *What about me? Am I going to stay cooped up in this car all day?* Kiana smiled at him. He was a handsome beast. He was well-behaved, too. Unlike his randy master.

Once she and Gabriel were seated in the Wagoneer, she turned to him. "Let's get one thing perfectly clear, Mr. Merrick. I'm not in the market for a hot love affair. A man I was very much in love with just broke my heart. Your advances are not welcome. In fact, I find them distasteful, rude and downright disrespectful. If you think I'm the type of woman who'd jump into bed with you without hesitation, you are sorely mistaken." She said this slowly so there would be no need to repeat herself.

"It's the hair, isn't it?" Gabriel asked with a humorous glint in his dark eyes. "You don't like the dreads."

Kiana had been willing to let it drop if he'd been decent enough to apologize. But here he was childishly egging her on. So she let him have it. "You know what I think?" she asked, looking him in those smug eyes. "I think you enjoy teasing women. But when push comes to shove, and they call you on the mat, you run and hide like the big baby you are!"

Gabriel leaned close to her. Their mouths were mere inches apart. "Care to test your theory?"

Kiana breathed in the citrus aroma of his aftershave. And his clean warm breath. She wondered what his lips would feel like on hers. How his sculptured jawline would feel to her wandering fingers. Was his hair as soft as it looked?

Gabriel only knew one thing: Physical contact with Kiana Everett was inevitable. It was only a matter of time. And if it didn't happen in the next few seconds, it would happen before he left Damascus, Florida. That was a promise he meant to keep.

Kiana slowly turned her head, breaking the nearly

mesmerizing hold he had on her. As calmly as you please, she turned the key in the ignition. "I wouldn't spit on you if you were on fire."

"Daniel was right, southern women can say anything and make it sound sexy."

Kiana couldn't help it. She laughed.

The Everett home was a large southern-style bungalow with wraparound porches. No matter what door you came out of when departing the Everett house, be it front, back or side, you stepped onto a porch. And since Evelyn Everett had never tended a plant that didn't sprout luxuriant green foliage just to please her, there were hanging plants, plants in pots and every imaginable flower growing along the yard borders and along the walk leading to the front porch, and climbing roses trailing along the matching whitewashed trellises flanking the front porch steps.

So when Gabriel saw the house, the first thing he said was, "Who tends the garden here? I'd like to hire him."

Kiana smiled as she put the Wagoneer in park and reached for the door's handle. *"Her.* It's my mother, who's never met a plant she didn't like. And vice versa."

Evelyn must have heard the car pull into the yard because by the time Kiana and Gabriel made it halfway up the walk, she was standing in the doorway with an apron on over her smart pantsuit.

Coco, adept at squeezing her small body around adults, slipped right past her grandmother, ran and catapulted her compact body into Gabriel's arms. "Uncle Gabe, Uncle Gabe, you came!"

A lump formed in Gabriel's throat as he hugged Courtney to him. She smelled of bergamot hair oil, perspiration and sunshine. A heavenly combination. Mounds of black hair fell in braids down her back, and her eyes, too dark and intense for someone so young, were so like Kevin's that he felt like crying.

Laughing, he said, "Of course I came, Coco. I had to see my best girl, didn't I? You didn't believe I'd stay gone forever, did you?"

Courtney's brows furrowed in a frown. "I don't know . . . You've been away a *long* time, Uncle Gabe. I almost forgot what you looked like." She looked him straight in the eyes.

Feeling guilty, Gabriel hugged her tighter. "I'm not going to go away and stay away that long ever again!"

Courtney smiled her pleasure. Then she suddenly began looking all around them. "Where's Max?"

"He's in your aunt A . . . Kiki's car."

Courtney wriggled out of his arms, and once her feet were on the walk she started running toward the Wagoneer. "Let him out!" Remembering the proper protocol when she was at her grandmother's house, she paused in her headlong rush and looked back at Evelyn, who was smiling at her handsome guest.

"Grandma, may Max and I play in the backyard?"

Evelyn, not wanting to appear stern in Gabriel's presence, relented, although normally she wouldn't allow dogs in her yard, front or back.

Courtney ran on to the Wagoneer where she opened the back door and Max carefully jumped down and licked her face. Giggling, Courtney took him by the collar and they ran around the house to the fenced backyard.

Kiana hastily made introductions. Her attention was on Courtney and whether the little girl would be able to get the heavy gate unlatched and hold onto Max's collar at the same time.

"Mama," she said, "this is Gabriel Merrick. Gabriel, my mother, Evelyn." She turned away and began jogging in the direction of the backyard. "He's tired and hungry, Mama. You know what to do."

Evelyn did, indeed, know what to do.

When Kiana finally came through the back door ten minutes later, Gabriel was at the kitchen table devouring a heaping plate full of Evelyn's smothered oxtails over rice, collard greens, corn bread and sweet potato souffle.

Gabriel paused long enough to smile at Kiana before lowering his head again and giving the delicious food his undivided attention.

Kiana smiled back. Maybe he wasn't so bad after all if he could appreciate good southern cooking.

Evelyn was at the stove looking into the dutch oven that the collards had been cooked in, making certain the pot liquor was at an acceptable level. To cook tender collards she had to be sure they were simmered long enough in sufficient liquid, otherwise they came out tough and chewy.

She hadn't tested them for tenderness before dishing up a serving for their guest and was loath to ask him how they were. She surreptitiously glanced at him. He was eating them as if they were not only good, but mighty tasty. She gave a satisfied little sigh.

Kiana interrupted her train of thought with a quick peck to her cheek and a whispered query, "What do you think of him?"

There was little chance of their being overheard by Gabriel since Evelyn had the radio on low and tuned to her favorite R & B station, and since they were standing several feet away from him.

"He doesn't look a thing like Kevin," was Evelyn's considered opinion. "They must each take after a different parent. He's *black*, isn't he? Beautiful skin. And that face! I wonder why he isn't married."

Kiana humphed. "I just wanted to know what you

thought about him, not a list of his physical attributes."

Her mother laughed softly. "You asked me what I thought of him, and, at this point, all I know about him is that he looks darn fine to me! I suppose I'll get to know what he's like personality-wise if he hangs around long enough."

"If you're done whispering about me," Gabriel said, rising with his plate in hand, "I'd like to get a little bit more of those collards if you can spare them. I haven't had collards that good since my mother passed away over two years ago."

Evelyn laughed delightedly. "I like that boy!"

She moved around Kiana and took the plate from Gabriel, whereupon she handed it to Kiana. "You heard the man, more greens." She wiggled her eyebrows suggestively at her daughter, and Kiana knew her mother wasn't beyond a bit of matchmaking if the occasion arose.

Inwardly sighing, Kiana accepted the plate. The last thing she needed was for her mother to be in *Gabriel's* corner.

Turning to Gabriel, Evelyn asked, "Is it all right if I give your dog . . ."

"Max."

". . . Max some leftover roast beef and a bowl of water?"

"That's very kind of you, Mrs. Everett," Gabriel said with a grateful smile.

"Oh, it's the least I can do," Evelyn said modestly.

She went to the refrigerator to get the treat for Max, and Gabriel took the opportunity to peruse Kiana up close.

"You can tell so much about a woman just by observing her parents. What her values are, how she'll look twenty years from now."

His dark eyes caressed her face. "You've got great

parents. And your mother's a very attractive woman. Your worthiness quotient just shot up quite a few points."

Kiana behaved as if she hadn't heard a word he'd said. She dished up another serving of collards and placed a slice of cornbread next to it on the plate. Then, as she handed him the plate, she allowed her gaze to seductively scan him up and down. "Must you be so clinical, professor? Why don't you just admit you like the way my jelly rolls and you'd like to sop me up with a biscuit?"

The expression on Gabriel's face told her she'd struck a nerve.

His mahogany eyes searched her face and settled on her mouth.

The screen door slammed shut. Evelyn had gone outside to take Max his dinner.

Gabriel placed the plate on the countertop and gave Kiana his full attention. "All right," he said, answering her challenge, his eyes boring into hers. "I like the way your jeans fit and I'd like to be the one who helps you out of them tonight."

"And then what?" Kiana asked, feeling her power over him surge. Gabriel sighed as he moved closer still. "And then I'd like to slowly kiss every inch of your body starting with your belly button . . ."

"Oh, you've got a thing for bellybuttons?"

"Not particularly. It's just close to a favorite spot, found further south."

Kiana's face flushed. She'd intended to tease *him* to the point of arousal and he'd turned the tables on her.

Hastily walking away, she said, "Your food's getting cold." The screen door slammed shut for the second time that afternoon.

Come On In My Kitchen

"That meal was . . ." Gabriel closed his eyes a moment, ". . . stupendous, Mrs. Everett!"

They were all sitting around the table in the kitchen eating Evelyn's sweet potato souffle, washing it down with cups of her rich Colombian coffee.

Kiana smiled to herself. She thought Gabriel was laying it on a little thick. The food *was* delicious. But, really! When she saw the sublime expression on her mother's face though, she knew he had made a fan.

Evelyn reached over and placed a hand on top of Gabriel's. "Sugar, you're always welcome in my kitchen." She gave a quick nod in her daughter's direction. "Hers, too. She can *burn* when she wants to."

"Mama, I don't think Gabriel's interested in whether I'm a good cook or not," Kiana protested mildly.

She reached over and wiped a bit of the dessert from the corner of Courtney's mouth with a napkin. Courtney was contentedly swinging her legs. It had been a wonderful day for her. Her uncle was here. He'd brought Max with him. Max had found a grassy spot beneath the pear tree in the backyard. He was snoozing there now.

She observed her uncle, who was watching her auntie. Smiling at the turn of events, feeling almost happy for the first time since learning she'd never see either of her parents again, she felt safe and protected in the bosom of her family. It would be nice if Uncle Gabe could stay forever.

"Don't be fooled, child," her grandmother was saying to her auntie. "Men are still interested in what a woman can do in the kitchen."

Courtney knew there was some underlying "adult thing" they were discussing. She didn't concern herself with trying to figure it out though. She was consumed with the way Uncle Gabe was looking at Auntie Kiki. And how Auntie Kiki wouldn't look him in the eyes.

Auntie Kiki leaned over and whispered to Uncle Gabe, "You know where this is leading. Help me out here!"

"Mrs. Everett," Uncle Gabe spoke up suddenly. "Your daughter has already informed me that she isn't a woman to be trifled with."

"Kiki, you didn't!"

Auntie Kiki frowned at Uncle Gabe. "That isn't the kind of help I was asking for." She looked at Grandma. "Yes, Mama, I did tell him that."

Remembering that her niece was at the table, she smiled at Courtney and suggested, "Wouldn't you like to finish that on the back porch, sweetie?"

Courtney looked up. She was perfectly content to sit there and listen to the rest of the conversation. But she knew by the tone of her Auntie Kiki's voice that it was best not to lodge a complaint, so she picked up her dessert plate and fork and left the table. Maybe Max would like a taste of the sweet potato souffle.

Kiana waited until Courtney was out of earshot before turning her wrath on a smiling Gabriel. "I can see you're not going to play fair." She beseeched her mother with her eyes. "Honestly, Mother, I can't believe you're buying this. I've already explained to Gabriel that I recently broke up with a man I was in love with and he won't listen. Now you're trying to push us together? I'm just *not* interested."

Gabriel regarded Evelyn. "She's not interested."

"Oh, come on, Kiki," Evelyn said, pushing her dessert plate aside and pausing to take a sip of coffee before continuing. She swallowed. "You didn't see fit to tell me everything that went on between you and Carter. But you know small towns. People talk. He isn't worth all this self-pity and self-evaluation on your part. I say go on with your life and forget about him!"

"I second the motion!" Gabriel put in.

Kiana just glowered at him.

"And furthermore," Evelyn said, getting her second wind. "Kerry told me about Miami . . ."

"What about Miami?" Gabriel asked, cocking his head toward Kiana.

"It's none of your business!" Kiana cried, pushing her chair back and rising. She directed the next words to her mother. "Are you so eager to see me married that you'd toss me into the arms of the next living, breathing male? You don't know a thing about him except that he's Kevin's brother and that he's good-looking."

Gabriel rose too, prepared to follow her if she should bolt. He looked her in the eyes. "You think I'm good-looking?" he asked incredulously.

But both Kiana and Evelyn ignored him as they got into the argument. He would learn to stay out of altercations between members of the Everett family.

"Carter was never right for you," Evelyn expounded. "For one thing he never knew the value of fidelity in a relationship. Some men never grow up. They go through their lives sampling woman after woman, never wanting to build a life with any of them. That was Carter Henderson. He led you along for nearly three years and you let him because you loved him. Well, love ain't that blind. And if you suddenly awakened to see him for what he truly is, then it's about damn time!"

Frowning, Kiana shot a glance at Gabriel. "Mama, can't we discuss this some other time?"

"Oh, he's family," Evelyn said dismissively.

Those southern mores again, Gabriel thought as he eased on out the back door. He would give them their privacy anyway.

Kiana met her mother's eyes. "You're right. Carter isn't worth my spending a minute grieving for what could have been." Her eyes glistened with unshed tears. "But I *am* grieving, Mama. I'm grieving for Dee and Kevin. And I know it's selfish, but I'm also grieving for the life I'd imagined Carter and I would someday have together. I'm wallowing in self-pity because I'm already missing the years we would have spent loving one another like you and Daddy have for the past forty years. I'm upset because I may never give birth, and one day stand in *my* kitchen trying to talk sense into a daughter who's getting over a broken heart."

Evelyn had pulled Kiana against her ample bosom before Kiana got out her last sentence. "I know all of that, baby. And I feel for you." She was hugging Kiana so tightly, Kiana had trouble catching a breath. "When any of my children are in pain, I'm in pain. The last few weeks have been hell on all of us. Life has a way of making you prioritize, whether you want to or not! Dee and Kevin getting killed like that was beyond our control. There's nothing we can do for them except remember them and keep them in our hearts." She paused, sniffing. "Their deaths taught us a lesson: we must keep our focus on what's important. Controlling many aspects of our lives is often out of our hands. However, we *can* control whom we choose to spend the rest of our lives with. Carter wasn't the right man for you. You would have either left him or shot him inside of five years." Her voice softened as she held Kiana at arm's length. "It was best to break it off, baby. You should be congratulating yourself and celebrating your freedom instead of depressing yourself over what *might* have been. Now, Mama has had her say. You go out there and apologize to our guest for our arguing in front of him. And on his first day in town no less!"

Laughing softly, Kiana went over to the paper towel rack over the sink, tore off a towel and blew her nose before going to do her mother's bidding.

Kiana joined Gabriel and Courtney on the back porch.

Evelyn strode over to the table and began removing the dirty dishes, transferring them to the sink. Of all her children, Kiana had the biggest heart, the most love to give, it seemed. And the problem with that was that the biggest heart was also the biggest target, and in danger of being broken more often. Now if Carter Henderson had broken *Kerry's* heart, Kerry would have taken her frustration out on his hide and gone home and slept like a baby, her conscience not bothering her one iota.

Sometimes, Evelyn worried about her baby girl.

"I'm sorry about instigating that argument between you and your mother," Gabriel said later as Kiana drove him out to do the repairs on the SUV.

Kiana didn't reply. She thought she'd let him stew in his own juices a while. To an onlooker it might appear that she and her mother were arguing, but in reality they never argued. They *discussed.* This particular discussion had helped her to get rid of some of the self-doubt she'd been experiencing since telling Carter it was over. Was a woman to be deemed ignorant or needy if she put her trust in a man who didn't deserve that trust? And was it lack of judgment on her part or was there something lacking in her makeup that made her love a man like Carter?

Did men like Carter create themselves? Or did enabling women build them from the ground up? Without women who were willing to look the other way and forgive them time and time again, cheating men would not find a safe harbor in a storm of angry women. She'd given him no welcome place this time. And never again would she allow another man to use her.

"So, you're not talking to me?" Gabriel asked quietly.

Kiana smiled. "Since you're a part of the family now you should know that we tend to get into heated discussions on a fairly regular basis. That argument you witnessed between me and Mama, I'd give it a one on a scale of one to ten."

"Really," Gabriel said in contemplative tones. "As a linguist I have to tell you, the passionate way you went at it was very intriguing."

"Not only intriguing, but cathartic," Kiana told him.

They arrived at the spot where the Expedition had blown a hose earlier. Kiana parked the Wagoneer facing the front of the Expedition in case they needed to utilize the Wagoneer's headlights.

It was dusk. The sky was purple. The sun, low on the horizon, sat like a huge orange ball suspended in the purple sky above.

They got out and the wind whipped about them as they walked toward the Expedition. Kiana carried the new parts, removed from their boxes, and Gabriel carried her red toolbox.

At the Expedition, Gabriel sat the toolbox on the

grass. He then raised the hood. A light automatically came on which gave them enough illumination to change the hose.

Beside him, Kiana was snapping on a pair of surgical gloves.

"You're going to operate now, doc?" Gabriel joked.

"Unless you want a go at her," Kiana replied, looking at him with a smug look on her face. City boys. They didn't know anything about cars except how to drive them.

"Well," Gabriel said casually as he moved around to peer down at the designated area. "I *could* give it a try. If you have the time to patiently give directions. But, if you're in a hurry . . ."

"Oh, no," Kiana assured him lightly. She wanted to see him in action. The experience might give her ammunition for future spats they were sure to have, since he seemed to take pleasure in provoking her.

She went to take off the gloves. "Would you like to use these?"

Gabriel smiled. "No thanks. I don't mind a bit of grease under my fingernails."

Kiana watched, amazed, as he competently removed the upper and lower radiator hoses, disconnected the coolant recovery hose and put the new clamps on. Lastly, he fitted the hose flush with the clamps and quickly tightened the clamps. It took him all of twenty minutes. He bent and placed the wrench back in the toolbox and straightened up, his eyes on her.

Kiana tried not to show it, but she was impressed. Their eyes met and held. The air felt electrified. The sound of the cicadas grew louder, it seemed. If she could just get her heartbeat to slow down, maybe she could get control of her breathing.

"I've had a little experience," Gabriel said, not bragging, just stating a fact. "When I was a teenager,

I worked at a service station. It was my first after-school job."

"Well, you haven't lost your touch," Kiana said, complimenting his skill. She walked up to him.

Gabriel's thigh touched hers. "I try to keep in practice."

Kiana tilted her head up. "It was thrilling to watch," she said huskily. She offered him her mouth.

Gabriel swallowed hard. He was suddenly nervous. What if this woman was the one who'd be hell to get out of his system once he was back in Bridgeport? Daniel had told him that when it happened, it would be out of his control, and he'd been right. Ever since she walked up to his car that afternoon, all he'd wanted to do was touch her. Now that seemed a real possibility, and he was hesitant.

Lourdes' betrayal hadn't been able to get to the core of him because he'd gone into that relationship with his eyes wide open. He knew she'd chosen him only because of his position at Baylor and his inheritance, which was substantial. But this woman . . . This woman was a different story. Even in the space of only a few hours, he knew she was real. Not hiding behind pretensions. She was warm and wonderful. She cared deeply about her family. Vibrant, sexy. With a body that a man could spend a lifetime getting lost in.

But there was one problem. She was Courtney's aunt. Was it wise to take a chance on alienating a member of Courtney's family should things not work out between them? *Sex on the brain.* Besides, she'd already told him not to trifle with her emotions. You should listen when a woman speaks. She invariably tells you what you need to know about her. And Kiana Everett had told him she wasn't interested in a love affair. Unfortunately, he wasn't looking for anything *else*.

But she smelled so good, and the warmth of her

body and the scent of her cologne, coupled with the promise contact had to offer, was making him crazy.

He sighed and the night sounds around them were barely noticeable. Against her mouth, he said, "I've monopolized enough of your time for one day. Why don't we call it a night?"

Kiana dared not moved her lips at that moment because she would have kissed him if she had. So she sighed and took a step away from him, instantly chagrined by her wanton behavior.

The whole while they'd been together today she'd been rebuffing his advances, stating how her heart was still recovering from a relationship gone bad. Now look at her. About to lay one on him that he wouldn't soon forget. About to place her soft body against his hard form and exult in the sheer sensuality of it.

Her stomach muscles contracted painfully at the thought.

"Of course! It's after seven and you've had a long trip. You've still got to check in at Moore's Inn."

She knew her voice sounded overly cheerful, but she couldn't help it. She bent and closed the lid of the toolbox and locked it. Then she gripped it by its handle and easily lifted it. Turning toward the Wagoneer, she tossed over her shoulder, "You can follow me back to town."

Gabriel closed the hood and held a regretful sigh until he saw Kiana climbing behind the wheel of the Wagoneer. Then he got in the Expedition and started it.

What had he been thinking anyway? For God's sake, hadn't he always avoided emotional entanglements? What was wrong with him? He attributed his uncommon behavior to losing Kevin. Now that Kevin was gone, he was afraid he'd be alone in the world for the rest of his life. Was he attaching too much credence to this physical magnetism Kiana Everett seemed to hold over him? Was he subconsciously *willing* himself to fall in love with her because she seemed to represent all he'd ever hoped for in a woman? That had to be it.

As he followed the red taillights of Kiana's car onto Highway 441, he wondered how he'd be able to survive an entire month looking at her face, coveting her body, melting whenever he heard her speak? He wished there was some kind of pheromone repellent on the market. One spray and he'd be immune to Kiana Everett's charms.

It was Kiana's idea to stop by Moore's Inn on their way back into town. Then, Gabriel could go back to her parents' home with her and pick up Courtney and Max. After that, they'd go to her place down the street and later that evening, when Courtney was snug in bed, Gabriel and Max could head to the inn for the night.

So they were both surprised when after Gabriel signed in and gave his credit card to Mrs. Edna Moore, a middle-aged black woman with salt-and-pepper hair worn in a bun and glasses suspended on a chain around her neck, she began to explain the rules of the establishment. "No pets allowed."

"But I have a dog," Gabriel began.

Mrs. Moore gave Kiana a disapproving look. "You didn't tell me that when you came to reserve Mr. Merrick a room."

Kiana smiled apologetically. "I didn't think to tell you, Mrs. Moore." She smiled hopefully. "He's a very *nice* dog . . ."

"I'm sorry, but no pets," Mrs. Moore reiterated sternly. "I like you, Kiana. Your parents have been friends of mine for nearly forty years, but I can't bend the rules. The Board of Health would close me down. This inn is our only livelihood. You know ever since Matthew suffered the stroke, he hasn't been able to work any place else."

Kiana knew Matthew Moore's case history like the back of her hand. She gave him physical therapy every Thursday evening at the Health Center.

She and Gabriel looked at one another, trying to figure out what to do next.

She pulled him aside. "Max can stay with me. I have a fenced backyard."

"Are you sure?" Gabriel said skeptically. "He can whine like a baby if he gets afraid at night. And being in a strange place, he might keep you up all night."

"The only other solution is for you to stay at my house," Kiana said half-jokingly.

After what had almost happened between them a few minutes before, Gabriel knew that wasn't a logical option.

"All right," he said to her first idea. "Max can stay with you."

"Good. Courtney would love having him there. I'll tell her he's her baby. She can groom him and play with him."

"And I'll come over and take him for walks every day," Gabriel said.

They returned to the front desk where Mrs. Moore had been patiently waiting. "I'll take the room," Gabriel said with a warm smile.

Mrs. Moore looked relieved. They could use the patronage.

" 'Once upon a time, in an African land strange and wonderful and long forgotten by modern man, there lived a young woman who loved butterflies . . .' "

"Her name was Lirah!" Courtney exclaimed. She

placed a tiny hand atop the book her uncle, who was sitting on the edge of her bed, held in his hands. Her brown eyes danced as she related, "Lirah loved Prince Deocles. But she was poor and he was rich. Read, Uncle Gabe!"

Chuckling, Gabriel continued, " *'Her name was Lirah, and she lived in a small village where her parents worked as tailors.'* "

"Do you know what a tailor does, Uncle Gabe?"

"They make clothes," Gabriel answered, loving this child whose mind was so sharp and inquisitive.

"Yes!" Courtney said excitedly. Sitting up in bed, she pointed at the colorful picture of a golden carriage. "Read how Lirah and Deocles met. It was a beautiful spring day . . ."

Yawning, Courtney lay back down.

" *'One fine spring day, there came riding through the village the young Prince Deocles. Prince Deocles was unhappy with his lot in life. He could attend only so many feasts, woo only so many princesses without becoming bored out his royal skull. So for a change of pace, he instructed his coachman to ride through the village and the adjoining countryside. After leaving the village they came upon a field of wildflowers and in the middle of the field was a beautiful maiden chasing a lone butterfly.'* "

Gabriel paused to peer down into his niece's slumbering face. He'd never seen her sleeping before. How innocent and peaceful she looked, as if nothing untoward could ever touch her. And yet the reason he was here was because she'd undergone the most brutal brush with life's unfairness a child could have visited upon her, that of losing both parents at once.

Quietly closing the book and rising, he walked over to her bookshelf by the window and put the book back in its spot, then went back over to the bed and stood watching her sleep for a moment. Would he be a worthy guardian for this child? When she cried out in the middle of the night, missing her parents, would he be able to comfort her?

"How did it go?" Kiana asked from the doorway.

Gabriel turned toward her, a look of alarm on his face.

Kiana smiled. "Oh, you can speak normally. When she's out, she's out."

Gabriel strode out of the bedroom, pulling the door closed after him, leaving a crack in it.

"She decided last night that she could sleep in her own bed again," Kiana told him as they slowly walked down the hallway to the kitchen. Max was bedded down on the back porch. Gabriel had brought Max's bed in from the Expedition and Kiana had placed an old blanket in it to provide extra warmth. It had been getting down in the forties at night. "She told me that she'd dreamed of Dee and in the dream Dee told her there was no reason to be afraid of anything, and that she and her daddy were watching over her and whenever she felt afraid, to remember that."

In the kitchen, Kiana smiled up at him. "What do you make of that?"

Gabriel was having trouble concentrating because after arriving at the house earlier, Kiana had gone to her room and emerged several minutes later with her hair out of the ponytail and dressed in a short dress that cinched her waist and fell three inches above her well-shaped knees. He'd thought she was delectable in jeans. But her legs—long, fairly muscular but not too muscular, unmarred golden-brown skin— were every leg man's fantasy come true.

"The dream you mean."

"Of course I mean the dream."

Her luscious lips parted, revealing short, straight, white teeth as she continued to gaze up at him, expecting a lucid, intelligent reply from an educated man who taught English to college students and wrote papers on linguistics for major literary magazines. And all he could come up with was, "It's her way of compensating for the loss."

"Yes!" Kiana agreed, smiling broadly now. "She's mending." She walked over to the stove and lit the fire under the kettle, which she'd earlier filled with tap water. "How about a cup of coffee? All I have is instant, but it's pretty good." She gave him a sympathetic grimace. "Unless you'd like to go on to the inn. You must be tired . . ."

"No!" he said too quickly.

He shoved his right hand into his pocket. A nervous habit. He removed it and ran it through his dreadlocks. "I'm too keyed up to sleep anyway." He casually went to the breakfast nook and sat on one of the stools while Kiana went to the cabinet above the stove to get the jar of Maxwell House instant coffee. He watched as the hem of her skirt raised an extra three inches and he caught a tantalizing glimpse of soft inner thigh.

"Tell me about Baylor College," Kiana said as she put heaping teaspoonfuls of coffee crystals into mugs.

"It began as a small, black technical school back in the thirties. You remember Booker T. Washington and his teachings about blacks needing to learn how to be of service to whites in order to get along in society? You know, how to be Pullman porters, maids, farmers. Baylor started out on that premise. But in 1945, after the war, a new president took over and decided it was time blacks started training for jobs that would help them *compete* with whites for jobs. It became a liberal arts college. Soon after that a college of dentistry was added, and a college of medicine. Today Baylor has students from all over the world getting degrees in English, computer science, law, medicine, and more! It's still a small college. But it can compete with any Ivy League school in the state of Connecticut, including Yale."

Delighted, Kiana smiled at him as she set a steaming cup of coffee in front of him and slid onto the stool next to him. "You have a note of pride in your voice when you talk about Baylor." She shyly met his eyes. "A man *should* be proud of what he commits himself to."

A man should be proud of what he commits himself to. The words played over and over in Gabriel's mind. As he sat watching her sip her coffee, he thought he'd be proud of *her*. He'd be proud to introduce her to Daniel and Deborah. He'd be proud to have her on his arm at one of those boring faculty functions. In fact, he might just stay awake through one if she were there with him.

"Stop. I'm blushing," he joked, admiring the way her long, thick lashes lay on her cheeks a fraction of a second whenever she blinked. He inwardly chided himself for noting such unimportant things about her when he should be committing to memory the sound of her laughter and the unconscious nervous habit she had of shaking her legs when they were crossed, as they were now.

His eyes drifted downward and Kiana caught herself in mid-shake.

She gave him an apologetic grin. "You make me nervous," she said of her fidgeting.

To halt the shaking, she modestly sat with her legs together.

"Why do I make you nervous?"

"Because I almost forgot myself and kissed you today," she replied, looking him in the eyes again.

Gabriel's eyebrows shot up in surprise. "I don't believe you have that right. *I* was the one who nipped that kiss in the bud, not you. *You* didn't do a thing except agree with me that it was best to leave before we did something foolish."

Kiana stood, her chin defiantly thrust out. Her dark eyes flashed when she begged to differ, "Wrong! I was the one who pulled away from *you!*"

Gabriel rose and looked down into her upturned face. "May I demonstrate?"

"Please do," Kiana haughtily replied.

He bent his head as if to kiss her and just as their lips touched, he said, "This is torture, Ana."

It was the first time he'd called her Ana in hours. He'd not had the opportunity. Not when they were around her parents or Courtney, not when they were headed back out to Highway 441 to repair the radiator hose. The setting hadn't been intimate enough.

Kiana softly moaned deep in her throat. "You're right," she whispered against his mouth. "You *were* the one to end it, because I want you to kiss me, Gabriel."

And with that, their mouths met in consensual bliss. Tasting, teasing. Made even sweeter because both of them had been anticipating it ever since they laid eyes on one another.

Kiana had never done anything so reckless. She was a woman who measured her actions against probable outcomes. She always looked before leaping. Well, now she was jumping in headfirst! Giving heed only to the voices in her head that said, *Touch him, hold him, feel his body against yours. It's all right. Let yourself go.* Gabriel knew he was lost when her lips parted and their tongues met. It jolted him down to his toes. It was as if he'd been given an electric shock, only the pain was tempered by pleasure of such a magnitude that he was crying out for more. Hit me again!

And she gave him more. Answering his need with her own.

When they parted to gaze into one another's eyes,

in hers he saw the confusion he'd caused, and it wounded him because he was clear-headed and sure of himself. He wanted her.

"I'm sorry," she said, a sob in her voice.

He offered her comfort. "There's nothing to be sorry about. It was just a kiss. Nothing to feel guilty about."

He knew to what she was alluding. How could she kiss another man, a stranger, like she'd kissed him, when she'd just ended a three-year union with Carter Henderson? What did her actions say about her as a person? That she was easy? Desperate? Or both?

Women imposed tougher moral standards on themselves than many men did. A kiss wouldn't make the average male regretful.

He felt bad for having not been strong enough to resist her.

"Listen," he said in a low voice. "You're not a loose woman simply because you sought comfort in my arms. We're both hurting now. Sometimes grief makes you behave irrationally."

That explanation seemed to make sense to her. She sniffed and sighed and her swollen lips looked so enticing to him, he was tempted to kiss her again.

But he didn't. Smiling, he said, "I'm going now. The kiss'll be our little secret."

In silence, they walked to the front door, where Gabriel looked into her eyes for a long while before reaching for the doorknob and pulling the door open. With one final glance at her, he left.

Something's Got A Hold On Me

Gabriel's goal was to fit into Kiana's and Courtney's everyday routine without disrupting it too much. So in the mornings, Kiana continued to drop Courtney off at St. John. However at around ten o'clock Gabriel would come by the church, pick up Courtney and take her on outings. Sometimes they would walk around the small town and Courtney, with her limited child's knowledge, would point out interesting landmarks or, as was usually the case, interesting people.

The Friday of his third week in Damascus, Gabriel and Courtney were downtown when lunchtime rolled around. They'd brought Max with them on their walk and Gabriel tied Max's leash to a limb of a young dogwood tree growing a few yards from Percy's Diner.

A bell jingled over the door when Gabriel pushed it open. Courtney preceded him into the homey place of business and, immediately, several folks called hello to them. The air was redolent with the smells of burgers cooking on the grill and freshly sliced onions.

Gabriel's stomach growled. He'd skipped breakfast.

They found a booth near the front and sat down.

Courtney liked the feel of the cushioned seat and the fact that her jeans-clad bottom easily slid on the surface of it. She tested it a couple of times, grinning when she nearly slid right off it onto the floor.

Remembering what a thrill it used to be to go to a restaurant with his parents when he was a kid, Gabriel smiled at her antics, but admonished her to be careful.

Gabriel picked up the colorful menu. "Mmm, let's see. What can we order for a little girl who has ants in her pants?"

"I don't have ants in my pants, Uncle Gabe," Courtney said, giggling. "You're silly!"

"Little girls who can't sit still most certainly do have ants in their pants. It's the ants that make them wiggle so much. Didn't you know ants like to dance?"

"That rhymes!" Courtney quickly noted with a gape-toothed grin.

Then something caught her attention directly ahead of her and she sat staring straight ahead. Gabriel followed her line of sight and spotted a couple exchanging fervent kisses in a booth in the back.

"Uncle Gabe, are they married?"

Oh, no, Gabriel thought. *Are we going to have the first facts of life talk at the age of four and a half?*

In a low voice he explained, "A man and a woman don't have to be married to kiss one another. Couples kiss when they're in love, or when they're getting to know one another. But, yes, kissing does sometimes lead to marriage." He thought he'd done well. Nothing too detailed. Just the facts. Short and sweet.

Courtney leveled her big brown eyes on him and said, "Well, are you and Auntie Kiki going to get married?"

If it were possible, Gabriel would have gone pale. What could've possessed her to ask that question? Had she noticed the way he and Ana looked at each other? Because since the first night of his visit he and Ana hadn't spent much time alone together. He'd wanted to, but she was a hard woman to pin down. When she wasn't working, she was at the Health Center. A new physician from Shands had agreed to take over where Kevin had left off. She (thank God the new doctor was female) had started work a bit over a week ago. Ana was doing everything within her power to make the doctor's transition as smooth as possible. So she was at the Health Center early to make certain everything was organized and the doctor would find no confusion and be able to do her job quickly and efficiently.

He saw Ana mostly in the evenings when he came by the house to read Courtney a bedtime story. She'd given him a key so he could check up on Max in the daytime. Saturdays she found some excuse not to go with him and Courtney on their shopping excursions. The most often used one was, "You came here to spend time with Coco, not me. Besides, I've got plenty to do around the house on Saturdays since I'm so busy during the week." Truer words were never spoken.

"Uncle Gabe?"

Gabriel grinned. "Guess I zoned out, baby girl." Then he remembered her question. "Why would you ask if your Aunt Kiki and I are going to get married?"

Courtney raised her brows as if her reason should be obvious to him. She explained nonetheless. "Because I saw you and Auntie Kiki kissing."

Gabriel needed a moment of silence to digest this bit of news. Courtney had apparently awakened and gone to the kitchen, perhaps for a drink of water, come to the doorway, seen him and Ana in a passionate clinch and decided not to make her presence known.

He wondered if Ana was aware Courtney had witnessed the kiss. Probably not. She would have more than likely mentioned it to him by now. The question was, who else had Courtney spoken with about what she'd seen? The scene might have been so disturbing to her that she could have needed to hear a reasonable explanation for the cause of it from a trusted adult.

"Sometimes when two adults . . ." he searched for the right words, ". . . *like* each other a lot, they express their feelings with a kiss, Coco. Your aunt and I haven't talked about getting married. We're friends."

"Grandma . . ."

Oh, God, Evelyn Everett knows!

"Grandma," Courtney said again, "says that it's all right for you to kiss Auntie Kiki because even though you're my uncle and she's my aunt, you and Auntie Kiki are not really kinfolk."

She *had* been confused about what she'd seen. Gabriel could kick himself. He'd behaved irresponsibly. He and Ana had to have a talk. *Tonight.*

Luckily the waitress, a petite blonde in her early thirties, appeared beside their booth with a pad poised in her hand, ready to take their order. She looked down at Courtney and beamed. "Hey, don't I know you, you little charmer?"

Courtney's head bobbed up and down in the affirmative. "I play with Jamie at the Health Center."

"That's right!" the waitress exclaimed. She turned dark gray eyes on Gabriel and offered him her hand. "Hi, I'm Doreen Wilkins. Are you her father?"

Smiling, Gabriel shook her hand. "No, I'm her uncle."

"Well, you've got a sweetheart of a niece. My son Jamie loves to play Chutes and Ladders with her every Tuesday night at the Health Center. I leave him in the playroom while I have dialysis. Bad kidneys. But the dialysis has helped. And Nurse Everett has such a gentle touch and warm bedside manner that I almost don't mind the time I have to spend on that machine."

Gabriel hoped the surprise didn't show on his face. Doreen Wilkins looked like the picture of health. Not like a woman fighting for her life. The only telltale sign of her illness was that the whites of her eyes weren't as bright as they should be. But that could be from lack of sleep.

"I'm sorry you have to go through that," he said sympathetically. Doreen laughed shortly and said, "Those are the breaks!" She clicked her pen, preparing to write. Looking down at Courtney she asked, "What can I bring you, sweetie pie?"

"May I have a cheeseburger with ketchup?"

Kiana turned the volume up on the cassette player. Van Morrison's soulful voice helped her come down from a very stressful day. They'd nearly lost a patient. Mrs. O'Halloran had a history of gastrointestinal bleeding. But they'd never seen it as bad as it was today. The poor woman had passed huge blood clots from the rectum. Kiana seriously feared they'd lose her but, by some miracle, the bleeding stopped and her condition stabilized. Kiana knew it had been a combination of medical expertise and God's grace that had saved the woman. She could tell by the expressions on her colleagues' faces that they held out little hope of survival. Kiana had been praying so hard throughout the entire ordeal that the severity of the situation didn't hit her until she was clocking out to go home. While in the midst of it, she'd felt as if she were operating on automatic pilot. Years of training made her perform her duties competently and without emotion. Emotion got in the way when you had to maintain a clear head in an emergency. You simply had to act without hesitation.

She rolled down the driver's side window as Van Morrison began *Into The Mystic.* The early November air had a touch of frost in it. Next week, Damascus Springs High School would celebrate their homecoming. The entire Everett family would be in the stands with just about the whole of Damascus cheering the kids on. Last year they'd had to bring blankets and thermoses of coffee, it had been so cold. She used to get a thrill out of watching Carter shouting directions from the sidelines. This year she'd go simply to support the team.

Since their breakup, Carter had tried to get her to talk to him, but she erased his messages on her machine before listening to them and deleted all e-mails with his address attached.

Since he knew her schedule, last night he'd shown up at the Health Center. She'd been putting Mr. Moore through his paces in the therapy room when Carter had, as confidently as you please, sauntered into the room. "Authorized Personnel Only" the sign on the door read.

Mr. Moore was using the treadmill. Kiana glanced down at her watch. Mr. Moore had five minutes left to go on the treadmill. Carter had to be gone by then.

He'd come by right after leaving football practice. He had on the Damascus Springs Fighting Rams team jacket, a purple fleece garment with a picture of a ram boldly emblazoned on the back. The rest of his attire consisted of gray sweats and black athletic shoes. Even under loose fitting athletic gear, Kiana could see the muscles of his fit body straining against the fabric.

"Hello, Mr. Moore," Carter spoke to the elderly man. Carter had grown up in Damascus, too, and he knew everyone she knew, which made it even tougher to have any kind of private life at all.

Kiana had folks walking up to her pleading Carter's

case. "He loves you, Kiana. Won't you at least talk it over with him?" That from Mr. Moore not fifteen minutes before Carter's appearance.

For once, Kiana despaired of living in a small town.

Going up to him and grabbing him by the sleeve of his jacket, Kiana jerked him toward the door. "You're not welcome here, Carter."

"I'll go if you promise to meet me somewhere so we can talk like two rational adults," was Carter's stipulation. His feet were rooted to the spot and Kiana wasn't strong enough to move him.

Letting go of his jacket, Kiana said, "It's over. So leave me alone before I'm forced to call Kerry in on the case. And you don't want Kerry hassling you."

Carter laughed shortly. "If you were going to sic Kerry on me, you would've already done it." He leaned in, peering into her eyes. "I'm sorry, Kiki. Please give me . . . us . . . another chance."

"No!"

"You're becoming as hard as your sister," he groused.

"Thanks for the compliment. Now get out!"

He wouldn't leave until she walked across the room, picked up the phone and dialed the number straight through to the sheriff's office. Then he walked through the door with the idle threat, "I'm going. But I'll be back."

"Yeah, and I'll keep throwing you out until you learn to stay away from me!"

Now she reached over and rewound the cassette. She liked side one best. *And It Stoned Me* came on and she sang along. After that, she harmonized on *Moondance* with Van Morrison. In a perfect world, she and Van Morrison would be as popular a duo as Ashford and Simpson.

By the time she pulled into her driveway she was feeling pretty mellow, that is until she saw the familiar late-model Ford Expedition parked on the street in front of her bungalow.

In the house, Gabriel was putting the finishing touches on a romantic dinner for two. He'd driven to Gainesville after dropping Courtney back off at St. John and gone to the restaurant Evelyn had recommended. They catered full-course meals. Plus they offered a delicious selection of desserts. What's more, customers didn't have to order the food days in advance.

He walked from the dining room to the living room to greet Ana, hoping all the while that his turning up in her house without permission would be welcome. Courtney was spending the night with Evelyn and Buddy. It had been Evelyn's suggestion, but he hadn't turned her down. He and Ana needed their privacy. He had things to say to her that were not fit for small ears.

The door was unlocked so Kiana slipped her keys back into her purse and pushed the door open. Music was playing on the stereo; Keb' Mo', his new CD. She looked around. Her living room was just as she'd left it, neatly picked up. But there was a vase of red roses on the cherrywood sofa table. She paused next to them, pulled one from the two dozen in the vase, brought it to her nose and sniffed appreciatively. The fragrant, velvety petals still had droplets of water on them. Oh, God. It had been years since a man had given her flowers. Carter thought the practice was a frivolous expense since the flowers died a few days later anyway.

"I'm glad you like them," Gabriel said.

He had been standing in the doorway watching her as she shyly approached the flowers and chose one. He walked up to her and seductively ran a finger along her arm. Kiana slowly raised her eyes to his and the next thing she knew, Gabriel had swooped in for a kiss that made her insides quiver.

He was smiling when he raised his head and peered into her astonished eyes. "There's no longer any reason to pretend we don't want to do that, Ana."

Still a bit dazed from the kiss, Kiana asked, "What do you mean?"

"Courtney saw us that night in your kitchen."

Kiana suddenly didn't know what to do with the rose she held in her hand. She tried to put it back in with the others but, for some reason, it wouldn't fit.

Gabriel calmly grasped her hands, took the rose from her and slid it back into the vase. "I can see that upsets you."

In a huff, Kiana shot him an irritated look and walked past him, heading in the general direction of her bedroom. See what he'd done? Coming here and causing upheavals in people's lives. In *her* life! What made him think she'd welcome the news that folks all over Damascus would be talking about her behind her back? Saying things like, "It *sure* didn't take her long to find someone to replace Carter, did it?"

"Ana, try to see the positive side of this," Gabriel pleaded with her.

Kiana turned to stare at him stonily. "What's the positive side? If you had to live in Damascus, you'd be upset, too. Believe me, people are already talking about the inordinate amount of time you spend at my house." She tapped a finger in the palm of her left hand as if she were about to give him examples of what the residents of Damascus had been saying about them. "Mr. Moore, a Carter supporter, asked exactly when you would be going back to Connecticut. And then he made the comment that northerners were always poking their noses in where they didn't belong down south. I politely told him that it really wasn't any of his business. And then, not twenty minutes later, *Mrs.* Moore, with a certain twinkle in her eyes, said you were a wonderful man and she hoped you'd stay a while."

"One for, one against," Gabriel joked. He went to her and pulled her into his arms. "Ana, don't you see? We're *made* for each other. Forget about other people. Concentrate on us!"

He gently kissed her lips.

Kiana languidly turned her head. His touch sapped the will to resist from her, but she had to fight him. His mouth rested on her cheek. He went lower and nuzzled the side of her neck. "Admit it, Ana. You want me, too. Just let me hear you say that. I've been in pain, just wanting to hear you say those words."

Kiana's breasts swelled, the tips hardening. Her female center began to throb. What was it about this man that aroused her so? Even with Carter, who was a fine specimen of manhood, her pleasure points weren't disturbed in such a riotous manner.

There they were standing in the hallway, both in jeans and soft cotton shirts. He held her firmly against him. Her soft feminine curves fit so nicely in his embrace. His tongue trailed along her neck, his breath clean and hot on her skin. She wanted to turn into him and give him her mouth. She wanted to come out of her clothes and let him take her right there on the floor of the carpeted hallway.

She found the strength to push him away. They were both breathing erratically with pent-up desire. Backing away from him, she said, her voice hoarse, "I don't understand what's going on here, Gabriel Merrick. You make me want to do things I know I shouldn't. And I don't think properly when you're near."

He took a step toward her and Kiana held her hand up in a warning gesture. "Just stay where you are. And let me finish."

Gabriel stood still. He felt unusually giddy. As if he were high on something. Something had a hold on him and he wanted to—*had* to—express how he felt. "I love you, Ana."

There, it was out. And it was just as Daniel had told him. Once love hit him, it'd be right between the eyes and he'd be a fool for it. An unapologetic fool. "I love you, and I want us to be married. Once Coco said the words today, I've been thinking of little else. I love you and it would be the perfect solution. For Coco. For me!" He was rambling now but he couldn't stop himself. "But what of you, Ana? How do *you* feel?"

Kiana's answer to that was to run into her bedroom, slam the door in his face and lock it with trembling fingers.

"You're nuts!" she shouted through the door. "You're a crazy man if you think I'd marry you just to solve a logistical problem."

Confused, Gabriel leaned his forehead against the door. "I don't understand what you mean, baby."

"Logistics. The steps one takes in order to solve a major problem. Courtney needs parents. You see asking an old maid to marry you as the perfect solution. Courtney gets a surrogate mother and you get a wife in name only. You can go on with your life safe in the knowledge that Courtney is being well taken care of when you can't be there."

"If you'd come out of there, I'd show you how I really feel about you. Old maid, indeed! You've got me salivating over you! I haven't been this turned on by a woman since I was sixteen, and you know what a teenaged boy's hormones are like!"

"Don't try to persuade me to open this door, because I'm not going to do it!" Kiana cried, sounding as if she were close to tears. "Damn you for coming here and upsetting my life. I was perfectly fine until you showed up."

"You had just broken up with a cheating fiancé," Gabriel reminded her of the cold facts. "A man you had settled for. Why you did that, I can't fathom. He never deserved you."

"Oh, you know me so well? After only three weeks? I loved him!"

"You didn't love him. You just fell into a routine. Carter was safe. Well, not too safe. But safe enough for your needs. You wanted a husband and children. You wanted to live out the small town dream. Just like your parents before you. But things don't work out the way you want them to all the time, Ana."

His "Ana" was said breathlessly. The sound of it filled Kiana with longing. She stood with her hands pressed against the door. Wishing he'd go away. But, then again, wishing she had the guts to open the door, let him in and ravish him.

"Please go, Gabriel. I can't face you now. All right," she said in conciliatory tones. "If you won't go away until I tell you how I feel, then okay. I want you, Gabriel. There, I said it. But I'm afraid. What if what we're feeling turns out to be a very strong case of lust? After you've had enough of me, you might not feel so sure about your decision to share custody of Coco. Our acting on our feelings could jeopardize that agreement," she said reasonably.

Suddenly she realized Gabriel hadn't interrupted her in quite some time. "Gabriel?"

"I'm right here," he said, from behind her.

The wind whipped the sheers about at the open window.

"You don't lock your windows. A very bad habit, young lady," he admonished as he approached her. "What kind of an example is that for our niece?"

Kiana moved around the bed, away from him, her eyes never leaving his face. "And what of her uncle?

Climbing into unsuspecting women's windows like a common thief!"

"I love you, Ana," was all he'd say.

"If you love me, you'll leave now and let me *think.*"

He slowly followed her around the bed. "And then what? You'll wind up *thinking* me right out of the picture. No, I should stay and plead my case."

He stopped walking.

Kiana paused too, leaned against one of the posts and eyed him suspiciously. She waited for him to speak next.

"Do you have faith in God, Ana?"

Kiana wondered where he was going with that line of questioning. Faith in God? Of course she believed in God. She sometimes wished she could lay in bed on Sunday morning. But more often than not she was in church.

"Yes, I have faith in God," she said in a low, wary voice.

"Well, let me tell you a story about what happened to me in Kenya. A group of us set out to scale Mt. Kirinyaga. It's the second highest mountain in Africa . . ."

"Mt. Kilimanjaro being the highest," Kiana provided with a smile.

Gabriel smiled back, glad she was relaxing a bit. "So there we were in the Great Rift Valley. All of us imagining ourselves intrepid explorers. On the second day of the ascent, I was in the process of driving a piton into the rock, creating another foothold, when we felt a rumbling. Slight at first. But there. We continued on. An hour or so later, however, there it was again, only more so. Our guide then began speaking in rapid Swahili. I translated for the others as best I could, given that I was scared out of my wits, too. Anyway, what the guide said was, " 'God has spoken. We should listen. Let us get off his mountain.' "

Kiana forgot herself and went to him and put her arms around him. "You're lucky to be alive," she said wonderingly.

Gabriel was gazing into her upturned face. "When that dormant volcano came to life, in some ways so did I. I made a promise to God, Ana. I told him that if he got me back home alive, I'd stop seeking thrills all over the world. I'd begin to see the miracles in my daily life."

He held her head against his chest, his hand in her hair. "When I got the news of Kevin's and Dionne's deaths, I forgot my promise to him. I forgot everything that had happened to me. All I could see was that, while I was in Kenya making a vow to God, *he* allowed my brother to die. I know it sounds silly, my feeling as though God had failed me personally because he didn't see fit to intervene and save Kevin and Dionne. But that's how I felt. He had betrayed my trust in him, therefore my promise became null and void. But that's not how it works, Ana. And he reminded me of that fact the moment I laid eyes on *you*. Just like, in the Bible, where it says Paul was converted on the road to Damascus. Well so was I. I met you on the road to Damascus and my life changed for the better."

Kiana kissed his chin. "Gabriel, I don't know what to say . . ."

"Who *would* know what to say to a preposterous tale like that?" Gabriel joked. "But it's all true, Ana. I love you and I'm as sure of that as I am that the sun will rise in the east tomorrow and set in the west. But I'm a patient man. I know you need time. How much time, Ana?" He eagerly searched her eyes. "Just give me a round figure. Three months? Six? Nine? A year? How much time do you need in order to be sure of what you're feeling?"

Kiana massaged his back as they pressed closer together. "I thought you were a patient man."

"Patient. But extremely horny. And I'll not make love to you until I know you love me, Ana. I'll not have you feeling guilty about that, too!"

Kiana parted her lips to say something and suddenly there was a loud boom from the living room. The house literally shook, and Kiana was reminded of Gabriel's story about the rumblings on Mt. Kirinyaga.

Frowning, Gabriel placed Kiana behind him in case the sound had been that of some homicidal maniac breaking the door down to get at them.

The sound didn't repeat itself, and a few seconds later they heard the sound of someone leaning on the doorbell, followed by a voice like a foghorn yelling, "Damascus Police Department!"

Kiana and Gabriel gave one another knowing looks, then burst out laughing.

Kiana led the way down the hall. She swung the front door open to find her five foot ten inch sister standing there in her khaki policeman's uniform, her long, thick hair in a bun underneath the long bill hat that she had turned backwards, and wearing mirrored sunglasses.

"What is the meaning of this, Kerry?" Kiana demanded. She might be smaller, but age gave her a certain amount of rank in the sisterly hierarchy.

Kerry pulled off her glasses and with barely concealed laughter said, "Mrs. Banks, you know her, she's your neighbor, telephoned the office to report she'd seen a prowler climbing through your bedroom window."

Her eyes rested on Gabriel before she continued. "I was patrolling Sycamore Street with my eyes peeled for drug dealers when I got the call. Dispatch sent it directly to me since she recognized the address as belonging to my sister." She looked Gabriel straight in the eyes. "It was *you*, wasn't it, professor?"

"Yes, it was," Gabriel replied without hesitation.

He felt Kiana's elbow in his side for that confession.

Kerry sputtered with laughter. "I guessed as much when I saw your vehicle parked outside."

"Then why did you try to break the door down?" Kiana yelled.

"Oh, that," Kerry said with a wave of her hand. "I didn't even put my shoulder to it!"

"Well, you rattled my windows. I wouldn't be surprised if one or more of them were cracked!"

Smiling, Gabriel turned away and went to the kitchen. The dinner he'd gone to such pains to have waiting for Ana was in the oven staying warm. He'd better turn the oven off before the food dried out. He knew better than to get between two Everett women when they were in the middle of a discussion.

In the living room, Kiana told Kerry, "If any of my windows are cracked, the sheriff's department is going to pay for it."

Kerry stepped closer to her and said in conspiratorial tones, "I hope I interrupted something interesting."

Kiana laughed. Shaking her head in amazement, she said, "If you don't get out of here, I'm going to throw you out. Hitting my door like that when you *knew* it was nobody but Gabriel who'd come in through my window."

"Nobody but Gabriel," Kerry mirrored her words. She gave her sister an entreating stare. "Come on, Kiki," she whined. "You know I live vicariously through you. I haven't had a man since I broke Dwight Loomis's jaw." Her tone was nostalgic.

"All right," Kiana conceded just to get rid of her. "You interrupted a very intimate moment. You'll have to survive on that tidbit for a while. Now, out!"

With the weight of her department-issued .38 police special making her belt hang low on her hips, Kerry resembled a gunslinger as she turned and walked back through the door. "I'm going. But I want a play-by-play description of the big event."

"And not a word of this to anybody!" Kiana warned as she closed the door.

She waited until she heard Kerry's heavy footfalls on the front porch, then she went to find Gabriel.

He was bent over the oven pulling aluminum containers of food from it. Kiana grabbed a pot holder made in the shape of a frog from a hook next to the stove and went to help.

They worked companionably side by side as they filled plates with the savory dishes he'd chosen.

A few minutes later they were seated across from one another in the dining room.

"This is delicious," Kiana complimented him. "Where did you get it?"

"Connager's in Gainesville. Your mother recommended them."

"Six months," Kiana said.

Gabriel had to think a moment before he recalled what his last question to her had been before Kerry had shown up acting like Barney Fife on steroids.

Looking at her mouth as she placed a small piece of chicken inside and slid the fork out between those juicy red-brown lips of hers, he replied, "Six months, huh? Whew! My water bill is going to skyrocket!"

Kiana smiled slowly. "You can always try to persuade me to change my mind."

Gabriel was looking forward to it.

Tell Everybody I Know

The town of Damascus was in the throes of football fever. Everywhere a person looked downtown, banners were waving in the wind proclaiming the inevitability of the Rams' victory Friday night over the Santa Fe High School Raiders. The Rams were ranked second in the state, the Raiders first.

The Everetts were making the occasion a family get-together.

Kiana was able to get off work early on Friday afternoon and when she, Gabriel and Courtney arrived at her parents' home, Eddie's and Jorja's pickup truck was in the yard.

She hadn't seen her big brother, who was a floor manager at a local plant that manufactured lids for aluminum drink cans, since the funeral. Eddie lived in Ft. White, which was about thirty miles from Damascus. He and Jorja had been married seven years and had two children, Deja, three, and Edward, Jr., five, called E.J.

The Amoco station was closed for the occasion. To Buddy, homecoming was a holiday. His employees were grateful they had such a big sports fan for a boss. They'd been invited to the Everett home to partake of Buddy's special barbecued ribs and Evelyn's mouth-watering sweet potato pies.

"Hello in here!" Kiana called as she walked through the front door.

Gabriel began coming out of his coat as was his practice when entering Evelyn's home. She had a large rack next to the door for her guests' coats.

"Better stay in that for the time being," Kiana cautioned him. "They're probably all in the backyard."

Gabriel laughed shortly. "It's fifty degrees out there."

Courtney had hold of her uncle's hand. She'd been sticking to him like glue recently because she knew this was his last week in Damascus. She missed him already. He reminded her so much of her daddy. Not so much the way he looked. But her daddy was in his voice and the way he smiled. He made her feel close to her daddy when he told her stories from their childhood. Nobody else could tell a "daddy" story like Uncle Gabe.

"We're back here!" Evelyn's voice rang out.

They followed the sound to the back porch where Evelyn, Buddy, Kerry, Eddie, Jorja and the kids were all either sitting on chairs or on the edge of the porch.

Eddie and Jorja rose to give Kiana and Courtney generous hugs.

Eddie was around five eleven and stocky. He had warm brown skin and black, curly hair that was already going gray at his widow's peak. Whenever anyone asked him why he had gray hair at thirty-six, he told them it came from growing up with three outrageous sisters. Eddie was the quiet one in the family. Strong, compassionate. There was nothing he wouldn't do for his friends or family.

Kiana adored him.

She reluctantly let go of him to introduce him to Gabriel.

"Eddie, this is Kevin's brother, Gabriel. Gabriel, my big brother, Eddie."

Courtney squeezed past the adults to get to her cousins.

The two men shook hands.

Eddie smiled into Gabriel's large dark eyes. "It's a pleasure to meet you, man. I'm sorry about Kevin. He was a good friend. He and I used to go fishing together."

"You don't say," Gabriel replied, rubbing his chin with the fingers of his right hand. "What's biting down here?"

"Trout, catfish. You and I ought to go down to the Suwanee River one of these mornings. How long you gonna be here?"

Gabriel paused for a second because Kiana was standing right next to him and he knew the subject was a sore point for her. She wanted him to stay longer now that they'd confessed how they felt about each other. He needed to get back to Baylor for the winter quarter, he explained. Secretly he hoped she'd miss him terribly and get on a plane to join him. "A few days longer," he answered.

Kiana smiled to herself and turned to Jorja.

She and Jorja were close in age. Jorja hailed from Louisville, Kentucky. She'd met Eddie while on spring break from the University of Kentucky, where she was majoring in education. They corresponded for two years before she moved to Florida, where the relationship heated up and Eddie proposed marriage. She taught high school level science.

Jorga wrinkled her nose at her husband and Gabriel as the two men stepped to the side, discussing the intrinsic superiority of a cane pole when angling for catfish.

"So that's Gabriel Merrick," she said to Kiana. "Kerry has been filling me in."

Kiana's brows knitted together in a frown. "What did she say?"

"She said she nearly ran him in for climbing through your bedroom window," Jorja answered in a low voice. She knew never to let Buddy overhear anything about his daughters' relationships with the male sex. He was fiercely protective of his daughters and liked to believe they were all virginal. If he heard about Gabriel's impulsive act, he'd probably insist upon a shotgun wedding. Either that or Gabriel would wind up with buckshot in his posterior.

"Well, let me give you the lowdown," Kiana said in equally low tones. "Nothing happened. I just let Kerry think something had because she was looking for some juicy gossip. And I gave it to her."

Jorga turned her dark brown eyes on Gabriel. "He's *fine.*"

"That he is," Kiana agreed, feeling proprietary.

"I like those dreadlocks." She returned her attention to her sister-in-law. "So, what really *is* going on between you two? I could feel the tension in the air."

"That's just it, a lot of tension."

"You mean you haven't . . ."

"No, I just said we hadn't."

"Yeah, but I thought you just meant *that* time. You know, when Kerry showed up."

"Don't you think it's a bit reckless to consider that step so soon after breaking up with Carter?"

"Carter again!" Jorja said, tossing a flyaway lock of burnished copper hair out of her eyes. She pursed her lips. "I love you, Kiki, so I never spoke ill of Carter while you were with him, but now that you're not, I see no reason not to tell you I'd heard rumors about him from several of my girlfriends. He made the rounds, girl. And all of his stops weren't done *before* you, if you know what I mean." She gave Kiana a serious look. "Do you think some men are genetically predisposed to cheating? Do you think Carter just couldn't *help* himself?"

Kiana guffawed.

Kerry chose that time to walk up to them. She rubbed cheeks with Kiana. "Hey, sis."

Kiana met her eyes. "Jorja just posed the question: Are some men genetically predisposed to cheating? What do you think?"

Kiana didn't mention that Kerry had blabbed about something she'd specifically asked her not to. When she'd issued the warning, she'd known Kerry would talk at the first opportunity. Her sister was an inveterate gossip. But, she *did* limit it to family members. She never put their business in the streets. Kiana could respect that.

Kerry only had one thing to say on the subject of men cheating. "If some men were born to cheat then some women were born to cut it off!"

"Amen!" Evelyn said, coming in on the tail end of the conversation.

She and Kiana hugged briefly.

"Hey, baby," Evelyn said. She gazed in Gabriel's direction. He, Eddie and Buddy were engaged in a lively debate about the Rams' chances of defeating the Raiders. "So, Sunday's the day." She regarded Kiana. "I'd say his visit was a huge success, wouldn't you? Coco gets to live here among us most of the year and then go to him during the summer months. And he'll fly down on special occasions, I suppose?"

"He said he would," Kiana said, not as forthcoming as her mother no doubt wished she'd be. She knew what her mother was fishing for. Evelyn wanted to know if she and Gabriel were romantically involved. Well, she wasn't telling any of them anything until she and Gabriel made a real commitment. She'd learned her lesson with Carter. She wasn't making any announcements until she had the actual ring on her finger and the chapel booked! Let them all wonder.

"Then I'm sure he will," Evelyn said, letting it drop.

Curiosity was eating her up, but she didn't want to push Kiana. She still felt a bit guilty for forcing Kiana to face up to the reality of her doomed relationship with Carter that day a month ago in her kitchen. With Gabriel right there!

Besides, Kiana didn't have to *tell* her how she felt about Gabriel Merrick. Evelyn had but to look at Kiana while she was looking at Gabriel. That told her everything she needed to know. Kiana could eat that man alive.

The doorbell rang.

Evelyn turned away, "That's probably George Freeny and the gang from the station. Your daddy invited them. You girls can start bringing the food out to the table." That's all she had to say. Kiana, Kerry and Jorja were all schooled in what needed to be done at family gatherings when a passel of folks needed to be fed.

Soon, the back porch's boards were creaking under the weight of nearly thirty people as they devoured the ribs, potato salad, garden salad, baked beans and slices of sweet potato pie.

After Kiana had made certain everyone's plates were filled to overflowing, she went and slid next to Gabriel on the bench of one of the wooden tables. Courtney was sitting at the table next to them, the children's table. A couple of the station's employees had brought their children. So now the number totaled six, where there had been only three with Courtney and her cousins.

The excited voices of the guests were so loud, Gabriel had to bend close to Kiana's ear. "Is homecoming always celebrated in this fashion?"

Kiana's wavy hair fell across her breasts as she leaned toward him. It smelled of jasmine and fresh

air and Gabriel had an impulse to bury his nose in
it. She flashed her lashes at him. "You haven't seen
anything yet."

The stadium was crowded. The stands on the visi-
tors' side were as packed as the ones on the home
team's side. The temperature hovered in the thirties
and the wind was cutting. But no one seemed to mind
because their boys were on the field fighting for the
honor of their respective schools.

First the Santa Fe High School marching band took
the field, moving across it with perfect precision. The
majorettes flanked the tall, lean drum major, a black
kid with moves Michael Jackson would have been en-
vious of. They played a lively rendition of *Boogie
Nights,* then the announcer stepped up to the microphone. "Good evening ladies and gentlemen. May I
present the 1999 varsity football team of Santa Fe
High School, the Raiders!"

The crowd went wild. The team ran onto the field
with the team captain leading the way and jumping
through a paper hoop with the Raiders' emblem
painted on it. They were followed by the team's athletic, energetic supporters, the cheerleaders, all of
them glowing with pride. Several of them did spontaneous somersaults, their short, striped red and white
skirts coming up to reveal red pants underneath.

After the visiting team and their cheerleaders ran
to the sidelines, the Damascus Springs High School
marching band took the field. Never had the purple
and gold looked so wonderful. Their uniforms fit
beautifully, the spats on their shoes sparkled white!
Their knees came up high and came down with a
snap. The brass horns shone in the stadium's bright
lights. The drum major's routine put the visiting
team's drum major's moves to shame. And the ma-

jorettes in their sequined gold and purple swimsuits and white tasseled boots didn't miss a beat as the band played *Another One Bites the Dust.*

The home crowd gave them a standing ovation. They howled and stomped their feet. The racket was deafening. So loud that they almost missed the announcer when he said with an obvious lilt of pride to his voice, "Ladies and Gentleman, it gives me great pleasure to introduce the 1999 Damascus Springs High School *mighty* Fighting Rams!"

The crowd erupted in a frenzy of thunderous applause coupled with shrill screams of fervent adoration.

The Fighting Rams ran onto the field amidst the clamorous spectacle of support, and the team captain, who was also the quarterback, broke the paper in the hoop followed by his brothers, leaving the two sides of the Rams' emblem flapping in the wind.

The cheerleaders brought up the rear, entering the field while performing difficult gymnastic feats that made the oldsters in the stands wish they were still young.

"Now please stand for the national anthem, sung by our own Mrs. Tracy Newbold."

Mrs. Newbold was Damascus Springs High's music teacher. She was also the lead soprano in the St. John choir. She belted out the patriotic song a cappella. A hush fell over the stadium, and with her voice alone, she moved many to tears.

In the area of the stands occupied by the Everetts, middle section, seven rows up, Kiana stood near Gabriel with Courtney between them. After Mrs. Newbold's performance ended, Courtney peered up at her aunt with hopeful eyes and asked, "May I go sit with Deja and E.J., auntie?"

Eddie, Jorja and the kids were sitting right down the row. Kiana stood up and allowed Courtney to get past her. She tapped Courtney on the colorful knit hat she was wearing. "Keep that hat on," she admonished. Courtney didn't like wearing hats and removed them whenever she was out of her aunt's eyesight.

"Yes, ma'am," she said resignedly.

"You know what she's doing," Gabriel said as he put his arm about Kiana's shoulder and pulled her a bit closer.

They were both wearing thick overcoats, so there was nothing remotely suggestive in his gesture, but Kiana knew her family had their antennae up, looking for any sign of what was really going on between her and Gabriel.

"What is she doing?" Kiana asked, smiling.

"Giving us time alone together."

"In a crowd of four thousand?"

Gabriel grasped her hand in his. He gently rubbed it between his. "Your hands are cold." He looked down at the blanket lying folded on her lap. "Why don't you get under that blanket with me?"

Kiana suddenly found the action on the field riveting. "Kick off!" she exclaimed.

Gabriel chuckled softly. He would let that slide. He held on to her hand though.

At one point during the game, after observing Carter Henderson on the sidelines, he whispered, "So, that's Carter."

Carter had been in his element all night, ever the ferocious leader, inciting his players to victory. Kiana had looked away whenever he looked in her direction. He knew the stands like the back of his hand, so it hadn't taken him long to spot her. "Yeah, that's Carter." Her tone was nonchalant.

"Powerfully built."

"Like a bull," she agreed. Where was he going with this?

"He could probably break my neck like a twig."

"Scared?"

"Terrified."

"I'll protect you."

At halftime, her best friend Veronica Brown showed up with her husband, Gil, in tow. "I thought I heard your mouth from up there," Veronica joked, sitting down next to Kiana on the right, forcing the woman next to Kiana to move down a little.

"Ronnie, you haven't met Gabriel Merrick," Kiana said. "Gabriel, this is Veronica Brown and her husband, Gil. Veronica's a physical education teacher."

Veronica playfully raised an arm and made a muscle. "Being bigger and tougher than they are is the only way to survive the students of today!"

Gabriel arched a brow. Looking at Gil, he said, "Give them a few more years and women will rule the world."

"I hate to disillusion you, my brother," Gil said, sitting next to Gabriel. "But they *already* rule the world."

"Are you going to the after-game bash at the school?" Veronica asked Kiana. Seeing that her husband and Gabriel were engrossed in conversation, she said in Kiana's ear, "Did you notice Carter down there 'bout to break his neck to impress you? I thought he'd pop a vein, the way he was carrying on. I have it on good authority that it's over between him and Pamela. She assumed he was all hers after you threw him over. But apparently your ghost still haunts him."

"I'm sure she'll recover and give it another try," Kiana said. She looked Veronica straight in the eye. "You look a bit flush and you've picked up a few pounds. Is there anything you'd like to tell me?" She already knew Veronica was pregnant. She'd seen her test results in the lab at the Health Center.

"We're *finally* pregnant," Veronica exclaimed happily.

Other spectators around them heard the outburst and craned their necks in order to hear the rest of the story.

Kiana hugged Veronica. "I'm happy for you, Ronnie."

Veronica and Gil had been trying to have a child for the past five years. They'd become so discouraged, they'd seriously begun to consider artificial insemination. So Veronica's pregnancy, accomplished without artificial insemination, was a minor miracle.

Her arms still around Kiana, Veronica said, "You're next, girlfriend." Veronica knew how much Kiana wanted children.

"Not without a husband," Kiana said.

"It's done quite often nowadays without the benefit of a husband. You could have a close friend donate sperm," Veronica said as she sat up straight and her gaze swept past Kiana and settled on Gabriel. "The Merrick men make beautiful babies. Look at Coco."

Kiana would never admit it, but she'd been thinking the very same thing. She and Gabriel would make beautiful babies together.

The last band to perform left the field and the teams returned.

Veronica reluctantly rose. "Gil, we'd better get back to your parents. They're going to think we've forgotten about them."

She rubbed her cheek to Kiana's. "Remember what I said, he's the perfect specimen."

Kiana merely smiled. "Take care of that bun you have in the oven. No more seven-mile jogs. You hear me?"

"Girl, I'm looking forward to vegetating for a while," Veronica assured her.

When they'd gone, Gabriel expressed sympathy for Veronica and Gil's long struggle to have a child. "I knew that some couples have problems. But I never imagined what they had to go through. All sorts of tests. Painful operations." He blew air between his lips. "I just hope I haven't waited too long to have a child." He looked down into her upturned face. "You *do* want to have children, don't you?"

Kiana nodded in the affirmative. She'd been shy about broaching the subject. It amazed her that he'd brought it up. "Yes, I want children." She laughed softly. "And believe me, you haven't waited too long. You're probably extremely fertile."

She was glad the rest of the family had gone to raid the concession stands. She and Gabriel had stayed behind to watch the others' belongings.

"I *could* have a test done," Gabriel proposed, looking into her big brown eyes. "I'd rather do it the old-fashioned way, though."

"You frighten me, Gabriel Merrick," Kiana said a bit breathlessly. "You seem so sure of us. As if you're on a speeded-up time schedule. Slow down. Enjoy the moment. There's plenty of time for babies."

But her heart was playing a staccato rhythm in her chest and her stomach felt as though she'd just drunk a cup of hot cocoa, all warm and satisfied.

When Gabriel pulled the blanket over both their heads and leaned in to kiss her, she passionately gave him her mouth.

The Rams beat the Raiders by three points, reclaiming a title they hadn't held since 1989, that of state champions.

Gabriel had to carry a sleeping Courtney to the waiting Expedition. He gave Kiana the keys so she could unlock the car and she hurriedly did so, then opened the back door and watched as he gently buckled Courtney onto the back seat.

When they were inside the car themselves, he turned to Kiana before starting the car, "You know I'd stay if I could. But I have responsibilities."

"I know," Kiana assured him.

"I'd rather be right here with you and Courtney."

Those words would resonate in Kiana's mind as the months passed.

He came again for Christmas. This time he flew, leaving Max with Daniel. Kiana met him alone at the airport in Gainesville. She didn't want any of the family witnessing the sheer relief that would cross her features when she finally saw him.

She didn't think it was possible, but he looked even better than she'd remembered. His tall, sinewy body was clothed in button-fly jeans, a thick, brown cable knit sweater and his favorite pair of Rockports. Kiana wanted to run her fingers through his dreadlocks, and did.

She didn't care that they'd become the center of attention in the small airport.

Gabriel allowed a big hand to roam from the back of her head to the nape and hold her there while he kissed her breath away.

"Has it only been a month and a half?" he asked against her mouth. "It feels like it's been much longer. God, I missed holding you." He kissed her again for good measure.

Holding her away from him so he could get a good look at her, he perused the forest green cotton knit dress that clung to her luscious curves in all the right places. "You look good, girl." And then he joked, as he so often did, "Six months, huh?"

This time, raised eyebrows or no raised eyebrows, he stayed in her guest room.

On Christmas morning he and Courtney were in the living room watching the various parades on TV. Courtney, who'd matured considerably in his absence it seemed, no longer climbed into his lap. He missed that. She sat beside him like a young lady, wielding the remote as adeptly as her grandfather did when watching his sports events on Sunday mornings.

Except for her father's eyes, she could have been a miniature clone of her mother, with the same rich, warm, dark brown skin with a reddish tint to it. Unruly black hair that her aunt tried to keep under control by putting it in small braids that fell midway down her back. But it was the uncanny knowledge that the little girl already possessed the defiant spirit passed down from one Everett woman to the next that unnerved him. When she looked him in the eyes he could see her future. She'd grow up to be a strong, confident woman. He realized he'd done the right thing when deciding to leave her in Ana's care.

Now why did he have to go and think of her when he was trying to spend quality time with Courtney? He glanced at Courtney, who'd changed the channel to WGN and a rerun of *Imitation of Life*. It was the funeral scene where Mahalia Jackson was singing with heartbreaking intensity, "Soon we'll be done with the troubles of the world . . ." One of his favorite scenes, he must have viewed it a dozen times over the years. Still, he sat with Courtney and watched it again.

Later when the hard-hearted daughter ran down the crowded street, trying to catch the wagon that carried the body of her long-suffering mother, he looked over at Courtney and saw tears in the little girl's eyes.

He pulled her into his arms.

"I would never be that mean to my mama," Courtney said against his chest. He knew then she'd seen the film before and had stopped at that station because she'd been interested in seeing a favorite scene unfold.

"Of course you wouldn't be," Gabriel consoled her.

"Grandma says an ungrateful child is sharper than

a serpent's tooth," Courtney said. Evelyn had a saying for every occasion. And Courtney could quote all of them.

She frowned as she raised her eyes to his. "What's a serpent, Uncle Gabe?"

Later that day, they drove over to Buddy and Evelyn's home for Christmas dinner. The Everett women had a tradition of making the meal a potluck affair. Evelyn baked a ham and her daughters and daughter-in-law prepared the various side dishes.

So when Kiana, Gabriel and Courtney entered the house whose air was filled with the sweet fragrance of slow-baked ham, each of them was carrying a covered dish: Kiana, baked macaroni and cheese; Gabriel, green beans cooked with onions and red peppers; Courtney, the crescent rolls.

Kerry had phoned Kiana the previous night and pleaded with her to make the rolls this year. Kerry would have normally prepared them but she was swamped at work. She always told them the crazies came out during the holidays. People drank too much and drinking led to irrational thinking, as the family well knew. This year Kerry had arrested seventeen drunk drivers from December first to December twenty-fifth, a record for the small town. Kerry was afraid crime in general was on the increase. Drug crimes had doubled in the past year. She'd bent Kiana's ear for nearly an hour the previous night before pleading with her to step in and help her out by preparing the time-consuming yeast rolls for Christmas dinner. Kiana, in a great mood due to Gabriel's presence, immediately agreed to do it.

After the family was gathered at the big table in the dining room, Evelyn asked Eddie to say the prayer. She would have preferred that Buddy, as the head of the family, do it. But her husband always refused the job. Why, he'd asked her on a number of occasions, would you want the only member of this family who never sets foot in church to petition God on its behalf? Evelyn swore that by the time the Lord called her home, her husband would be a regular churchgoer.

After the prayer, the family dug in and the chatter around the table commenced as they caught up on what had been going on in their lives since the last time they'd had a gathering.

Kiana was on Gabriel's left, Kerry on his right. Courtney sat on the other end of the table next to her cousins. Every now and then she looked over at her aunt and uncle and smiled.

The dress was semi-casual. It was the one gathering of the year that Evelyn insisted the men wear ties and the women a dress or nice pant suit.

Kiana's dress was a sleeveless royal blue sheath with a mandarin collar. Gabriel could hardly keep his eyes off her. Her hair was upswept with tendrils escaping on the sides of her exquisite face, and she had diamond stud earrings in her lobes. And her musky cologne, mixed with the heat of her body, smelled so wonderful he wanted to bend over and kiss the side of her neck.

To compound his state of arousal, she'd removed her stockinged foot from her pump and was slowly and sensuously running it up and down his leg. When he looked her in the eyes, she innocently smiled at him. "Something the matter, professor?"

She knew it got to him when she called him professor, the little tease. He swallowed hard. "Not a thing."

Buddy suddenly pushed his chair back and rose. His hand went to the knot in his tie, automatically loosening it a bit. "I'd like to say something," he announced.

The assemblage quieted down.

Buddy leveled his gaze on Kiana and Gabriel. "Now some folks in this family might think the impact of what's happened recently hasn't hit me." There were murmurings. Had Buddy imbibed too much beer? It wouldn't be the first time he'd held forth after getting a good buzz going. He was never belligerent when he was in his cups, but sometimes he could bring up embarrassing subjects. Things from years ago that other members of the family would just as soon forget.

They waited in tense anticipation.

"Our beautiful Dee and her husband, Kevin, a good man, are gone. Evelyn and I have only three children left and . . ." He had to pause because a lump had formed in his throat. "And I just wanted them to know how much we love them, and will always love them."

Kiana had tears in her eyes. She knew it had been difficult for her father to stand up and say those words. Gabriel held out his clean cloth napkin. But Kiana was already off her seat and moving swiftly around the table to throw her arms around her father and kiss her mother's proffered cheek. She was followed by Kerry and Eddie. Buddy looked embarrassed as he gruffly told them to get back in their seats, he wasn't finished.

When his children had returned to their seats, he regarded Gabriel with keen eyes. "I suppose this is as good a time as any to say welcome to the family, son."

"Thank you, sir," Gabriel said gratefully. He looked at Kiana, and none of the adults were left wondering how he really felt about her after that. "It's good to have a family again."

At Last

Springtime was Gabriel's favorite season in Connecticut. The trees were turning green again with new leaves. The mornings were cool and crisp, the afternoons generally warmer with clear skies.

He and Daniel were in their old routine. Now, though, their favorite topic of conversation was not Lourdes and Guy Ledoux. Lourdes had divorced Guy, who'd gone back to Paris to lay a trap for the next unsuspecting romantic fool (Lourdes' opinion, not theirs) from America. His literary success had been short-lived when his publisher found that many passages from his best-selling novel were "borrowed" from several other best-selling novels. They had lawsuits pending well into the year 2005.

"You know," Daniel said as they rowed toward the shore, "with Lourdes divorced, she's liable to return to familiar ground."

Gabriel chuckled. He'd broken a sweat and his lungs were beginning to burn, which meant he was getting a good workout. "Oh, are you trying to say I'm like her old, faithful dog, Shep?"

"You *did* stop avoiding her when you returned from your trip to Florida last November," Daniel reasoned. "That might have given her hope."

"When I returned from Florida, I was in love with Ana. I saw no reason to hold onto wounded feelings."

"She confided to Deborah that she'd been a fool to let you go," Daniel came out with it. He'd been dying to pass on the news the moment Deborah had told him about her phone conversation with Lourdes the previous night. "Deborah told her you're involved with Kiana, but she shrugged it off. How serious can you be about her when she lives in Florida and you live in Connecticut?"

"Serious enough to buy an engagement ring," Gabriel answered, trying to keep the smugness out of his voice. He didn't want to hurt Lourdes. She'd been through enough with Guy. But he couldn't help feeling a bit of satisfaction at the knowledge that she wanted him back. He supposed it was only human nature.

"With the faculty dinner party coming up next week, and you and Lourdes being two of the few unattached faculty members, you know who she's going to make a beeline for the moment you step into the room."

"I don't think I have to worry about that," Gabriel said. "Because I won't be alone."

Kiana bent and placed the fresh tulips in the vase on Dee's headstone. Yellow tulips had been Dee's favorite flower. She used to joke that God had created them so perfectly that they looked artificial.

Courtney squeezed her hand. Kiana knew visiting her parents' graves made Courtney uneasy. But this time Courtney had suggested they get the flowers and take them out to the cemetery in honor of her mother on Mother's Day. With her father's assistance, she always got her mother a gift on the special day. She didn't want this day to go by without her mother having a gift from her.

"We can go if you like," Kiana said.

"Are Mama and Daddy in heaven, Auntie?"

"Yes, baby," Kiana immediately answered. She was not going to get into a philosophical, religious debate with a grieving child. Some folks might not believe departing human souls went to heaven. But now wasn't the time to explain the differing views on the subject. "Yes. Heaven is a wonderful place God built especially for his children. Your grandmother has probably told you that already."

Courtney nodded in the affirmative. "She said I should remember Mama and Daddy exactly the way they were when they were alive. Because that's how they'll stay. Forever."

"That's right."

They were slowly walking toward the exit now.

"So that's how I'm going to remember them."

"Shouldn't you be out rounding up the usual suspects?" Kiana joked, placing a folded satiny nightgown in the open suitcase on her bed. Kerry had shown up while she was in the middle of packing.

Courtney had gone to her Uncle Eddie and Aunt Jorja's for the weekend. Gabriel generously sent a large check in addition to the one he sent monthly for Courtney's living expenses, with a notation on it, "This is for Coco and the kids' trip to Disney World." Kiana had told him of Eddie and Jorja's plans to take the three children to Disney World for the weekend.

Dressed in a pair of shorts and a tank top, she hurried about the large room, collecting items to put in the suitcase.

"I had a minute and I just wanted to run something by you," Kerry said of her unexpected visit. "You remember Chuck Reeves . . ."

"Yeah, you had that brief fling with him your senior year in high school."

"Uh huh," Kerry grunted as if the memory hadn't been a pleasant one. "Well, he works for the sheriff's office now."

"I already knew that, Kerry."

"Which means we'll be working closely together . . ." Kerry said, almost getting to the point.

Sighing, Kiana placed her hands on her hips and stared at Kerry. "Will you get to the point already?"

"He came on to me last night," Kerry said. "I need a little advice. Should I file sexual harassment charges against him? Should I handle the problem in my own inimitable fashion? Or should I jump his bones and get it over with?"

Kiana laughed. "Do you want to jump his bones?"

Screwing up her face, Kerry said, "I felt a sentimental tug when he kissed me."

"He's not ma—"

Kerry promptly set her sister straight. "Married? No way. If he were married, I would have punched him out if he'd tried that on me. No, I checked him out. He's single, thirty-three, a great body. And he earns a decent salary."

"Then what's the problem?" Kiana wondered. "If you liked that kiss, why are you confused about what to do next?"

"There isn't supposed to be any fraternization between members of the police department and the sheriff's department."

Kiana knew the depth of her sister's dilemma then. Kerry was a by-the-book peace officer. She had to play by the rules or not at all. "You *do* have a problem," she said sympathetically.

"I could compromise myself and have a man in my life," Kerry said thoughtfully as she paced the floor of Kiana's bedroom, her black athletic shoes leaving slight indentations in the plush carpeting. "Or I can ignore him."

THE KEYS TO MY HEART 117

She stopped walking and looked Kiana in the eyes. "It's going to have to be the second choice because if we got caught, that would be a black mark on our records. And you know I can't have that."

She smiled at Kiana. "Thanks for helping me figure that out."

Kiana walked her to the door. She didn't believe she'd done anything except listen to Kerry gripe. Kerry always found her own answers. Just as *she* came up with *her* own.

"No sneaking around for you, then?"

Kerry rolled her eyes. "And you could bounce a dime off his butt, girl." She sighed regrettably. "Ah well, you and Gabriel have fun. From what Dee used to tell me about Kevin, the Merrick men are extremely good in bed."

"And good night, for K-E-R-R-Y news," Kiana joked, referring to her sister's love of spreading gossip.

"I'm telling you, you're gonna be pleasantly surprised," Kerry said in parting.

Kiana closed and locked the door. She didn't need Kerry to tell her Gabriel would be good in bed. She knew he would be good. He had all the qualities of a seasoned lover. He was patient. He was kind. He was healthy. And, most important of all, he loved her. As much as she loved him.

He couldn't believe it. She was wearing the exact outfit she'd had on the very first day they'd met. A pair of jeans and a short-sleeved sweater set. No, the other sweater set had been green. This one was sky blue. The color made her vibrant golden-brown skin look even more alive. His heart thumped as he walked up to her in the busy terminal.

Kiana braced herself for his powerful male sensuality to hit her full force. But no amount of preparation could save her. When he was within three feet of her, she dropped the carry-on bag onto the floor, and when he was within two feet of her, she leaped into his open arms.

He lifted her off the floor. "Damn, girl. These long separations are bad on my heart."

Then his mouth claimed hers in a deep, slow, passionate kiss that left her knees weak and her body tingling. They were oblivious to the other commuters moving around them.

They parted at last. "You cut your hair," Kiana said, fingering his dreadlocks.

His dreads were six inches in length now. And the burnished brown color caught the sunlight, streaming in through the glass doors behind them.

"Didn't want them getting out of control," he joked. "Gotta maintain my conservative image."

Kiana smiled at that. The first time she'd heard him speak, she'd thought he'd sounded like an insufferable snob. But that was because he'd been putting on an act. Now his cadences were so familiar to her ear, they were like much-loved music. The kind you enjoyed listening to over and over again.

As they jogged out to the waiting car, Gabriel asked, "How is my niece? Was she very upset about not coming with you?"

"Upset?" Kiana asked. "She was so busy anticipating meeting Minnie Mouse that she could think of little else. They all told me to express their thanks for your thoughtful gift."

Gabriel handed her in, then opened the back door and placed her bags on the seat. "I just hope they have a good time."

Once in the cab, Kiana immediately felt Max's absence. She'd grown to like the friendly Lab. "I see you left Max at home."

Gabriel leaned over and planted a kiss on her lips.

"No, I left him at Daniel's for the weekend. His kids love playing with him." He gave her a blatantly suggestive look. "Besides, I wanted my girl all to myself this weekend."

Kiana shyly lowered her eyes and fastened her seat belt. She could see *he* wasn't experiencing any stage fright whatsoever. She had painful knots of tension in her stomach. And her palms felt moist. Here she was a thousand miles away from home. About to spend the weekend with the man she loved. And she was terrified! Okay, not *terrified* terrified. But nervous. Yes. Because, and she hadn't told him this yet, Carter had been the only lover she'd ever had.

Gabriel had cooked this meal. He'd planned it a week in advance. He'd grilled the lemon-pepper chicken to a tender, juicy consistency with just the right amount of spices, tossed the garden salad, and washed and stir-fried the green beans. The Pepperidge Farm sourdough bread was store-bought, but that had been his only concession.

They sat at a tiny round table on his patio. The night air was unseasonably warm, around seventy degrees. Kiana wore a white, sleeveless linen dress with a hem that fell several inches above her knees which, he was happy to note, were as sexy as ever.

He'd dressed in a casual pair of black slacks and a black polo shirt left open at the neck. He wore black, highly-polished loafers, and was sockless. Socks were so uncool when you were coming out of your clothes at that long-awaited moment. And he was already mentally undressing Ana as he watched her face, with the aid of candlelight, at that very moment.

She suddenly yawned. And he remembered it had already been dusk when he'd picked her up at the airport. Now it was dark. He wondered how long she'd been up. She could be tired.

"Want to make it an early night?" he innocently asked.

"No!" she said too quickly.

He laughed. "Ana, there's nothing to be nervous about."

He grasped her hand and pushed his chair closer to hers. "I want you to know that, for whatever reason, if you should decide you don't want to make love tonight, you don't have to. I mean I'm not going to *force* myself on you. And I certainly don't want to rush you if you still haven't decided . . ."

"It's not that," Kiana said softly. She met his gaze. "I don't have a lot of experience, Gabriel. Besides Carter, I don't have *any* experience."

"So you're nervous about pleasing me?" Gabriel asked, leaning so close to her their heads touched. He trailed a finger along her jaw line. Then he tilted her chin up so that she was looking into his eyes. "Ana, do you know where sexual satisfaction lies?"

Kiana looked down at his crotch.

Laughing softly, Gabriel shook his head in the negative. "No, little girl, it lies right here." He placed her hand over his heart. "You already have the key to my heart. That opens a host of other doors, among them the ability to entice, inflame and generally drive me insane with need. I want you so badly, I can taste it. The only true sex organ is the brain. And, baby, from the moment I saw you, I've had sex on the brain."

As she listened to his words, Kiana's breath was coming in short rasps. Her nipples hardened, pressed against the material of her bra. Her right hand had found its way to Gabriel's chest where it was now pulling frantically at his shirttail.

Gabriel, gentleman that he was, pulled the shirt

out of the waist of his slacks. No need for her to overexert herself.

They rose and Kiana lifted his shirt and began kissing his smooth, muscular bare chest. She ran her fingers over his pectorals, past the six-pack and down to his bellybutton. Her exploration ended at his belt buckle where she slowly undid it and then unbuttoned his slacks.

"I'd rather move this inside before we give the neighbors something to talk about," Gabriel said next to her ear.

He opened the patio door and allowed her to precede him. Then he paused long enough to close the blinds.

Kiana had pulled out the comb that had been holding her heavy fall of hair up, and it cascaded down her back. She stood a few feet away from him and blew him a kiss. "There's more where that came from." And she turned and ran in the direction of his bedroom.

Gabriel grinned and followed. *Now* she was talking!

His bedroom was large and airy. He'd had the furnishings handcrafted by an artist who did amazing things with pine. The bed was a sleigh bed, king size, and sat high off the floor.

When Gabriel entered the room, he was in a state of undress. His shirt was somewhere down the hall. His belt hung loose at his waist and the shoes had been left at the bedroom door.

Kiana was nowhere to be seen.

He walked farther into the dim room. "Ana?"

Silence.

Kiana appeared, framed in the bathroom doorway, dressed only in a white teddy. A very *sheer* white teddy.

Gabriel's already tumescent member hardened to an even greater extent at the sight of her.

He'd known she had a full, lush figure. But he

never imagined how wonderfully put together that figure was until now. Breasts that were just right for cupping in his hands, round and full, with the nipples pointing north. He walked closer. Her thighs were firm and uniformly golden brown. Muscular, yet feminine. Curving into a bottom that needed to have his hands molding them, right now. He couldn't stand it any longer. He went to her and kissed her full on the mouth while Kiana playfully held his hands at bay. "No fair," she said, her voice husky. "You've got to come out of those pants."

He didn't have to be asked twice. He stood before her in a pair of black briefs.

Kiana went to him then and kissed his chin. "I love you, Gabriel." She held his gaze. "I'll always love you."

Gabriel dropped to his knees and hugged her about the waist. "Thank you, God!" He rose. Looking into her eyes, he explained, "One should always thank him for his bounteous gifts."

Kiana kissed his clavicle. "Thank you, God," she whispered.

Gabriel lowered his head and found her mouth. She was soft, warm and inviting. And as hungry for him as he was for her. Lifting his head, he kissed the tops of her breasts then reached up and pulled down the straps of her teddy. The garment fell to her waist. He wondered if the skin on her flat belly was as satiny as it looked. He knelt and kissed it. Yes. His tongue tasted her there.

Kiana remembered what he'd said about bellybuttons. But that was before they knew one another. Surely he had only been kidding. No, he hadn't been kidding. He pulled the teddy all the way down and she stood before him as naked as the day she'd come into the world. He buried his face in her crotch and Kiana moaned.

"No!"

"Yes!"

He gently but insistently spread her legs and as she stood, he slowly and methodically kissed her inner thighs, his tongue inciting her to near orgasmic heights. She knew she'd be lost if he probed any farther. Any deeper.

She was lost.

She collapsed to the carpet in the aftermath of the most mind-blowing, purely sensual orgasm she'd ever experienced.

Gabriel still hadn't come out of his briefs.

Kiana lay on her back, her hair spread out, forming a halo around her head. Gabriel lay next to her. "You all right?"

"I'm . . ." She was so mellow, it was as if she were floating on a cloud. "I'm still here."

"Good, because my brain isn't done with you yet."

They were on their sides facing one another. "I never thought it could feel that good," she said wonderingly.

Gabriel kissed her and their tongues danced until Kiana felt drunk with desire. Then Gabriel sat up and turned her onto her back. Smiling, he lowered his head and took one of her nipples into his mouth and manipulated it with his tongue. After he was done with that one, he took the other and did the same thing. "You want to stop here?"

"No! Don't you dare stop," Kiana said, her hands on his briefs.

"You sure?" he teased.

"Yes, I'm sure." Her eyes were smoky with pent-up passion.

Gabriel rose and went to the nightstand next to the bed.

Kiana sat and watched his progress across the room. Sighing, she thought, *A butt you could bounce a dime off of.* He returned and handed her the condom.

She tore it open and removed the latex sheath. Gabriel doffed the briefs.

Kiana went still with awe when she saw him fully erect.

Now she was so ready for him to take her, she felt as though her next orgasm might not wait for his penetration.

But she held onto her composure as she placed the condom on him and rolled it toward his belly until it was properly in place.

Gabriel laughed. "You act as if it might bite."

"It might," Kiana joked as she lay back on the carpet.

Gabriel rained kisses on her flat belly and partook of the delight between her thighs again before sitting up, pulling her legs apart and pushing himself inside of her.

Kiana breathed in sharply and then released a slow, satisfied sigh. A sound that said she was finally where she belonged.

Gabriel had to rein in his desire to let go. He'd been anticipating this moment for so long. He was so excited that he feared he'd have a premature ejaculation. So he slowed down. But that only intensified the sensation. He felt her muscles tightening around him and he knew if she kept that up, then it would be the end of it for him. At least for a good twenty minutes. "Marry me, Ana."

He felt her body relax. That was good for him, because he no longer felt the need to come right away.

"What?"

"I said, marry me."

"Can we discuss this later?"

His thrusts were more fierce now.

He was getting into the rhythm, could enjoy her at his leisure.

"Marry me and make an honest man out of me. You've already had your way with me."

Kiana moaned deep in her throat. "Oh, God. Can you give me a minute to *think?*"

He felt her quiver. It excited him even more.

"No, Ana, I want your answer now. You know what happens when you take the time to think. You make me wait six months!"

Several more thrusts and they were both shouting.

"Okay, okay," Kiana said breathlessly. "I'll marry you."

Elated, Gabriel pushed deeper. Suppressing screams of pleasure, Kiana held onto him as their bodies developed thin layers of perspiration from the effort.

Moments later, breathing hard, Gabriel asked, "When?"

Kiana leveled an askance look on him. She was close to orgasm and frantically asked, "What?! What?!"

"When are you going to marry me?"

A deep thrust that left her quivering.

"I'll marry you *tomorrow.*"

"Yes!" Gabriel shouted as he felt his impending release.

Kiana reached her peak a second later, and wrapped her legs around him, holding him there until she came down.

Spent, they lay side by side on the carpet looking into one another's eyes. Gabriel reached out and gently took her right hand in his and brought it to his lips, kissing each finger. "My brain and I both think you're the most delectable creature ever to grace the planet, Ana. And we plan to remind you of that fact as long as we're both functioning properly."

"Is that your way of saying you enjoyed that, professor?"

Gabriel kissed her slowly. He felt himself stirring.
She *knew* what she did to him when she called him
that!

Epilogue

The wedding was held three months later at St. John A.M.E. Church with Reverend Benjamin Darton officiating. It was a simple affair. The bride had one bridesmaid and a rather tall maid of honor who insisted that her gown itched. She had the presence of mind, however, not to scratch during the ceremony. The groom's best man was his best friend from Connecticut.

Nearly five hundred people attended the wedding, some without an invitation. But that was how they did things in Damascus. And nearly that many were at the reception. It was a good thing that every church mother in town had been baking cakes and frying chicken for a day and a half prior to the festivities.

After the wedding, the couple resided in Bridgeport, Connecticut. They maintained a summer home in Damascus, Florida. Mindful of her parents' wish for Courtney to be raised in Damascus, they spent many idyllic summers there, where they watched her grow into a bright, spirited young lady.

In the second year of their marriage, Kiana gave birth to a boy. They named him Kevin.

In the fourth year, she gave birth to a girl. They named her Dionne.

For some reason, Kiana had a penchant for giving birth every two years.

A MOTHER'S LOVE

Courtni Wright

One

Jackie Peterson awoke to the sound of birds singing in the trees. The sun shone brightly and the petunias in the window boxes outside her bedroom bloomed in a mad profusion of reds, purples, and pinks. The grandfather clock in the downstairs hall chimed nine o'clock as she stretched lazily across the queen-size bed.

Listening to the sounds of silence from the empty house, Jackie began to plan her day. With her husband out of town on business and her son away at college, Jackie had the entire day to herself. She could come and go as she pleased. She would not have to cook dinner or drive anyone to the airport or a ball game. She would not have to consult anyone or take someone else's preference into consideration as she planned her activities. The day was hers to do with as she pleased.

Yet Jackie was not happy. She had the gift of leisure that most women craved, but she was feeling very blue. It was Mother's Day, and no one was home to wish her a happy day, bring her burnt toast and too strong coffee in bed, tell her about a disastrous date, or share the details of a business deal. No one would sit in the chair outside her bathroom door and talk while she showered and asked an occasional question. No one would read newspaper articles to her while providing a running commentary. She was completely alone, and Jackie could not have been more miserable.

When the clock downstairs struck ten o'clock, Jackie forced herself to get out of bed. The day would be long enough without spending it on her back thinking about the solitude she had once craved and now had in abundance and no longer desired. After her shower, she would dress and get on with her day. She would not continue to indulge in self-pity.

Rinsing the fragrant shampoo from her short, brown hair, Jackie muttered, "I'm not the only woman in the world who's spending Mother's Day alone. Besides, it's a commercially motivated day anyway. I'm above all this sentimentality. I know that my guys love me. I don't have to have them with me every minute telling me of their feelings."

Feeling self-confident and proud of being able to fend for herself, Jackie toweled off standing in front of the full-length mirror in her bedroom. It was not often that she was alone and could take the time to examine her body. At forty-eight, she still had a trim figure; having their son almost nineteen years ago had not caused too much damage. Her long, shapely, brown legs were still well-muscled from the hour each day she spent on either the treadmill or the stepper. Her arms were still firm from the weights she lifted on alternate days. Her small, almost perky breasts had been spared the damage of gravity. Her hair, although graying subtly, contained much of its former shine. In all, Jackie was aging well.

Pulling on a pair of apricot linen slacks and a matching short-sleeved blouse, Jackie gave her reflection one last look as she worked her fingers through her curls and slipped her feet into soft, brown sandals. The color was perfect with her complexion and brought out the rose in her skin. The silk hugged her hips and buttocks perfectly. Her husband had selected the outfit for her, saying that she should not hide her body from view. He thought that people who worked hard to chisel their physiques should be proud of them and show them off. Seeing her reflection, Jackie had to agree.

Satisfied with what she saw, Jackie fastened a diamond pendant on a thin gold chain around her neck and eased her watch over her newly manicured fingers. She added a gold bracelet to her right wrist and her favorite watch to her left. Before turning off the light, Jackie sprayed herself with her husband's favorite perfume. She smiled as she thought about his usual reaction every time she wore it.

The ringing of the telephone tore Jackie away from her pleasurable reflections. Rushing across the room, she picked up on the fourth ring as the recorded voice of the answering machine began to intone its message. Jackie shouted into the receiver over the sound of her husband's voice, "Wait! Don't hang up. The message will finish in a minute."

Jackie waited impatiently until the bodiless voice stopped. Then she added, "Hello? Who is it?"

"Hi, babe! Happy Mother's Day!" answered the same voice as on the recording.

"Thanks, honey, I'm glad you called," Jackie answered as she sank onto the rose-colored bedspread.

"You know I wouldn't have missed the opportunity to wish my favorite lady a happy day. I'm sorry that I couldn't be there with you, but you know how things are. What do you have planned?" Jackie's husband Bill asked. He was a pharmaceutical representative for a major firm and had to attend a briefing on the newest treatment for high blood pressure.

"Don't worry, Bill, I understand. I don't really have anything planned yet. I think I'll just go with the flow," Jackie replied, trying to hide the disappointment at not having him at home with her.

"Don't forget that you wanted to watch the documentary on perennials this evening. I think it comes on at eight o'clock," Bill reminded her as the time slipped away.

"I'll be home long before then. You know I don't like being out at night by myself. Unless I have a friend with me, I always get home before sunset. But, just in case, I'll set the VCR," Jackie assured him. They lived in a lovely suburb of Washington, DC in which the crime rate was wonderfully low. However, Jackie did not believe in pushing her luck.

"Did you get my flowers?" Bill asked, hoping that he had at least done that part correctly. Since he could not physically be with Jackie, he wanted her to know he was mentally at her side.

"Yes, and they're lovely. So is the card you sent me. The message is very sweet. I think I'll keep it so that I can remind you occasionally," Jackie said, smiling. She had already decided to stash the card in her night table in case Bill needed reminding that he considered her special.

"I'm glad you like it, but I don't need a card to remind me that you're special. The things you do every day to make our lives richer do that just fine. I just wish other husbands could have wives as wonderful as you. Well, I'd better run. The session is starting again. I sure hate being away from you. I miss our leisurely Sunday together. I love you, Jackie. I'll be home tomorrow night around seven. Will you hold dinner for me?" Bill asked as the noise in the background increased. Jackie could tell that the other conferees were already returning for the next session.

"I love you, too, Bill. We're having pepper chicken, rice, string beans, and salad. I don't mind waiting. You can tell me all about the session over dinner,"

Jackie responded. She did not want to hang up, but she knew that Bill had to return with the others.

The silence in their bedroom was even greater as the phone line went dead. Returning to her dresser, Jackie fastened a chain with the emblem of their son's college around her neck. She needed to be close to her family even if they were far away.

Walking down the stairs, Jackie marveled at the sense of peace and tranquillity that filled their home. The subtle sponged paint patterns on the walls coordinated beautifully with the tapestry in the upholstery of the living room sofa and dining room chairs. Landscapes and portrait prints continued the cheerful color scheme. Flowering plants bloomed gaily on every table and invited guests to inhale their sweet perfume. Her husband always bragged to his friends that Jackie was the best wife a man could ever have. Not only was she an equal partner in their lives, but she managed the house, tended the flowers, and cooked gourmet meals.

The house was so quiet that, for once, Jackie could hear the soft clicking of her heels on the highly polished oak floors. She and Bill had removed the carpet years ago when their son, Doug, developed a dust allergy. Now, all Jackie had to do was run a dust mop over the floors to keep the dust bunnies at bay. She loved the warm glow of the wood and wondered why she had ever spent the money for carpet.

Today, however, the lack of happy laughter, the absence of big thundering feet, and the silence made their home seem empty despite the beautiful furnishings and blooming plants. Her son did not sit at the piano composing a new song. Her husband was not in the family room watching whatever show related to sports happened to be on the television. Jackie was alone, and she did not like it one bit.

Wandering through the empty rooms, Jackie

fluffed a pillow here and picked off a spent bloom there. By the time she made her way to the kitchen, she had finished all of her little jobs. There was nothing left to do. The automatic coffee brewer had produced perfect coffee that Jackie sipped with only a small amount of sugar as she gazed out the kitchen window. She watched the sparrows playing in the birdbath, the chipmunk darting under hosta leaves, and the hummingbirds drinking nectar from the feeder for as long as she could. When she turned around, Jackie was still alone and the house was still silent. She and it were waiting for life to return.

Suddenly, the telephone rang, breaking the silence. Picking it up, Jackie heard the perky voice of her sister Dee. Dee was a successful corporate attorney who was between husbands and always on the go. She thought Jackie should put aside her red pencil, leave the classroom, and join her in the world of big business. Jackie, however, loved teaching, long winter and spring breaks, and the glory of summers to herself. She would not be able to spend long, leisurely days tending to her flowers if she joined Dee in her hectic lifestyle.

Jackie and Dee were close and growing closer. Since their mother's death, Jackie had hovered over her little sister like a mother hen. Their sisterly affection had grown with each year until they shared most holidays and important events.

"Hi, Jackie! Happy Mother's Day! What have you planned to do today? Do you want to go to the mall with me? I saw the most fabulous pair of leather slacks that I'm just dying to buy. Come with me and give your big sisterly advice on my selection," Dee cajoled brightly.

Chuckling, Jackie replied, "Heaven only knows why you'd want another pair of leather slacks. You already have black and brown ones. How many could one woman possibly need?"

"I know, but I don't have that wonderful shade of burgundy. Actually, it's almost a claret. You'll love them," Dee continued as she tried a little harder to convince her sister to accompany her. Since Jackie was not a shopper for anything except flowers, Dee knew that she had to pitch hard to win her over.

To Dee's surprise, Jackie agreed, saying, "Sure, I'll go with you. With Bill and Doug out of town, I really don't have anything else to do. I'll be there in about two hours. I have to go to Mass first."

"Well, if I weren't your sister, I'd be offended. There's nothing like being the consolation prize," Dee teased gleefully. She did not care if she won Jackie's company by default. Dee was happy to have it.

"You know what I mean. You're not going to make an issue out of this are you? If you are, I'll stay here. I'd rather be alone than picked on. Maybe I should drive myself just in case you decide to spend your entire day at the store," Jackie responded a bit angrily. Although she loved Dee, her "little" sister always seemed to know exactly what to say and do to get on her nerves. Despite their close relationship, Dee was still very much the annoying little sister.

"Only joking, Jackie! Fine, I'll meet you at the mall. I'll be the beautiful little sister standing at the center fountain!" Dee chirped as she hung up the phone. She always liked to remind Jackie of the three-year age difference. Not that it mattered to Jackie, whose skin was still smooth and tight. She had inherited her father's genes; Dee had their mother's. Long after Dee had gone under the knife for plastic surgery, Jackie would still be looking fine.

Collecting her purse, Jackie headed toward the family room and the door to the garage. Just as she turned the key, the telephone rang again. Thinking it was Dee with a change of plans, she answered, "Yes, Dee, what is it?"

"Hi, Mommy. It's me. Happy Mother's Day!" the youthful male voice replied. Even though Doug sang bass in his college choir, his speaking voice still carried the lilt of a teenager. Jackie could hear the chuckle in her son's voice at her mistake.

"Doug, I'm surprised to hear from you. I thought you'd be sailing on the bay today with your team," Jackie replied as she smiled broadly in pure delight at hearing from her nineteen-year-old son.

"Nah, I didn't go. I have too much studying to do. Exams start next week. I couldn't afford to take the time off," Doug replied with regret in his voice. He was a sophomore at one of the best colleges in the country and was a very dedicated student.

Jackie replied proudly, "You always were a sensible kid."

With a wry chuckle, Doug responded, "Yeah, well . . . Did you get the balloons I sent you?"

"Your friend Peter brought them over last night. You should see them bobbing around in the family room. When the moonlight hits them just right, they look like three little ghosts floating around the room," Jackie commented, enjoying the sound of her only child's voice. They were a very close family and the separation of college was difficult on all of them. Doug's freshman year had been especially trying.

"What are your plans for today?" Doug asked as he laughed at the image of the helium-filled silver and red balloons floating over the sofa and television.

"I'm on my way to Mass and then to the mall to meet Dee. Your aunt wants to buy a pair of leather slacks," Jackie answered as she picked a spent bloom from a nearby plant.

"Another pair?! Her closets are already bursting at the seams," Doug responded incredulously.

"That's what I said, too, but you know your aunt," Jackie laughed at her sensible son's reaction to his spendthrift aunt.

"Give her a hug from me. Well, I better get going. Enjoy your day. I'll come home immediately after my last exam next Friday," Doug said reluctantly. He enjoyed the stolen time he spent in conversation with his parents.

"Any special requests for when you come home?" Jackie asked, although she already knew the answer. In many ways, her son was very predictable.

"Yeah, tuna and macaroni salad and blueberry pie," Doug responded with enthusiasm.

"Got it!" Jackie stated. "Be good and study hard. I love you, Doug."

"I will, Mommy. You know what? You're the best mom in the whole world! I love you, too," Doug informed her, then promptly hung up before Jackie could say something mushy.

"Bye, my baby," Jackie whispered to the silence as she returned the portable phone to its cradle.

Wiping the tears from her overflowing dark brown eyes, Jackie again gathered her things. She was almost looking forward to spending the day shopping with Dee as a distraction from her loneliness. This time, the phone did not ring as she closed the door on the silent, empty house.

Two

Climbing into the family's sports utility vehicle, Jackie headed to church. Running her hand along the smooth silk of her trousers, she could remember the time when she had to wear a veil and skirt to service. Now, she went hatless and in slacks. Times had definitely changed.

The church parking lot was packed with cars. Families that Jackie had not seen since Easter and, before that, Christmas filled every pew. Squeezing into the last space in the last row, she looked through the missal. Well, at least some things remained the same. The service had not changed since she was a teenager and the ecumenical movement had swept through the religious community.

Looking at the sturdy Gothic architecture, Jackie saw that many things remained the same here, too. The building was only four years old, but the basic structure dated back many years. The light from the stained glass windows and the patina of the dark brown wood of the pews combined to give the church an atmosphere of solemnity. Incense filled the air from the last Mass, and a mixture of red and white carnations and roses overflowed on the altar beside the snow white candles.

Pinning on the red and white carnations handed to her by the usher at the door, Jackie thought about the mother and grandmother in whose memory she wore the flowers. Her grandmother had been a pillar of her church in rural Virginia, the impetus behind the building of the school building, and the owner and driver of the school's bus. Her mother had worked devotedly at church when Jackie was a child, keeping the choir robes clean and pressed. She had volunteered on Wednesdays to help with the weekly mailings until the day she died.

As the priest droned on about the Biblical mothers and the contemporary role of mothers and women, Jackie daydreamed about her family. Only a few years ago, they had sat together in the pew now occupied by a woman and her family. Doug had been young enough not to mind if people saw him resting against her shoulder during the service. She had happily sat between her two guys with one leaning his head against her and the other holding her hand.

They had walked to the communion rail together as a family, with Jackie leading the way and Bill bringing up the rear. Even in church, they had formed a protective barrier around their son. Jackie had felt the eyes of the other parishioners on them as they had guided Doug's movements in the ancient ritual. The same priest who had baptized Doug and welcomed him into the family of the church had blessed their son as he had knelt between them.

That was years ago when Doug had still been young and lived at home all the time rather than only on vacations from school. That was before Bill had been promoted to vice president of his division and had to attend conferences on new products so that he could share the information with his managers and sales force. That had been when Jackie still had them at her side for Mother's Day. Now, Jackie was alone. The other mothers with young children sat contentedly in mom sandwiches between squirming kids who would rather be outside playing than in church on this lovely day, while Jackie sat among strangers.

Jackie smiled as the memories flowed over her. She remembered one particular Mother's Day. She had dressed Doug in his little navy blue double-breasted jacket with the anchor buttons and charcoal gray slacks and had told him to sit quietly while she had finished dressing. Being an energetic boy, Doug had decided as soon as he had heard Jackie run the water in her bathroom that he had sat still long enough. He had left his bedroom with his dog, Ginger, in tow. Together, they had slipped out of the house and into the backyard.

When Jackie had finished her shower and had gone to look for Doug, he had not been in his room. Bill, who had been in the kitchen making coffee and reading the sports section of the newspaper, had not noticed their son ease out the laundry room door and into the sunshine. Bill also had not seen the dog dart behind him. However, Jackie had seen them as soon as she had looked out the window that over-looked the backyard.

As Jackie had opened the door, her eyes had popped at the sight of her formerly clean son rolling around on the ground with his dog. Jackie had only been able to shake her head as the boy and dog had cavorted on the lawn. She had called both of them into the house and had cleaned them up as much as possible. She had quickly brushed the grass from Ginger's coat and Doug's hair. With a damp cloth, Jackie had done her best to remove the dirt from Doug's jacket and trousers.

All through the church service Doug had giggled and pulled bits of grass from his pockets and socks. Jackie had looked sternly at him but with little suc-cess. However, when she had given the soft skin on the underside of his arm a little pinch, Doug had quickly turned his attention to the homily. Suddenly, the grass on his clothing had become unimportant.

Sitting alone at the back of the church, Jackie only wished that her fidgety little boy were beside her. Now that Doug was away in college, he seldom joined her in worship at their family church. He had been christened in this church. His confirmation and first Holy Communion had taken place in front of that altar. Doug had sung in the choir and served as an altar boy. Now, he only joined her in worship here on holidays. The family feel of the church had changed, and Jackie had begun to feel like an outsider.

As the Mass neared an end, Jackie watched as the family that sat in what had always been their pew exited the church. The children had been still for as long as they could and were ready to leave. The mother mouthed words of warning to her son. In the nick of time, the priest intoned the final blessing and the organist struck up the chord of the recessional. Immediately, the little boy jumped to his feet. He sang the familiar song with great gusto and grabbed his mother's hand as soon as the cross passed their pew. Dragging her into the aisle, the little family was among the first to leave the church.

Jackie smiled as she picked up her purse and followed them. She remembered times when Doug had led the charge to leave the church. Now, she gently blended into the crowd that lingered on the steps, chatting and exchanging greetings. She had no real reason to hurry. She only had to meet Dee at the mall. No one waited for her at home.

Driving to the mall, Jackie listened to the oldies but goodies station. Now that Doug no longer rode in the car with her, she was free to select from the myriad of offerings. He was not there to grumble and change the station to his choice of music. She hummed and sang along to the old favorites from

Motown greats. And she remembered a time not too long ago when she had to listen to hip-hop rather than the gentle sounds of soul.

Doug was a real music aficionado and loved every variety from rock to jazz to classical. However, while driving in the car, he loved to listen to the sounds that moved the teenage soul. He would change the station to his kind of music, and Jackie would change it back to easy listening soul. As a compromise, they often tuned in the classical station. Although they were very much alike, mother and son did not agree on everything.

Doug was a perfect blend of the two of them. His eyes, mouth, and forehead were the same as Jackie's, and his nose and ears were like Bill's. He had Jackie's slim build, but Bill's father's height. His hair was dark like Bill's and curly like Jackie's. People who saw the three of them together often said that he looked as if the Creator had deliberately selected an equal number of characteristics from each of them when He created Doug.

As Jackie turned into the traffic leading to the mall entrance, the music changed from Motown to a group of young men singing a cappella. Their voices caressed the lyrics of a song that pulled at her heart and caused tears to well in her eyes. It was the sweetness of the tribute to mothers that moved Jackie to tears, and the knowledge that Doug loved her with the strength of which the vocalists sang.

Pulling into the nearest parking space, Jackie allowed herself to experience the loneliness that she had tried bravely to suppress. It was Mother's Day and her husband and son were far away. She felt miserable and already regretted agreeing to meet her perky sister Dee. She should have pulled the covers over her head and stayed in bed.

Stop that, Jackie, she scolded herself as she dried her

eyes. *The guys couldn't help it. You're being silly and just feeling sorry for yourself. You know they would have been with you if they could. Bill had to attend the session and Doug has to study. Pull yourself together. You're not the only mother in the world whose family isn't nearby. It's not like you to become sentimental and weepy. Pull yourself together before Dee gets on your case.*

Straightening her shoulders, Jackie walked into the mall to look for Dee. She certainly did not want her little sister to know she had been crying. Dee was the antithesis of sentimentality. Nothing ever moved her. One of her former husbands had said that he had left her because she had never emoted, had never reacted to anything, and had never experienced life. Jackie knew that Dee felt everything very keenly but refused to show her feelings. Dee considered emotional outbursts to be signs of weakness and prided herself on being above the show of sentimentality.

As Jackie scanned the faces for her sister, she thought about the last time she had seen Dee cry. She had not cried at any of her dissolved marriages. In fact, Dee had been particularly relieved when the last one had ended. Scott had been an especially difficult man to live with. He had been demanding of all her time and attention and very jealous of Dee's devotion to Jackie and her family. Dee had been relieved when Scott finally agreed that the marriage should end.

Dee had not even cried at their mother's funeral. She had sat dry-eyed and stoic during the entire service and burial. She had refused to allow anyone to see her break. However, later that night when Dee was alone, she had broken down. She had called Jackie so choked up that Jackie had barely been able to understand her.

The last time Jackie remembered seeing Dee cry was when Doug had broken his leg. Dee had been so upset at the sight of her favorite and only nephew in the mechanical device that had held his shattered bones together that she had broken down and sobbed. Dee had felt responsible for the break since she had been taking care of him at the time while Jackie finished the last night of the last course for her masters degree. Dee had not been able to stop the energetic little boy from climbing up the drawers of his dresser in search of a preferred pair of pajamas. The four-drawer dresser had fallen forward under the five-year old's weight and had pinned his left leg against the pine floor. Pulling the dresser from his body, Dee had practically fainted at the sight of Doug's limp foot lying flat on the floor.

Dee had remained sufficiently calm to call the pediatrician and transport Doug to the hospital. She had held him on her lap while they waited for the doctor to examine him. She had patted his hand as the physician applied the soft cast. Dee had stood beside Jackie as they listened to the physician say he was sure Doug would require surgery to reconnect the shattered bones. She had even been Jackie's strong support and comfort as they waited with Bill during the surgery.

However, when Dee had seen the metal device, she fell apart. The sight of the pins in her nephew's leg had proved too much for her. She had cried like a baby. Jackie had found herself having to take care of two children that night in Doug's hospital room.

Smiling, Jackie marveled at the nature of the memories that surfaced unexpectedly. She could remember so many of the little things in her marriage to Bill and in her parenting of Doug. Little things that seemed so insignificant at the time were now of the utmost importance.

Watching Dee rush toward her with a shopping bag in each hand, Jackie could hardly believe that this confident, savvy woman was the same one who dissolved into tears in Doug's hospital room. So much had happened in the almost fourteen years since the accident and surgery. Doug had grown up and entered college. Dee had divorced husband number four. Their mother had died. Bill had been promoted three times. And Jackie had received her doctorate in counseling.

"Hi, Jackie!" Dee shouted happily as she crossed the distance between the last row of shops and the fountain in the middle of the mall. "You're late and I've gotten started without you. However, I waited until you came before buying those leather pants. I want you to be the first to see them."

Taking one of the heavy bags, Jackie replied, "Why? Will you change your mind and not buy them if I don't approve?"

Smiling like a little girl, Dee responded, "No, I'm still going to buy them. I just want you to be the first to see them on me!"

Chuckling at her sister's childish ways, Jackie followed Dee into the trendy shop in which the least expensive item was a pair of fifteen-dollar underpants. Dee loved designer clothing, something that Jackie never bought. Dee believed that having someone's name on her fanny made the pants better. Jackie knew that the logo on the pocket only meant that she would be paying for the company's advertising rather than assuring she would get a better product. While Dee purchased clothing by the most famous designers, Jackie spent her money on brand X, stretching her budget to include more items for Doug and Bill. Even if they had been tremendously rich rather than comfortably situated, Jackie would not have spent her money on designer items.

"Here they are!" Dee enthused as she held the

buttery-soft wine leather slacks to her body. "Aren't they wonderful? Feel that leather."

"You're right, they're wonderful, but so is the price. Fifteen hundred dollars for a pair of slacks! Dee, have you lost touch with reality?" Jackie exclaimed as she read the tag that said the pants were on sale at fifty percent off of that outrageous sum.

"Jackie, if I had a husband and kids, I wouldn't spend money like this, but I don't," Dee said, momentarily somber. "I only have myself. I give to the church and to charities. I don't see any reason why I shouldn't do this for myself. Besides, they look fabulous on me. You may borrow them if you'd like. I'll be right back. I want you to see them on me."

Laughing, Jackie settled into the Louis XIV chair and accepted the cup of cappuccino that quickly appeared on a tray carried by a very solicitous saleswoman. Flipping through a fashion magazine and sipping the perfect brew, Jackie remembered the first time she had gone shopping with Bill as he had searched for the perfect suit for their honeymoon. She had sat patiently as he tried on one suit and sport coat after the other. Bill had broad shoulders on a five foot ten inch frame. Not being especially tall, he had wanted the jacket to optimize his shoulders while adding the illusion of inches.

As Jackie waited, Bill had tried on black and charcoal suits that made him look like his father. Brown or subtle plaids either washed out his complexion, blended with it, or made him look too round through the middle. She had scanned the last magazine on the table by the time he finally found the right one. It had been golden brown with very subtle blue stripes that added the required height, slimmed his shoulders a bit, and worked beautifully with his complexion.

The first night Bill had worn the jacket, Jackie had

seen the heads of numerous women turn to look at him. He had walked proudly as he escorted his new bride into the hotel's famous restaurant. Displaying his most gallant manners, he seated her and kissed her lovingly on the forehead before sitting beside her.

All through dinner, Bill had not been able to tear his eyes from Jackie's face as he gazed lovingly at her reflection in the glow of the candlelight. He had secretly hired the strolling violinist to stop at their table and had been barely able to contain himself with the anticipation of her reaction. As the first notes of their song had floated on the air, Bill had reached across the table and enfolded Jackie's hand in his. Jackie's reaction had not been a disappointment. She had cried happily as she smiled lovingly at Bill. The evening had passed in a rosy glow of love.

Two years later, it had been Bill's turn to wait. He had paced the floor, whispered encouragement, and watched the monitor as Jackie had labored to give birth to Doug. He had panted with her, had tried to share the pain, and had gone without food until he looked faint. Jackie had insisted that he eat the scrambled eggs that had arrived for her since she did not have the stomach to face them. Bill had taken them into the hall, wolfed them down, and returned to her side. When Doug had finally been born, Bill cried happy tears as he held his son.

And Jackie had waited as her two boys had gotten their hair cut. It had been the occasion of Doug's first time in the barber's chair. Jackie talked to him gently as her father, a retired barber shop owner and master stylist, had cut Bill's hair first. Doug had watched wide-eyed and nervous as his father's curls fell onto the floor.

When it had been his turn, Jackie watched as the proud grandfather had slipped the cloth around

Doug's neck and adjusted the height of the chair. Doug had hardly moved as the scissors and comb had performed their magic and had transformed him from a baby with a mass of curls to a sophisticated little man of three.

Jackie had held the camera that had recorded every snip. She had waited for any sign of the tears that never came. She had watched as her baby had taken another step toward growing up and becoming independent. She had recorded the momentous occasion on the newly purchased video camera and in her heart.

Now, Jackie waited for her men to come home and enrich her life once again with their laughter.

"How do I look? Don't they hug my butt great!?" Dee cried as she interrupted Jackie's reverie.

"They look wonderful, Dee. I just don't know if they're fifteen hundred dollars worth of wonderful," Jackie replied as she studied the perfect fit of the magnificent leather on her sister's bottom.

"I think they're fabulous. Just what my ego needs. To make you happy, I'll try to get a little more off the price," Dee winked as she returned to the dressing room.

Shaking her head, Jackie returned to her chair. A woman and her teenage daughter stood nearby looking at prom dresses. Picking up the magazine and studying the photo of the landscaping effort around a backyard pool, Jackie remembered the first time Doug had gone for a swim. She had sat on the side watching and waiting for him to need her, but, fortunately, he never had.

Doug had taught himself to swim. He had been assigned the project of writing a book report on a sport or craft when he had been in the third grade. He had selected swimming since he had known nothing about the skill required to propel a swimmer through the water. He had read the book, had made a model from craft sticks suspended by very thin wire, and had filled an aquarium with water. In discussing the skill he had learned, Doug had pulled the stick man through the water, moving his arms in a stroking motion. His teacher and classmates had been very impressed by the knowledge he had displayed through his presentation.

Doug had not been satisfied with making a stick man swim; he had wanted to apply his knowledge personally. Begging Jackie to take him to the neighborhood pool, Doug had slowly walked into the water first to his knees and then his waist. Waving to Jackie, who had stood nervously on the deck, he dived in and had swum across the width of the pool.

Jackie had held her breath as she watched every stroke of the long, thin, eight-year-old arms. The same boy who had climbed up his dresser now swam in five feet of water without instruction after simply reading books and applying the knowledge he had gained. Cautiously, she lifted the camera to her shoulder, steadied it, and filmed the feat. She need not have bothered since it had been forever engraved in her mind.

When Doug had returned to Jackie's side, he was grinning from ear to ear. Gone was the little boy who had clung to her hands as they had played in the surf at the beach. She saw no signs of the child who had nervously peered over the walls of the Empire State Building. Pride had shown in the set of his thin shoulders as he had climbed up the steps with the water dripping from his body. He walked with a new assurance and confidence as he joined her on the deck. And Jackie fought back the tears that welled in her eyes. Her baby had taken the steps to becoming a man much too fast.

"I'm ready," Dee chirped, holding yet another bag

in her hand. "I got another ten percent off the pants. Aren't you proud of me?"

"Very," Jackie replied as she took one of the bags from her sister and followed her to the distant end of the store. She put her memories of her family away as she waited for Dee at the perfume counter.

A smiling saleswoman handed Jackie a red rose as she sniffed the sample bottles. "Happy Mother's Day," she beamed.

"Thanks," Jackie replied as she slipped the flower behind her ear.

"Why didn't she give one to me? I'm certainly old enough to be someone's mother," Dee complained as she led Jackie out of the store and into the heart of the mall.

"Yeah, you're practically old enough to be a grand-mother," Jackie teased her pouting little sister. "I guess you just don't look like a mother."

Dee complained constantly as she led the way to a nearby restaurant. She kept up a steady tirade as they studied the menu about the woman's lack of sensi-tivity in ignoring her. Whenever possible, Jackie shot her a zinger, which only added more fuel to the flames of Dee's discontent. Finally, they stopped their gentle bickering long enough to order Caesar salads and iced tea. As soon as the waiter departed, they continued their sisterly jabs.

"Humph!" Dee snorted. "Maybe that's a good thing. At least I can still wear a bikini without stomach flab hanging out."

"True, but look at what I've got in exchange for the flab and stretch marks. I don't think I made out too badly," Jackie replied softly.

Smiling, Dee conceded, "Yeah, Doug is a nice kid. You made a pretty good exchange."

The two sisters ate their meals in silence, each one absorbed with her own thoughts. Dee mused about the wonders of motherhood that she had missed while Jackie relished the memories of a child's love freely given.

Three

Jackie allowed Dee to drag her through all the interesting stores in the mall. She even entered shops that would normally have little, if any, appeal, such as the hat shop into which they stepped. Looking around her, Jackie felt the flood of memories associated with buying church hats.

When Jackie was little, their mother had taken them to hat shops in the hopes of finding something appropriate for young girls who had to wear them to church. Their mother had thought that the hats in regular stores were too matronly for children. Besides, black girls could not try on department store hats because of the Jim Crow laws in Washington, DC.

They had shopped at the little millinery stores that had dotted the side streets as neighbors of the boot and record establishments. Jackie had dreaded entering the feather- and ribbon-festooned shops. Her long braids had always made her look silly in the frilly creations and corny in the more tailored styles.

Jackie would take a deep breath as she had entered the millinery shop in which hats of every possible description sat on white or black plastic heads. Everywhere she looked, Jackie saw a disembodied head sporting a lacy number appropriate for a member of the wedding party or a high crowned straw hat with ribbons down the back. She supposed that someone would consider them charming and romantic, but to Jackie they had simply been representative of styles that she had never been able to wear. Her round face and short hair demanded something else, something unique, something that did not exist.

Dee, however, had the perfect hat face. Her high cheekbones and red lips had looked perfect under a wide-brimmed garden hat or a soft, fabric cloche or a tailor man-style hat. In fact, everything that Dee had put on her head had looked terrific. Dee just had one of those faces.

After a time that had felt like an eternity, Jackie had finally found a passable hat. Her mother had reluctantly agreed that the little number with the upturned brim that had sat on the back of Jackie's head had more appeal than any other. Shaking her head, she had turned her attention to Dee, who had modeled almost every hat in the store and had finally settled on a cloche that had hugged her head as if it had been created just for her.

The three of them had left the store happy but for different reasons. Their mother and Dee had purchased fetching hats that would draw many compliments from their friends. Jackie had acquired a hat that was serviceable and attractive, which had pleased her mother. However, Jackie had been ecstatic to leave the little shop because, attractive or not, she had hated hats. Swinging the box, Jackie had silently wished for the day when she would not have to wear one.

Even now as a grown woman, Jackie carried the memories of the experience and refused to wear a hat on anything but the coldest days. She would pull an extremely ugly but soft felt hat from her closet and cram it onto her head. Somehow its ugliness added to its charm, and Jackie did not mind wearing it. She did not fool herself into thinking that the hat flattered her still full face.

Passing other women and their daughters, Jackie wandered the aisles of the store. She picked up and put down one hat after the other and found nothing to her liking. Nothing seemed quite right. Not one of them struck her as the perfect hat for her. She would not have been in the store if Dee had not pulled her inside. Looking at hats was such a waste of Jackie's time.

Jackie looked at the novelty baseball caps bearing the words "World's Best Mom". Smiling, she thought about the balloons in her dining room that bore the same message. No, that hat was not for her. Although she had done a good job of raising Doug, she would not say that she had been the best mom in the world. She had tried her best and was proud of the product, but Jackie would not proclaim herself to be superior to the other mothers who struggled to raise decent, law-abiding citizens who respected their elders and themselves.

Walking a little further, she found a cloche covered entirely with flowers. Jackie remembered the hat she had worn for Easter when she was eight years old. It was so similar to this one that Jackie felt as if she had stepped into a time warp. The hat had made her head look like a white bowling ball with her eyes as the finger holes. No, this was definitely not the hat for her.

At the back of the shop, Jackie found a little black beaded number similar to the ones that Princess Diana had made famous. It was designed to sit close to the head and hug the skull, while giving minimal coverage. The combination of beads and sequins was stunning. They were great hats for opening night at the theater or an elegant cocktail party, but, since she and Bill seldom attended those affairs, the opportunity to wear it would be limited. She replaced it on the Styrofoam head and moved on. Besides, the adorable little hat would have made her face appear too round.

Dee, however, had found the to-die-for hat. It was incredibly sexy, with a little black veil, yet elegant in design. The black ostrich feather that peeked over the top added a hint of sauciness as it curled into itself.

A tiny rhinestone rose glittered on the side of its velvet form as Dee turned and said, "How do I look? Isn't this the cutest thing! I have just the place to wear it, too. Joe is taking me on a cruise next month for my birthday. This is just the hat for the evenings on the boat."

Joe Walker was Dee's latest significant other, and in line to be husband number five. He was tall with deep brown skin and eyes. Joe's hair was a healthy salt and pepper. He worked out at the gym constantly and had a body that belied his fifty-five years. As the president of his own insurance firm, he was a great catch.

"I'm sure he'll love it. It really is attractive on you," Jackie commented honestly and a bit enviously. She wished that she could wear the darling little creation.

"Oh, Jackie, you haven't found one yet. This is Mother's Day and I'm doing all the shopping. You haven't bought a thing. Let's look for one for you while the lady wraps up this one for me," Dee replied with genuine concern that her sister had not found anything to her liking in the multitude of shops they had entered.

"You know that I'm not a hat person," Jackie said as Dee pressed another hat onto her head.

"You just haven't found the right one. Like men, there's a hat out there for everyone," Dee laughed as another hat joined the discard pile.

Eyeing her sister sideways, Jackie bit back the retort that immediately sprang to mind. Dee was trying to give her a good Mother's Day. There was little point in starting an argument.

After following Dee around the shop and trying on countless numbers of hats, Jackie looked at her watch. It was already four o'clock. They had been shopping since one. They had already spent an hour in the hat shop. She was ready to call it a day. Her feet and back hurt from standing. She was ready to go home. Empty or not, at least she would be able to sit down and put up her feet.

Dee was not the least bit tired and definitely not ready to leave. She was on a quest to find the perfect hat for Jackie. However, as the time ticked away, even Dee grew tired of the seemingly futile project. She was almost ready to agree with Jackie that she would have to remain hatless when she found what she had been searching for buried under a pile of wool flannel barrets.

"Voila!" Dee shouted as she waved the small cloth hat in the air.

"What?" Jackie asked hesitantly. She had already tried on every style of hat in the store and could not believe Dee could have uncovered anything new.

"This!" Dee replied as she rushed toward Jackie, happily waving the treasure in the air.

"I know that you don't think that I'd wear a barret. Mother made me wear those things when I was in elementary school. No way will I return to those days. I have too many memories of heavy oxford shoes and barrets," Jackie rebutted as she backed away and out of Dee's reach.

"Not the barret," Dee replied as she tossed the extra hat onto the counter. "This one. Try it, you'll love it. Stand still while I put it on you. I have to position it just right. There! Take a look."

Stepping hesitantly to the mirror, Jackie looked at her reflection. For once in their lives, her little sister had been correct. The little red silk circle sat nestled among her curls. It fit perfectly and looked as if it had been designed with her in mind.

"I'll take it," Jackie said to the saleswoman, who had watched the entire shopping spree with great humor. "I can't believe it, but we've finally found a hat that works for me."

"I told you!" Dee commented smugly, as if they were children again.

"Yeah, right," Jackie replied as she paid for her new treasure.

Jackie was so pleased with the way the little hat looked and its contribution to her outfit that she would not allow the saleswoman to put it into the box. Thanking her, Jackie carried the empty box from the store. The little hat sat jauntily on the top of her head.

They shopped in three other stores before making their last stop in an athletic shoe store in which a family was in the process of purchasing shoes for their three children. Dee needed a new pair of jogging shoes. Jackie was only too happy to sit and wait while her sister tried to make her selection from the myriad of styles. Her feet and back were killing her from following Dee all over the mall.

As Jackie waited, she thought about the first time she had brought Doug to the store for his first pair of real shoes. He had been only an infant and needed special orthopedic shoes to straighten his bow legs. Doug had sat quietly while the man measured his foot and laced up the shoes. However, as soon as his feet had hit the floor in the new, hard shoes, he had begun to bellow at the top of his lungs. Immediately, he had hated the feel of the confining shoes after wearing the soft fabric ones to which he had become accustomed.

Jackie had picked up the sobbing child and held

him close. Doug had looked into her face and cried even harder. Unable to express himself in more than a stream of no's, he had wanted to make her understand that the confining contraptions on his feet had not been to his liking.

"Maybe this isn't a good idea," Jackie had said to the salesman. "Maybe we should wait a little while longer."

"Don't worry, ma'am, he'll get used to them. After a while, he won't even notice the bar that you'll attach at night. At this age, they're very resilient," the man had replied with a knowledgeable smile.

"But what if he won't stop crying? What if they're hurting his feet?" Jackie, a new mother, had inquired. She had almost been in tears herself at her baby's unhappiness.

"They're not. They fit perfectly. If he doesn't stop crying by the time you get ready to leave the mall, bring them back. However, I know children, and I'm sure he'll stop before you can walk to the next store. The shoes are new to him, and I'm a stranger. He'll stop," the man had stated with infectious confidence.

As Jackie paid for the shoes, Doug's howling had changed to a whimper. He had clung to her and had eyed the man suspiciously. By the time she had pushed the stroller with Doug in it into the center of the mall, he had stopped crying and sat contentedly playing with the beads on the front of his stroller.

At that moment, Dee's voice penetrated Jackie's thoughts. "Ready?" Dee asked as she scooped up some of her packages and handed others to Jackie.

Rising, they exited the shop and headed toward the parking lot. Jackie had lucked out and found a spot two cars away from Dee. Turning, she said, "It's been fun, Dee, but I've got to go home. I'm hungry and tired."

3 QUICK STEPS
TO RECEIVE YOUR "THANK YOU" GIFT
FROM THE EDITOR

Send back this card and you'll receive 4 Arabesque novels!
These books have a combined cover price of $20.00 or more,
but they are yours to keep for a mere $1.99.

There's no catch. You're under no obligation to buy anything.
We charge only $1.99 for the books (plus $1.50 for shipping
and handling). And you don't have to make a minimum
number of purchases—not even one!

We hope that after receiving your books you'll want to
remain an Arabesque subscriber. But the choice is yours to
continue or cancel, anytime at all! So why not take us up on
our invitation to receive 4 Arabesque Romance Novels, with
no risk of any kind. You'll be glad you did!

Call us
TOLL-FREE
at 1-888-345-BOOK

Accepting the four introductory books for $1.99 (+ $1.50 for shipping & handling) places you under no obligation to buy anything. You may keep the books and return the shipping statement marked "cancel". If you do not cancel, about a month later we will send 4 additional Arabesque novels, and bill you a preferred subscriber's price of just $4.00 per title (plus a small shipping and handling fee). That's $16.00 for all 4 books for a savings of 25% off the publisher's price. You may cancel at any time, but if you choose to continue, every month we'll send you 4 more books, which you may either purchase at the preferred discount price. . . or return to us and cancel your subscription.

THE ARABESQUE ROMANCE CLUB
c/o ZEBRA HOME SUBSCRIPTION SERVICE, INC.
120 BRIGHTON ROAD
P.O. BOX 5214
CLIFTON, NEW JERSEY 07015-5214

AFFIX
STAMP
HERE

"No, you're spending the day with me. There's no one at home and I'm not going to let you sit alone. Let's go out to dinner. We'll take my car and leave yours here," Dee insisted as she dragged Jackie toward the passenger side of her car.

"But, Dee . . . ," Jackie began, to no avail.

"No, I won't hear another word. Get in the car," Dee concluded as she gave Jackie a little shove.

With a sigh, Jackie settled into the leather upholstery of Dee's car. The drive into the countryside was wonderfully relaxing and just what Jackie needed after being dragged around the mall by her sister. The farms that flanked the road were green with this year's crop. New calves and lambs frolicked in the warm sun. Breathing deeply, Jackie melted into the seat and left her cares behind.

Allowing her mind to wander, Jackie thought about the first time Bill had driven them into the countryside to Le Gateau for dinner. Doug had been about ten and more interested in playing with his buddy, Tommy, than in eating dinner with them. But it was Mother's Day, and he begrudgingly went along with them. Doug especially hated having to wear his Sunday clothes all day, preferring jeans and a T-shirt to trousers, a button-up shirt, a tie, and a jacket.

Doug had dozed all the way to the restaurant while Jackie and Bill chatted softly. Considering Doug's mood, they had been all too happy to have him silent in the back seat. He had already complained about having to take an hour and a half drive into the country when there were perfectly good restaurants closer to town. However, Bill had been determined. He had made the reservations months in advance. Nothing, not even his son's logical arguments, would have stopped him from taking Jackie to one of the area's most famous French restaurants.

The parking lot had been packed when they had

arrived. Families had overflowed the gardens as they had waited for their tables. They walked along magnificently manicured paths, stopped to admire flowers blooming in profusion, and chatted happily under the shade of spreading magnolias and weeping willows.

Doug had made a face as they had joined the crowd and commented that they could have been eating already if they had gone to a restaurant closer to home. Bill had shushed him with a parental stare that silenced Doug's laments for the rest of the day. Following his father's application of parental authority, Doug had even appeared to enjoy chasing the butterflies that drank from the phlox and watching the hummingbirds as they had played around the feeder.

Entering the stately old house that had been converted into the restaurant, they had been enchanted by the trellises overflowing with flowers in the dining porch. Jackie and Bill had been impressed by the fabulous artwork decorating the formal dining rooms. Even Doug had gaped at the display of Tiffany glass glistening in the former living room that had been converted into a reception area. As they followed the hostess to their table, they looked wide-eyed at all the natural and man-made treasures that had filled the rooms. Reaching their table in the garden room, they stared in fascination at the fountain and aviary that stood at the center of its décor.

Doug had sat mesmerized by the flight of the colorful little birds, just as Jackie did now. By luck or design, she did not know which, Dee had managed to secure a table in the same room in which they had sat that Mother's Day years ago. Nothing in the restaurant had changed. It still contained an air of casual elegance that oozed from every pore. Patrons still filled every table and waited in the garden for their reservations. Mothers with their toddlers in their arms mingled with the older women whose children had grown up and moved away, just as they had when Jackie first visited the restaurant. Even the waitresses in colorful dresses and the men in matching cummerbunds walked with a serenity uncommon in the restaurants in town in which the rich and famous of the nation dined just as they had years ago. Jackie relished the respectful, leisurely service and the chance to study the menu without feeling rushed by a member of the serving staff with pad of paper in hand.

"Well, what are you going to order?" Dee inquired as she scanned the pages of delicacies.

"I don't know yet. There's too much selection. You know I have trouble with more than three or four entrées. That's why I let Bill do all the ordering at Chinese restaurants," Jackie responded as she flipped to the pages devoted to fowl of every description. The restaurant served chicken and turkey cooked in various country and elegant French dishes. In addition, they specialized in wild fowl such as pheasant in a burgundy sauce, Cornish hens with portabello mushrooms, and duck in the ever-popular orange sauce.

"I know what I'm having for dessert. I've been dreaming of their thick, rich chocolate cake. Only the French can make a cake that sinfully delicious," Dee drooled as she read the selection of more than fifty desserts, ranging from pastry to pie to ice cream and mousse.

"You're still a kid, Dee. When you were little, you would always select your dessert first and then decide on your entrée. You haven't changed," Jackie chuckled at her almost salivating sister.

"That's the best part of the meal!" Dee rebutted with a big smile. She was thoroughly enjoying having her sister all to herself for the day. They had not hung out together in years. Both of them were always too busy with their jobs. When Dee had a few minutes to spare, Jackie was occupied with her family. Now that Doug was in college, Jackie had enjoyed a bit more freedom, although Bill found a way to fill her spare time with projects for them to share.

"In that case, it's up to me to order first," Jackie volunteered as the waitress approached them with a smile. "I'll have the house salad, onion soup, and the game pie. I love the combination of venison, duck, and rabbit."

"Oh yuck! You're going to eat Bambi, Donald, and Thumper! How could you?!" Dee exploded in mock surprise. She knew that Jackie shared their father's love for wild game and ordered it whenever it was on the menu. Doug and Bill would rather starve than indulge, which limited Jackie's ability to serve it at home.

"And you'll probably have something with oysters or even steak tartar," Jackie scoffed mockingly, knowing that Dee always ordered one or both of her favorites.

"You're absolutely correct." Dee answered merrily as she grinned at the waitress. "I'll have oysters Rockefeller, the house salad, and filet mignon rare with a baked potato."

After the waitress left, Dee commented, "Isn't this fun? It's been ages since we've spent any real time together. It's nice not having the guys with us. Don't get me wrong, Jackie, I love our family, but I like having you all to myself sometimes."

Patting her sister's hand, Jackie replied with a grin, "I'm really enjoying being with you, too. Thanks for keeping me from sitting around the house feeling sorry for myself because my guys are away. For a little sister, you're not too bad."

They spent the rest of the meal chatting about old times, arguing in the amicable way that sisters do, and relishing each moment together. Occasionally, Jackie felt sadness at not being with her guys on Mother's Day, but she quickly pushed the feelings away. Dee was working so hard at giving her a good time that she did not want to put a damper on the day. Besides, she had been blessed with eighteen wonderful Mother's Days with Doug. She could relive any one of them in her memory and feel happy.

While Dee kept up a steady stream of conversation about work and men, Jackie let her mind wander to a time not too long ago that had filled her heart with warmth. Doug had just been accepted to college, one of the nation's prestigious service academies, at which he would train for an officer position in the armed services. The family had been invited to an appointee reception by the congresswoman whose district Doug would represent. The affair had been held in one of the conference rooms on Capitol Hill. Doug, Bill, and Jackie had attended along with special family friends, an older couple who had been like second parents to Jackie.

At the beginning of the ceremony, the congresswoman had given each one of the appointees the opportunity to have a photo taken with her in front of the mural on the wall of the Science and Technology conference room in the Rayburn building. Then, each one of the newly commissioned servicemen and women and the appointees had been invited to say a few words. The new junior officers had been appropriately mature, but most of the appointees had been typical teenagers. They had talked about their dreams of playing soccer or baseball in college, of serving the country as pilots or sailors, in a very childlike way appropriate to new high school graduates. Jackie had been sure Doug would do the same. When it was his turn, Doug had taken his place at the podium and had thanked Jackie and Bill for their support in the application process, for raising him to manhood, for providing him with a loving environment, and for being the best parents in the world.

As he talked, Jackie had dissolved into tears, as did all the other mothers and many of the fathers in the room. The congresswoman had even wiped away tears. When she had returned to the microphone to introduce the next appointee, she had to struggle to speak. Everyone had said later that Doug had spoken the best, had shown incredible maturity for a seventeen-year-old, and had shown that he would make a wonderful addition to the armed forces. Her other parents had been equally proud of their surrogate grandson. They had watched him grow into manhood and had liked what they had seen.

Of all the cherished memories, Jackie had held that one most dear. Doug, her usually reticent son, had told the entire population of that room that he loved her. She would live on those words forever.

Jackie and Doug had always had an agreement that he would not spend any money on birthday, Christmas, or Mother's Day gifts for her. All she had ever wanted had been for him to hug her and say that he loved her. Doug, who had been a very affectionate child until his teen years when he had decided that kissing was for babies, had been quick to accept the arrangement. He had been able to save money and make Jackie happy at the same time. For a teenager without a steady job, Jackie's proposal had contained a great deal of merit.

Each holiday or birthday, Doug had wrapped his arms around Jackie, had said the words with genuine emotion, and had given her a kiss. He had blushed and quickly left the room. Jackie had smiled at his retreating back, knowing that the handsome young man truly loved her.

However, when the six weeks of summer military

training separated them, the words, hug, and kiss had taken on an even greater meaning. During their time apart, Jackie had thought of Doug constantly and had missed him deeply. She had thought her heart would break from missing him and had relished the three short phone calls the service academy had allowed him to make.

When they had finally been reunited on Parents' Weekend, Doug had wrapped his thin body around hers in a bear hug that had nearly lifted Jackie off the ground. The young man who had never allowed public displays of affection had kissed his mother and father in front of his twelve hundred classmates and their parents. He had missed them so terribly that he had not cared who might have seen him.

For Jackie, that reunion had been the reprieve she had needed from the anxiety of the empty nest syndrome. She had found that she could laugh and enjoy life again. The separation that had prevented her from speaking with, seeing, and holding her son had at last ended.

"Jackie, are you listening to me?" Dee queried. "You look as if your mind is miles away. I don't think you've heard a thing I've said. You've only picked at your chocolate mousse."

"I'm sorry, Dee. I was thinking about Doug. I'll be more attentive, I promise," Jackie replied as she tucked away her memories.

"That's more like it," Dee said emphatically as she feigned jealousy. "This is my time with you, not his. I want you all to myself."

Laughing, Jackie forced her mind to stay with Dee's chatter rather than returning to the pleasant memories of her family. However, on the short trip to the movies, Jackie once again found her attention wandering to her first date with Bill, whom she had known since childhood.

Jackie and Bill had grown up in the same church and had seen each other every Saturday and Sunday. She had sung in the choir, he had served as an acolyte. She had been a Girl Scout, he had been a Boy Scout. Their families had known one another for years. Jackie and his sister were the same age, and for years Bill had considered her to be as much of a nuisance as his younger sibling.

One December day, Jackie and Bill had been invited to the birthday party of one of their mutual friends. Unfortunately for Bill, he had been the only boy whose mother had accepted the invitation. He had sat sadly alone on the window seat while all the girls had chattered happily about dolls and clothes. At nine years old, Bill had found the company of six-year-old girls to be extremely boring and beneath him.

Jackie had taken pity on him and had brought him something to eat. Although he had barely grunted his thanks as he had torn into the hamburger, fries, and potato salad, Jackie had been hooked. The shy, skinny little boy in the knee pants and matching navy blue blazer had won a permanent place in her heart.

When they had been teenagers meeting on the church steps, Jackie had tried to make Bill give up his cigarette habit. Every weekend, she had nagged him until he had at least stopped smoking on the church front. However, since they had attended different schools, he continued to smoke whenever she had not been around. Although they had seen very little of each other, for a few minutes every Saturday and Sunday, they had been an item.

Then one Sunday when Jackie was twenty-nine, she had attended church with her parents. Her boyfriend at the time, a much older man, had gone out of town on a hunting trip. Before Frank left, he had given Jackie instructions to behave herself. Jackie had taken his words as a challenge. No one, not even her father, had told her to behave herself since she had reached the age of majority. As Frank's car had pulled out of her driveway, Jackie had decided that if he could go deer hunting in Pennsylvania with his brother, she could go hunting, too. She had not been able to think of a better place to hunt for a new man to fill her life than at church where she would have no choice but to behave herself.

That Sunday Jackie had sat between her parents on the old familiar pew she had occupied ever since she had been a little girl. She had watched the acolytes light the candles and the crucifer carry in the cross. She had sung along with the choir to the old familiar tunes. She had listened to the same priest who had been delivering the homily since her youth as he spread his wisdom among his flock.

When the priest had called everyone's attention to the Sunday bulletin, Jackie had seen Bill's name on the list of the sick and shut-in. Smiling, Jackie had realized that she had her prey in her sights. She knew from her mother's gossip about the church members that Bill had not married. She decided between the doxology and the communion that she would rekindle their old friendship. Although they had not seen each other in almost ten years, Jackie had known in her heart that she would be victorious.

As soon as she had returned home, Jackie had telephoned Bill, who had been recuperating from an appendectomy. They had reminisced about the old days . . . the parties, the church services, and the nagging. Their conversation had been filled with warmth and laughter and the comfortable camaraderie of old friends. By the time the conversation had ended, Jackie had remembered that his birthday would have been the following Friday and had asked him out to lunch.

The week had passed more slowly than ever. Her

clients in the marketing department of a major tele-
communications firm had gotten on her nerves with
their constant demands. Unlike other days, Jackie
had not felt like humoring them. She had been
happy to honor their requests, but she had felt little
sympathy for their minor complaints.

When Friday had finally arrived, Jackie had checked
her makeup, straightened the wrinkles from sitting at
her desk from her skirt, and walked the two blocks to
the restaurant in the crisp October air. The sun had
felt good against her back after a morning in the office. The cool air had put a healthy glow in her cheeks.
The sound of her heels tapped a gay tattoo as she had
hurried past other members of the workforce on their
way to lunch. Nothing in Jackie's demeanor had betrayed her nervousness.

They had not seen each other since their high
school days. Every time Bill had returned from his
college in Virginia, he had made a point of getting
in touch with Jackie. She had usually been so busy
with her studies in hopes of matriculating at a top
tier undergraduate program that she had spent little
time with him. However, Bill continued to call. Only
when he entered the service after college did they
lose contact.

Bill had been waiting at the restaurant door for
fifteen minutes when he peered through the crowd
to see someone who had looked familiar. He had
liked what he had heard on the phone and had anxiously awaited their reunion. Not wanting to be late,
he had arrived early. He had wanted to arrive first so
he could check out the grown up Jackie.

Spotting him standing at the door as she crossed
the street, Jackie's heart had lurched. Her old friend,
the shy boy at whom she had sneaked peeks, the
young man whom she had nagged, the college man
with whom she had danced, had grown up. Bill had

become a handsome man who had smiled and waved at first sight of her.

Meeting her halfway between the restaurant and the corner, Bill had swept Jackie into his arms. Holding her close, he had planted a warm, firm kiss on her lips. Jackie had instantly felt comfortable and safe with Bill at her side. The crisp October afternoon had suddenly become warm and bright. Jackie had known immediately that she had found her soul mate.

Bill had felt the same immediate attraction. He had known from their conversation that they would have much to discuss. However, he had not been prepared for the heart-stopping lurch he had felt in his gut when he had first held Jackie in his arms. She had fit him perfectly, not like their teen years when she had been taller than he. His last growth spurt had made him a good two inches taller. The most amazing physical change had been the way in which they had fit so perfectly together. Jackie had slipped into the space against his chest that had been empty for so long. She had completed him.

Lunch had consisted of more conversation than food. Bill barely touched his shrimp scampi, and Jackie had only picked at her western omelet. When the birthday cake had arrived, Bill had asked the waiter to package it so he could take it home. They had planned to celebrate his birthday later that evening. They had too many years to catch up on to let food get in the way.

Jackie had barely kept her mind on her work the rest of the afternoon. She had planned to see Bill again that evening. They had arranged to have dinner together, take in a movie, and then sample the untouched birthday cake. She had been so upbeat that one of her coworkers had asked what liquid refreshment she had consumed for lunch.

That evening, Jackie had dressed in a black slip

dress with a matching jacket. She had taken special care with her short, curly afro. She had donned pearl earrings and necklace to accentuate her complexion and coordinate with the simplicity of her dress.

Jackie had run the vacuum cleaner over the sea foam carpet, had fluffed the cushions, had dusted the furniture, and had confined her cat to the basement. She had turned down the lights so they had the perfect lighting. She had mixed a batch of sangria for them to sip while eating the cake. And Jackie had waited.

When Bill did not arrive on time, Jackie had paced the floor, had looked out the window, and had walked down her lawn for a better view so many times that her feet started to ache in the cute, red heels. When Bill did not phone, she had thought the worst. After all the years of searching for the right man, she had finally found him, only for him to slip away.

As the clock on the mantel ticked away the minutes, Jackie had come to accept the reality that Bill was late for their first dinner date. Jackie had worried that he had become lost on the drive from town to her home in the country. Although the distance between Bill's condo and Jackie's house had not been that great, the twisting roads often became treacherous at night. She had phoned his home but not even the answering machine had picked up.

Finally, an hour and a half late, Bill had pulled his yellow sedan into the driveway. As he climbed out, Jackie had fought the urge to run out to greet him. She had watched from the living room window as he slowly climbed the stairs that led to the front door.

Jackie had not answered immediately. She allowed Bill to wait a fraction of the time that she had waited. She had not been exactly angry; her worry had prevented that. However, she not want to appear to be standing at the door. When she finally opened the door, she had been shocked by the sight.

Bill stood on her front porch with his dusty jacket over his arm. His shirt was streaked with dirt. His trousers were ripped at the knee. His face and hands bore multiple cuts and scratches.

Immensely worried, Jackie had pulled him into the house. Regretting having made him wait, she led Bill to the den. Along the way, she collected peroxide and bandages from the bathroom.

As she had ministered to his wounds, Bill explained that he had suffered a flat tire on the way. Hiking a far distance from his disabled car, he had been unable to locate a pay phone or a gas station on the deserted back road. Bill had been unable either to phone her or to call for help.

Returning to the car, he had undertaken the task of changing his tire, only to find that his spare had also gone flat. Half rolling and half carrying the flat tire, Bill had walked the two miles to the closest service station. He had not been sure when he had cut his hands, but he supposed it might have happened when the jack had collapsed. Bill had soiled his shirt when the tire had hit a rut, and he had fallen face down onto the shoulder of the road. He had ripped his trousers climbing into the tow truck for the ride back to his car. All this Bill had done to be with Jackie.

Bill had looked so pitiful that Jackie had immediately thrown her arms around him and had held him close. She had heard a lot of stories from tardy dates, but never had she listened to one like Bill's. Her heart had gone out to him even more. They were married six months later. Neither had seen any reason to wait. Doug had been born in November two years later.

Four

The movie theater was filled with families. To Jackie, it looked as if every father had decided to treat every mother to a day at the movies. Dee chatted merrily as if she did not notice, but Jackie felt a momentary surge of self-pity. Not wanting to put a damper on her sister's happiness at spending the day with her, Jackie pasted on a smile and joined in Dee's conversation.

Easing into the last two seats on the last row, Jackie and Dee shared a box of heavily buttered popcorn and their childhood memories of coming to the movies with their parents. They remembered sitting between their parents in a kind of child sandwich so that they would be protected from strangers. Their father had always bought them chocolate-covered raisins along with the popcorn. After the movie, they had indulged in their own critique sessions to see if their opinions matched those of the renowned critics.

Jackie had continued that tradition with her family. They always read the reviews before attending movies and then critiqued them on the way home. They even gave the films thumbs-up or thumbs-down ratings. Jackie and Doug almost always shared the same reactions, but Bill often went his own way. He liked films that they considered marginal at best.

As Jackie watched the previews of upcoming movies, she thought about the worst film she had ever seen. It was one of those movies that catered to the younger market or to those who enjoyed ribald humor. The main characters had lived in a shabby apartment, had worn poorly coordinated clothing, had barely any education, and had made inappropriate comments about women. Doug and Bill had laughed their heads off at their antics while Jackie had sat with her arms folded waiting for the movie to end. Not only had the film been one of the most distasteful she had ever watched, the spring in the seat had constantly stuck into her backside. Between the pain in her butt and the agony of having to watch that movie, Jackie had not enjoyed the outing that afternoon. Unfortunately, that distasteful film had been rated among the best by the critics. Jackie could only wonder at the quality of the worst that the summer had to offer if she had seen the best.

On the drive home, they had engaged in a heated justification of their ratings. Jackie's guys had said that the film was harmless, and the portrayal of women as sex objects had been comical since the men making the statements had been portrayed as buffoons. Jackie had objected on the grounds that the mentality of the males had not excused the inappropriate comments about women. Just because the characters had acted like sex-starved pubescent teenagers rather than grown men had not compensated for the insult to women.

They had argued all through dinner at their favorite Chinese restaurant, but they had been unable to reach either a compromise or an agreement. By the time they had finally returned home, they had agreed to disagree on the merits of the movie. Neither side had been willing to bend.

Doug had only been ten years old when they had seen that terrible movie, but even then he had held his ground in their discussion. Jackie had been very proud of his verbal abilities and had suggested that he might want to consider joining the school's debate team. Being a math and science person, Doug had decided that he would leave that to the kids who liked history. He had been content to work equations on his calculator and spend time in the science lab.

Bill had smiled proudly at their son every time he defended his position on the film. Although he had seldom told Doug of his appreciation of his intellectual skills, leaving that to Jackie, Bill had always swelled up every time he had watched his son excel one more time. He had enjoyed seeing the boy hold his ground against the formidable opponent, his mother. Doug had never once backed down, softened his attack, or given ground. When the debate ended with Jackie folding Doug into her arms, Bill had beamed with pride.

As a young child, Doug had always been more studious and intellectual than athletic. He had played softball for a while because all of his friends had joined teams. However, he had never really liked it. From an early age, his great joy had been making music and singing. Doug had played the violin and the piano and composed music for both. As he had grown older, he had sung in the church choir and then in his college glee club from almost the first day of plebe summer. He had taught himself to play the guitar because his college roommate had bet him that he could not master a very difficult piece they had heard on the radio. His friend had studied the guitar while in high school and still could not play the piece.

To win the bet, Doug had spent hours during his summer vacation listening to the song and playing it by ear. He had slowly picked out the chords and the melody. Finally, putting it all together, he had played along with the CD until his efforts blended perfectly.

Returning to his college, Doug had called the bet. Sitting on the edge of his bed, he had played the song perfectly. When the roommate had heard him, he had quickly paid up. That night, he had called home to share the news of his success with Jackie and Bill.

Forcing her mind to return to the movie, Jackie mentally prepared the argument points that she would not need. Still, from habit, she could not stop herself from critiquing the actors, plot, and direction of the remake of a 1940s love story. Maybe one of her guys would have seen it, too. She would store her review in her memory until they were together again.

Both of the guys were real movie buffs. Doug often went to movies as a break from his studies, and Bill frequented them when he traveled. Doug said that the ability to suspend disbelief relaxed him and helped him to focus when he returned to the books. Bill used them to fill the boring, lonely hours while at conferences. He had found that his single coworkers and some of the married ones liked to visit bars. Since he did not drink and had no interest in meeting women, Doug either retired early, exercised alone, or went to the movies.

Usually, when they were all together again, Doug, Bill, and Jackie would share their reviews of movies that the others had not seen. If the movies were still showing in local theaters, the family members who had not seen them would go. If unavailable, they would rent them. By swapping information, all members had the opportunity to see the good movies based on a family member's advice. If the guys had not seen this skillful remake, they probably would decide to see it based on Jackie's review.

As they walked from the theater, Jackie asked Dee,

"What did you think of the movie? I'd give it a thumbs up. I really like that actor, and he did a wonderful job of grasping the complexity of the character."

"Well, I think the female lead made the movie. Without her, the love scenes would have been flat. She had lovely sparkle," Dee replied as she fell into Jackie's customary movie analysis.

"Yes, but he played his part so well that his effort made hers credible. He was the perfect messenger . . . bold yet almost hesitant and naïve. He wanted to do his job, but, at the same time, he was reluctant. Milton Everett's handsome, youthful looks helped him capture the character," Jackie continued as they climbed into the car.

"I guess you're right. But I still think that her facial expressions made her a very believable character," Dee commented as she started the engine and pulled from the space. She carefully eased the car into traffic and headed toward their destination.

"You give up too easily. You're supposed to continue arguing until you convince me to change my opinion," Jackie added with a chuckle.

"I think you've made a valid point. I see no reason to argue any further," Dee replied as she eased onto the highway.

"Your point was correct, too. You shouldn't have given up so soon," Jackie said as she settled into the upholstery.

"I'm new at this. I'll do better next time," Dee conceded as she switched on the radio that put an end to their discussion.

They rode in silence as Dee drove out to her country club. She had joined the club because it was totally devoid of any of the pretensions of money. Everyone came to the picturesque country setting to play tennis or golf, not to hobnob with wealth. As a matter of fact, no one made a show of any kind about their positions in corporate America. Everyone simply enjoyed being in the country and playing sports.

However, Jackie knew that Dee traveled in well-heeled company. All of Dee's husbands had been more than comfortably well off, and, with each divorce, Dee's level of financial security had increased. Although she was a hard worker, Dee's wealth came not from her own efforts but from the money invested in the stock market. Wise investments had turned each one of the divorce settlements into gold. Dee was set for life.

Dee had been a generous child and continued to be a free-spending adult. She lavished Jackie and her family with gifts and always shared her good fortune with them. Jackie and Bill had comfortable jobs and did not need Dee's generosity for survival. However, the gifts of expensive leather handbags and briefcases for Jackie and Bill, the newest computer for Doug, and lavish vacations they took with Dee helped to enrich their lives.

Every summer, they traveled with Dee to exotic places. They had toured the world with her and enjoyed every minute. Each school year, she bought Doug outfits that would make the Rockefellers jealous. When he graduated from high school, Dee gave him a trip to England, Paris, Rome, and Barcelona, knowing that she would not be able to buy anything for him for a long time. The service academies supplied everything their students would need in terms of clothing, luggage, books, and computers in exchange for five years of service in the armed forces.

Dee had never been blessed with children and lavished all the attention and love she would have given to them on Jackie and her family. However, she knew when to give them space to be a family. Fortunately, they loved her as much as she loved them. The fabulous foursome was always together.

Maybe that was the reason for the failure of Dee's marriages. She always looked for the kind of happiness that Jackie and Bill shared, and, when she did not find it, she consulted an attorney. Her husbands had not been bad men; they had simply been more involved in their successful businesses than with her. Dee could not make them change and would not abandon her desire for more of their time. So the marriages ended. Her husbands, except for Scott who wanted to consume her, were not bad men; they had simply been more involved in their successful businesses than with her.

Dee and all her former husbands continued to be good friends. They exchanged holiday and birthday gifts and called each other frequently. They just could not be married to each other. When one of them remarried, Dee attended the wedding. When the marriage ended, she was the first to take the new bachelor out to dinner. The relationships were very friendly. Too close for Jackie's taste, but they suited Dee's personality perfectly.

Dee's personality fit the scene at the country club perfectly, too. Everyone knew everyone else. They partied together, played sports together, and commiserated with each other en masse. It was the perfect environment for someone who loved to be with lots of people, yet maintain a little distance between them and keep the sense of mystery alive.

The club, nestled in the woods and fields of Maryland's closed-in suburbs, was easily accessible from the Washington, DC, area. Members ranged from corporate bigwigs to judges to members of the Hill to physicians and teachers. They all enjoyed the fabulous food served in the dining room, the skillfully designed golf courses, the illuminated tennis courts, and massive swimming pools. The club even offered a pistol range for the firearms enthusiasts.

Buffy Mitchell, Dee's good friend and bridge partner, greeted them as soon as they walked through the door of the pine-paneled parlor. She had come to the club for dinner with her husband and two sons, who had become bored with devoting their attention to her on Mother's Day and had abandoned her. The children had joined the many others in a rousing game of pool while the husbands had assembled in the card room for few hands of bid whist. Buffy and the other mothers had gathered around the fireplace for a chat about their favorite topics, their children and their husbands. The glow of the fire took away the chill of the May evening.

The group opened its arms and embraced Dee and Jackie immediately. They all knew Dee and welcomed Jackie as if she were an old friend. After all, they shared the same complaints . . . husbands who worked too hard and had little time for them and children who grew up too fast and stopped needing them.

Settling into the deep blue leather wing chair, Jackie kicked off her shoes and curled into its protective embrace. The heat from the fireplace felt good against her legs and face. Looking at all of the incredibly open faces, Jackie felt a sense of contentment sweep over her.

"Well, where's your husband?" Buffy demanded without preamble. The congeniality of the group made small talk unnecessary.

"He's out of town on a business trip," Jackie replied, surveying the nodding heads of the other women.

"I guess he couldn't come home, right?" Bea asked with a knowing smile.

"That's right. He'll be back late tomorrow. This is the first time that Bill has missed a Mother's Day," Jackie responded, sensing an increase in the cohesiveness of the group.

"I remember when my husband missed my birthday. I gave him such a guilt trip that he never did it again," Phillippa added with a nod.

"Yes, and the bill to go with it. If I remember correctly, you bought yourself a diamond ring and charged it to his account for that trip," Buffy interjected with a hearty laugh.

"I sure did! It's the best present I ever gave myself. You can bet he never missed another birthday," Phillippa laughed uproariously at her own coup as she showed Jackie and Dee the ring that weighed down her right hand.

"It's not Bill's fault that he missed Mother's Day. The company sent him on this trip. As a matter of fact, I didn't even realize that Mother's Day meant anything to me at all until I woke up alone this morning. Anyway, he sent roses and a very sweet card," Jackie said, trying to clear Bill's name.

"Important or not, he shouldn't have gone on that trip. Men just never think about us. That's all," Bea commented as she ordered another rum and Coke.

"That's not true, Bea. Your husband is here. Bill just couldn't help it. He felt dreadful about not being here," Dee jumped in to defend her brother-in-law.

"Dee, you of all people should know how inconsiderate and unthinking they can be. Besides, Frank is here because we're leaving for the islands tomorrow. He had no choice but to be with me. Believe me, if I hadn't booked us into that trip, he'd be off somewhere, just like Jackie's Bill," Bea stated emphatically, lifting her perfectly arched brows for emphasis.

Buffy put down her empty glass and said, "I don't think that they're unthinking, really. I just don't believe that the things that interest us and are important to us mean anything to them. It doesn't matter how many times we tell them that we need for them to pay attention to us, they just don't understand."

"They pay attention soon enough when the court makes them. My sister's ex never misses one of those lovely alimony payments. I bet your last one doesn't either, Dee," Bea added cynically as she drained her glass.

"Look, I got mine up front. I didn't want to hear any excuses. 'The check's in the mail. The dog ate it. My new baby spit up on it. The mailman broke his leg.' I had heard enough while I was married," Dee replied with a chuckle.

"You're smart. We should remember that, ladies, should we decide to liberate ourselves one day," Buffy advised as she signaled to the waiter for another drink.

"Bill isn't like that. He's a good, decent guy . . . a wonderful husband and a good father. He couldn't help it, that's all," Jackie interjected as she sipped her diet soda.

"Whatever . . ." Bea commented. "Where are your children? Why aren't they with you since Mr. Wonderful is out of town?"

"Our son, Doug, is away at college and couldn't come home. He had one of his buddies deliver Mother's Day balloons," Jackie replied with a smile that soon faded under Bea's stare.

"His friend was home but he wasn't. How's that possible? Do they attend the same school?" Bea demanded with a slight slur in her speech. Whatever she was drinking had begun to take effect.

"Doug attends a service academy and his friend goes to a wonderful, historically black university. He doesn't have as much freedom as other college students. Besides, he has exams next week and couldn't spare the time from his studies," Jackie answered slowly. Suddenly, her family's reasons for not being with her looked like excuses.

"Really? You devoted eighteen years and nine months of your life to him. A few hours doesn't seem like too much to me. That's what I tell my kids. They don't listen, but I remind them just the same," Bea stated as she took a healthy swallow from her freshly filled glass.

Sensing Jackie's discomfort, Dee changed the topic by asking, "What are your summer vacation plans, ladies? Surely, Bea, you're not going on only one trip this year."

"Oh, no, honey. This is our trip without the kids. We take a husband-wife trip every year, leave the kids with my mother and go. No, we'll take a family vacation after school closes," Bea replied as she sank even farther into the sofa.

As the conversation turned to summer plans, Jackie reflected on her family. They had spent such lovely vacations together when Doug was a child. Now that he was in college, they had little time together. However, the memories would stay with her forever.

Jackie remembered the summer they had spent in Cancun. It had been one of the few vacations without Dee. Doug had been only six years old at the time and had helped plan the vacation. They had all been very excited about their first family trip to the beach.

Doug had been the first one out of the hotel room as he had charged across the white sand to the water's edge. Seeing the vast majesty of the Caribbean Sea, he had stopped in his tracks as the warm, frothy water tickled his toes. Jackie had quickly joined him to prevent the adventurous little boy from deciding that he could conquer the world beginning on that day and with that beach.

Rushing toward him, Jackie had stumped her toe on a rock buried under the sand. She had limped the rest of the distance to her son, who had stood still, mesmerized by the waves and the fish that had nibbled at the hairs on his legs. Her toe had throbbed and reflected a peculiar shade of deep blue-black through the shallow water. Yet, Jackie had said nothing. She had vowed to enjoy every second at the beach with Doug. She had been determined not to allow a visit to the hospital to interfere with their vacation.

Playing in the gentle waves, Bill and Jackie had swung Doug around in the surf as he squealed in delight. Then they had chased him and had splashed in the churning water. When they had become tired, they had stopped and built sand structures on the shore or searched for sea shells. Putting a conchshell to their ears, they listened to the sound of the waves crashing against the sand.

When dinnertime had come, Jackie had slipped a pair of thongs over her throbbing toe and accompanied her family for the walk to the restaurant. The concierge had recommended a delightful place overlooking the water about a half mile down the beach. The structure had been built on pylons set in the shallow water of the Caribbean. In the center of the dining room, the architects had left an opening through which the diners could watch the colorful fish of the Caribbean. As soon as they had entered the wood and glass structure, Doug had glued himself to the railing from which he had studied the antics of the creatures of the sea.

Jackie and Bill had stood beside him, not so much because they cared about seeing the fish, but to share the experience with their son. Doug had been so enthralled that they had to pull him away in order for him to eat his dinner. Between courses, he had returned to the rail and the fish gazing. Although not as impressed as her son, Jackie had admitted that the gentle voice of the sea lapping at the restaurant's undersides certainly added to the ambience of the establishment.

After dinner, they had walked back to the hotel, stopping along the way at an open-air market to purchase three pairs of haraches. Bill and Jackie had been able to find shoes to fit them immediately, but Doug's little feet had proven more difficult to fit. Finally, after searching every stall, Jackie had pulled out a pair that would fit him. With all three of them newly shod, they had continued their journey, with the guys wearing their new purchases and Jackie carrying hers. Her toe was much too tender for her to enclose it in the stiff leather of the shoe.

They had not gone far when they had encountered a creature they had never seen before except in the zoo. Jackie, Bill, and Doug had discovered a gigantic lizard meandering along the sidewalk. Its scaly body barely rustled the blades of grass as its massive feet trudged through the garden. The lizard had shown no fear of them as it had continued to poke under the leaves of flowers for insects in the nearby gardens. They had stood fascinated until the creature had padded away for more fruitful pastures without even turning its head in their direction. It had probably been accustomed to being stared at by tourists. The three of them had laughed and had continued their evening promenade.

When they had returned to the hotel, Jackie, Bill, and Doug had sat in the lobby listening to the mariachi band as it had played lively songs. The men had strummed their guitars and had sung spirited tunes as they walked around the lobby. The guests had sung along with the tunes and had clapped in time with the music.

Seeing a young boy in the lobby with his parents, the musicians had tried to make friends with Doug and had invited him to play the guitar with them. He had laughed and initially refused, but the more they pressured him, the less reluctant he became. Doug had studied the violin but not the guitar; however, when he had taken the instrument into his hands, it had come to life. Without knowing what he had been doing, Doug had managed to strum along with them in a manner that had exhibited a fundamental understanding of the instrument. When he had finished, everyone in the room had applauded wildly.

Jackie had been so incredibly proud of her little boy. Doug, a rather shy child, had taken the spotlight and had performed before an audience. He had become accustomed to the mandatory violin recitals but had never played for people he did not know. For the first time, Doug had felt the thrill of audience response. Working the crowded lobby, he had bowed deeply and had cast one of his most dazzling smiles around the room. Doug had been completely and comfortably in his element.

After the applause had died down, they sat among the hibiscus blooms and under the swirling fans until the crowd had begun to thin. The band had retired for the night and the lights in the lobby had dimmed. However, the bugs of Cancun had only just come to life.

Slowly, an army of insects unseen in the eastern United States had begun to appear. No-see-um mosquitoes had darted around the lights. Creatures that had sounded like amplified crickets had sung on the beach. And the largest cockroaches known to man had crawled from the gardens through the open lobby doors.

Jackie had been horrified at the sight of the four-inch bugs. She had imagined the difficulty she would have in exterminating them if one had happened to hitchhike a ride home with them. Bill had found them repulsive but had not reacted as strongly. Doug had discovered a new playmate.

Doug, without hesitation, had picked up one of the largest cockroaches and begun to study its sturdy body. The antennae had transmitted the bug's dislike at being held four feet above the ground by a little boy. Its legs had worked in a futile effort to escape.

Pulling a string from his pocket, Doug had tied one end around the cockroach's body. Holding to the other end, he had walked his new pet up and down the lobby floor. With each step, the ancient bug had tried unsuccessfully to run away from the inquisitive little boy. If Jackie had not been so appalled at the sight, she would have found it quite comical. Bill, despite his distaste for his son's new plaything, almost split his sides with laughter.

When Jackie had found that she could stand it no longer, she had instructed Doug to untie the cockroach, throw away the string, and follow them up to bed. Reluctantly, he had agreed, realizing from the stern tone in his mother's voice that there was little purpose in arguing. Leaving the bug to run for cover, Doug had joined his parents in the elevator for the ride to their room on the fourth floor.

As the country club ladies continued their amiable chatter, Jackie resumed her daydreaming about her family. The other women might complain about their untidy husbands and sons, but Jackie could think of nothing to add to the conversation. Although her guys had occasionally left a mess for her to clean up, they had always been delightful in every way and had enriched her life far more than they had added work to it.

The memories flowed in no particular order as Jackie relived the days of Doug's childhood. She remembered the time when she had taken him with her to a bath shop. She and Bill had planned to redecorate their bathroom and needed to purchase a new toilet, sink, and fixtures. Since Jackie hated to leave Doug with a sitter, she had taken him with them.

Doug had always been a very cooperative, agreeable, and patient child. He would happily amuse himself with a simple truck that he would push across the floor while his parents studied wallpaper samples, examined brass fittings, and selected appliances. This time had been no exception as he had built a little fortress from a deck of cards and had proceeded to park his truck in the garage.

After playing for a while, however, Doug had decided that he needed to use the bathroom. Not wanting to interrupt his parents and being a very self-sufficient three-year-old, Doug had planned to solve his problem by himself. Besides, he had been potty trained for six months and could take care of business without anyone's help, At home, he would climb onto the toilet, flush, and then tell Jackie proudly of his accomplishments. Doug had not seen any reason to change his ways simply because they had visited a store.

Placing his truck against the wall away from foot traffic, Doug had folded the cards and returned them to their box. Laying the box beside the truck, he had straightened his clothes and looked in the direction of his parents. Finding them busy, Doug had walked toward the nearest display of toilets. As he tugged off his pants, he announced to no one in particular that he had to use the toilet. Stepping onto the display platform, Doug had tried to climb onto the toilet seat but had found it too high for him to reach without the little stepladder that Jackie kept in his bathroom. With his pants around his ankles and his butt exposed to all in the store, Doug had yelled at the top of his voice that he needed to urinate.

Jackie, seeing her little boy standing butt naked to the world, had quickly pulled up his pants and carried him toward the restroom sign. Doug at first had not understood his mother's intentions and had tried to squirm out of her arms. After she had explained to him that he could not use the display toilets, Doug had quieted down. However, after that day, Jackie had paid more attention to him when she had taken him to a bath shop. Her independent little man had taught her an invaluable lesson.

However, Doug had not changed his ways. He had always been a brave, adventurous type who feared nothing. He had wanted a scooter when he was five. Despite Jackie's fear that Doug would fall, Bill had purchased one for him. Doug had been delighted and had immediately started riding it up and down the street. At first he had proceeded with caution, but as his coordination had increased so had his speed. Jackie had warned him not to whip around the grassy knoll at the end of the court for fear that the loose gravel would cause the scooter to tip over. Doug had listened, waved, and sped away.

One day, while Jackie was tending the flower garden in the front of the house, Doug had raced his scooter even faster than ever. After being cooped up in the house all winter, he had been invigorated by the crisp spring air to the point of recklessness. Doug had gotten up a good head of steam and had come charging down the street. As he passed their house, he had shouted for Jackie to watch him take the circle. Just as he had reached the top of the circle, Doug had hit the loose rocks. His scooter had slipped from under him, and he had fallen hard.

Doug had picked up his scooter and had begun the walk home as Jackie rushed down the street toward him. His knees had been badly scraped but it was nothing that peroxide, antibiotic cream, and bandages would not have solved. However, the skin of his chin had been badly mangled.

Jackie had taken him upstairs and had immediately treated the knees. However, under the bright light of the bathroom, she had seen that tiny rocks had become embedded in his chin. Using a nose aspirator, she had bathed the skin with water. However, unable to dislodge the pebbles, Jackie had decided to take Doug to the hospital.

Making the first of three visits to the emergency room, Jackie had sat patiently with Doug on her lap. Finally, the physician had called them into the cubicle. Staring at Doug's chin under a magnifying glass, he had pronounced that the wound would require stitches.

Doug had sat bravely as the doctor numbed his chin and gently picked out the stones. He had remained perfectly still as the skillful practitioner had stitched up the skin. Looking at himself in a mirror the doctor had handed him, Doug had chuckled at the black and blue lower part of his face. He had then declared that he would certainly have a trophy to show his friends as soon as he had returned home.

Jackie had driven her merrily chattering son home before the tremors began. Her knees had started to buckle and her heart had begun to pound wildly by the time she had entered the house. Bill, who had not been at home at the time of the accident, had looked up from his chair to see his frighteningly pale wife sink onto the sofa. He had been at her side in an instant and had listened attentively as Jackie had recounted the story of Doug's chin and the visit to the hospital.

Making sure that Jackie was comfortable, Bill had climbed the steps to the bedroom floor. Walking into his son's room, he had tried to sound casual as he had asked Doug about his afternoon. Immediately, Doug had poured out the story of his scooter, the fall, and the nice doctor. As he listened, Bill had felt his knees grow weak. Not being one who could handle the sight of blood with ease, he had been relieved that he had not been at home at the time of the fall.

He had been grateful that Jackie had been a strong woman who could cope with anything.

Those days seemed so long ago. Leaning back in her chair beside the fire, Jackie smiled to herself. She had a wonderful family and fabulous memories. In fact, she had everything that any woman could possibly want. Other than not having her family with her on Mother's Day, Jackie had been blessed with happiness and really could not complain.

She was not like the other ladies, whose children and husbands had spent the day with them out of obligation. As soon as they felt they could free themselves, they had left them alone, preferring the company of other men and children to that of their wives and mothers. At least when Jackie's guys were at home, they gave her their undivided attention. Bill spent all of his free time with her. They shared the same interest in antique cars, gardening, and marksmanship. They went everywhere together. Doug, although a young man with many friends, gave her time every evening during which they still watched television together. Jackie often heard her college man son tell his friends that he had plans to spend his limited time at home with his parents.

Looking around the room at the less-than-happy women, Jackie sighed under the comfortable weight of the love and affection of her family. She knew that she was on their minds as much as they were on hers. Despite their absence on Mother's Day, Jackie was a very happy woman.

"Jackie, you haven't told us much about your family. All we know is that they couldn't be here on Mother's Day. Tell us more," Bea cajoled in an intoxicated lisp.

Smiling, Jackie replied, "I guess there isn't much to tell, really. I have a wonderful family. We do most things together, at least we did until Doug went away to college. Now, we try to squeeze as much family time as possible into his short six-week vacations."

"Oh, so he's like my son. He gives you six weeks and then hangs out with his buddies. Jeff plans to backpack through Europe this summer. He's only here today because he wanted the check for his airfare," Buffy sneered as she adjusted her gold designer watch.

"That's not the case at all. Doug attends a service academy—you know, West Point, the Naval Academy, the Air Force Academy, and the Coast Guard Academy—and spends his time with us as much as possible. They only give their students six weeks of leave each summer. The rest of the time they spend in training. He comes home as often as he can during the academic year, but the demands on his time of a dual curriculum are heavy," Jackie replied with a proud smile at both Doug's accomplishments and his continued loyalty to his family.

"So his education is free? That should give you a lot of freedom to do whatever you want," Bea sniffed as she reached for yet another drink from the tray of the tired waiter, who wished that the bar would close and that the ladies would go home.

"It's true that we don't pay any of the normal college costs, but we do provide Doug with a monthly allowance. The students in the service academies are paid a very small salary from which the schools deduct their laundry, computer, books, supplies, clothes, haircuts, and all other items. They don't have much left. Actually, Doug only had forty dollars each month to spend on himself his freshman year. Not that he had much time to spend it. He was always standing watch and attending the mandatory sporting events. He carried an incredibly heavy academic load that he had to balance with the mandatory military training. And on top of the immediate loss of freedom, he will owe the government five years of his life once he graduates. So it's not really free. A life spent in a combat zone carries a hefty price," Jackie responded with a bit of sadness mixed into the immense pride she felt for her son.

"Well, I guess I'm glad that my nephew didn't go to one of those schools. I had always thought that they had a free ride with lots of cash to spend and plenty of free time. I didn't realize that the regulations were so strict. It must be especially hard on the kids who live on the opposite coasts from the schools. They must have a terrible time getting home," Bea commented while repositioning her lithe frame in the overstuffed sofa.

"Their families don't see much of them since they have no weekends to travel while freshmen and only three long weekends as sophomores. Having a kid matriculating at a service academy is a family commitment," Jackie replied as she studied the new expressions of understanding and empathy that filled the faces of the women.

"I guess I won't complain about not seeing more of my son. At least when I send him the airfare, he comes home. Sometimes, it appears as if he never goes to college. What's that they say about tuition these days? The more prestigious the school, the higher the tuition, and the less the kids attend classes," Bea added with an infectious laugh that spread throughout their group.

As the animated conversation continued, Jackie thought about all the parades she had attended at Doug's school. She remembered the time during his freshman or plebe training that she had marched along beside him without his ever sensing her presence. And then there were the numerous boxes of cookies and cheese crackers that she had delivered to the main office so that he would have something to eat before bed. She had had to endure the long six weeks of his initial training during which she could not have direct contact with him but serendipitously stumbled across him in the school's dining hall one Sunday after Mass. Those few stolen minutes would live with her forever. The joy that had illuminated his face at seeing her, the pride that had radiated from him at having survived the training, and the thrill that had overflowed from him for having a few hours to himself had been engraved in her memory forever.

Jackie remembered going to the football games, not to watch the action, but to catch a glimpse of Doug in the crowd of four thousand students. As a plebe, he had not been allowed to sit with her in the stands but had to stay in the pack. She had routinely prowled the stadium food stands searching for him. One of those times, she had been lucky and had found him as he purchased a hot dog at the concession near her seat. He had traveled as far from his assigned seat as he had dared in the hopes of having a minute with her. They had chatted as he smeared mustard on his hot dog. The moments had flown by too quickly, and he soon returned to his seat at the other side of the stadium.

She remembered, too, all the times she had picked him out in a crowd of students all dressed in the same uniform. Doug walked with a sway of his shoulders that made his tall, thin frame easy to isolate. As he paraded with his classmates, she could find him by that almost leonine movement. No one else had that unique movement.

However, Jackie had learned to recognize him in the dark, too, when she could not see the carefree movement of his body. She and Bill had attended a pregame bonfire at the service academy. The field had been populated by all of the twelve hundred plebes. As darkness filled the field, they had lit the five-story high piles of logs. Jackie had scanned the faces in the crowd for Doug, but she had not seen him anywhere. The light from the burning fire had not provided illumination for her to read the faces of the many students who cheered wildly for their team's victory over their arch enemy.

Feeling dejected as the fires had burned out and darkness had returned, Jackie had once again searched for her son, with the growing knowledge that she probably would not see him that evening. Suddenly, she had seen a thin figure walking through the crowd at a distance of twenty-five feet. Knowing there were hundreds of students as thin and tall as Doug, she had forced herself to remain composed. Walking toward him in darkness so thick she could not see more than a few feet in front of her, Jackie moved with the undulating current of the crowd.

Keeping her eyes on the young man's profile, Jackie had felt her heart begin to pound. She had sensed in a secret place in her soul that the youth in the blue and gold sweatsuit was her son although she could not make out his features. She had continued to close the distance between them as others cut into her line of sight.

Under her watchful eyes, the figure had suddenly reversed its direction and had started moving away from her. Afraid that she would lose him in the crowd, Jackie had called out her son's name. Only the darkness had answered.

Beginning to run on the field filled with divots, Jackie had again called his name into the milling students. Slowly, as if awakening from a deep sleep, the figure had turned in her direction. In the darkness of nine o'clock in late November, Doug had heard his mother's voice.

As they had closed the distance between them, Doug's features had become visible in the remains of the bonfire's glow. Wearing a smile from ear to ear, Doug had walked rapidly toward her. Immediately, Jackie had forgotten the crowds and thrown her arms around her son. For a few moments on that cold Thursday evening, Doug had allowed Jackie to embrace him in front of his classmates. He had been scouring the crowd in the darkness for her and had feared that they would not meet. For a few minutes, the school's strict rules about spending time with family had not mattered.

Jackie knew in her heart that she would never forget that moment when Doug had been her little boy again. Nothing and no one could separate their souls and their hearts. He would always be her son.

"Jackie, it's getting late. I'd better get you back home. We both have to go to work tomorrow," Dee said, intruding in her sister's thoughts.

"You're right, Dee. I was enjoying the company and the fire so much that I lost track of time," Jackie commented as she slipped her feet into her shoes. Rising, she stretched before thanking the ladies for a most enjoyable evening.

"Don't be a stranger here, Jackie. I'd be more than happy to sponsor you myself," Bea stated warmly as she stood unsteadily to hug Jackie good night.

"Bring that handsome son of yours with you next time. I have a niece I'd like for him to meet," Buffy added as she staggered over for a hug.

Chuckling inwardly, Jackie replied, "We'll return soon. I promise."

Walking to the car in the cool May evening, Dee asked, "Did you really like them? I know that Bea and Buffy can be a bit much sometimes."

"They were lovely. Thanks for bringing me here. I've had a wonderful Mother's Day," Jackie replied as she hugged her baby sister close.

Dee looked at Jackie with tears in her eyes. She had

adored her big sister when they were children, but, as the demands of family and work had filled their lives, they had drifted apart. Now that Dee was unattached once again and Doug had grown up, Dee hoped they could be close once more. Giving Jackie a memorable day had been part of her plan to reunite them.

"Good. I'm glad, Jackie. You deserve it," Dee responded as she kissed Jackie on the cheek.

They spent the drive home in animated reminiscing about the day. As sisters often do, they argued amicably about the fine points but generally agreed that they had made many wonderful memories together.

Their mother had died five years before, making Mother's Day a bittersweet occasion. Since her mother's death, Dee had divorced and discovered herself basically alone, despite her abundance of friends. Jackie and Dee had become closer as Jackie included her in more of her family's activities, in addition to their annual vacation trips. Often the two of them had gone shopping together or to the movies together while Bill and Doug had played golf. Jackie had done everything she could to fill Dee's life with happiness.

Now the tables had turned. Dee had rescued Jackie from the loneliness that she would have experienced in her empty house with both of her guys out of town. Jackie's Mother's Day had been a success because of her little sister's efforts.

Five

Jackie's neighborhood was silent when they returned at almost midnight. Bats fluttered around the occasional streetlight, and rabbits hopped across the street in search of better grazing in the neighbor's yard. Deer blinked in the headlights but continued munching the fresh buds off the dogwood tree. The lights had already gone out in the living room and dining room, and Jackie's house was dark and lonely.

"I'll go in with you," Dee offered as she turned off the car and picked up her bag.

"Don't be silly. You're tired and need to get your rest. I can make it just fine by myself," Jackie replied, always the big sister who had to face danger and dark houses alone to set an example for her sibling to follow.

"No, I'm going in with you. Your house is too dark for you to enter alone," Dee insisted as she joined Jackie on the flagstone walkway.

"And who will be waiting for you? I'm a big girl, Dee. I can go it alone, thanks. Good night," Jackie said firmly as she gave her sister a gentle shove in the direction of her car.

"I guess you've got a point. But at least I changed the timer. My house won't be this dark," Dee acquiesced as she hugged Jackie good night.

"I'm not used to going out at night without Bill.

I'll do better next time. Call me when you get home. Thanks again for a wonderful Mother's Day, Dee," Jackie replied as she kissed her little sister on her carefully made up cheek. Even this late in the evening, Dee still smelled of expensive perfume and looked so perfectly coiffed that she could have been going out on the town rather than home to bed.

Waving good-bye, Dee quickly backed her car down the driveway and into the street. The deer standing on the edge of the neighbor's yard barely lifted its head as she sped up the street and barely missed hitting a rabbit as it slipped under the hedge. She was out of sight before Jackie could get the key into the lock of her front door.

Dee was right. The house was too dark and much too empty. Jackie remembered a time when Doug would have bounded down the steps to greet her. Now, only the sound of the grandfather clock and the hum of the refrigerator in the kitchen met her as she pushed open the door and flicked on the hall light.

When Doug had been little, he had always waited for Jackie to come home before doing his homework. He had watched for her from the family room window while Bill had cooked dinner until she had pulled her car safely into the garage. Then, he had unlocked the door and had run to greet her. He had wrapped his thin little arms around her waist and had squeezed with all of his strength. Laughing, he had turned his happy face up to her for a kiss. Leading her into the house, he had fastened the door to keep the outside from intruding on their family time.

When he had grown older, Doug had stopped waiting for her at the door, but he had still listened for her return. As soon as he had heard her key in the lock, he had stopped his studying and had joined her in the kitchen. As Jackie had greeted both of them, they had shared their adventures and tribulations, with one trying to outdo the other.

Doug had followed her upstairs and had sat in the chair outside her closet door while Jackie had changed clothes. Through the closed door, they had continued their discussions. By the time Bill had dinner on the table, all the unhappiness of the day had been discussed, leaving them with pleasant dinner conversation.

Even when Jackie had taken the year off from work to spend with Doug during his senior year of high school, they had waited until they had reached the kitchen to share the news of their day. The drive home had given him time to relax but had not provided the peaceful environment he had needed. Then, as she had prepared his snack, Doug had told her everything that had happened to him before he had gone up to his room to study. There had been something comforting about being at home and safe that had caused Doug to let down his usual protective guard.

Bill, too, had loved for her to return home so he could unburden himself on Jackie's shoulders. He had the shorter commute and always arrived home first. While he had prepared the dinner, he had formulated the presentation for his concerns, selecting the items he wished to share with Jackie. As soon as Doug had finished his stories, Bill had begun his. Neither of them had ever really wanted her to solve their problems. All they had wanted was for Jackie to listen and share their lives.

Although more complicated and usually financial in nature, Doug's and Bill's stories had carried equal importance with Jackie. She had listened attentively to both of her guys as they had talked through the problems of the day, had arrived at conclusions, or had shared simple items of interest. When they had satisfied their need to unload, both of them had paid courteous attention to her activities. One of Jackie's favorite parts of the day had been the interaction between the members of her family.

With Doug away at school, things had changed. Bill still waited anxiously for her to return home, but the patter of a running child's feet no longer greeted her. She missed the big hugs that had not stopped even as Doug grew into young manhood. Jackie and Bill still shared their day's adventures although they usually talked over dinner. Gone were the lingering conversations with Doug.

Most of all, however, Jackie missed their family time. Regardless of the amount of work any of them had to do before going to bed, they had always met in the family room for an hour of television watching and snuggling. Nightly, Doug had stretched out on the sofa with his head in Jackie's lap while Bill had sat beside them in his favorite chair. They had either watched the national channels or old movies. It had not really mattered which one since the purpose had been for them to put aside everything and to spend time together. Just as they had never missed eating dinner together, they had always put distractions from their lives and shared their quality evening time together.

Even now when Doug came home from school, they still kept meal times and the hour of quality time sacred. Doug always planned his social time with his friends to occur after his dinner hour, and he always returned home in time for them to spend time together before going to bed. He still snuggled while watching television and sharing critiques of the movies he and his friends had seen with his parents.

Jackie could still hear the sweet sound of his childish voice of eight or nine ringing through the house as he had called to her that his kiss meter had run low. She had stopped whatever she had been doing and gone to wherever he sat and kissed him until he had laughed and begged her to stop. Usually, he had been playing the piano in the living room, but sometimes he had been in his bedroom. Jackie had never minded the walk up the long flights of stairs. Her son had needed her.

As he had aged, Doug had stopped saying that he needed her kisses. Instead, he had started draping himself around her shoulders and giving her bear hugs. Sometimes, he had merely teased her about being so short at five foot seven that he could eat soup off her head. The gentle teasing had become another form of affection.

And Jackie still tucked him in at night. Some things, thankfully, never changed in her life. Doug went away to school to be a man, but he came home to be her child. She hoped that none of his experiences in the service academy or the military would ever change the closeness of their lives.

Bill, too, demanded her time and attention. His favorite way of drawing her to his side was to call for his "wifey." When he thought that Jackie had spent enough time in the library doing work, Bill lured her into the family room with his resounding but pathetic bellow.

Now, walking through the silent rooms, Jackie missed the sound of their voices. Thanks to Dee, she had enjoyed a wonderful day, but she was still lonely for her guys. Her life was always so much richer when they were with her.

Jackie did not even mind doing the endless loads of wash that accompanied Doug's return from college. Unlike many mothers who insisted that their almost grown children assume the responsibility for their own clothing, Jackie liked the teenage, almost man smell of her no longer little boy. She enjoyed feeling needed by a young man who could very easily take care of himself and was being trained to be a leader of men. As long as Doug brought home his laundry, Jackie would wash it.

She enjoyed doing the little things that made their lives easier. Bill had lived for ten years as a bachelor prior to their marriage; however, he had forgotten how to sew on buttons and press creases in slacks as soon as they had married. Jackie knew that he could do these simple tasks if he really wanted to do them, but she did not mind when he asked her to help him.

Jackie would sew on his buttons or hem his trousers while watching television and talking with Bill in the evenings. She would do Doug's wash while preparing their meals. Maybe she was old-fashioned and out of step with the ways of the new working woman, but Jackie felt that her life was so enriched by their presence that she did not consider their requests an imposition.

When Doug returned to school after the weekends or one of his short vacations, Jackie would go into his room and inhale his smell as it lingered in his pillow and the clothes that he had hung on his coat tree. She would fill her soul with the fragrance of his scent, his natural body aroma since he did not wear colognes or aftershaves.

Jackie had been so distraught when he first went away to college that she had slept in his bed. As time had gone by, Jackie had been able to face the emptiness of her house without that crutch and had gone about her day with a heavy heart. Gradually, Jackie had learned she could live without Doug and had made a life as an empty nester.

Yet, every time Doug came home, Jackie felt a new awakening of herself. She became a mother again and loved every minute of baking his favorite pies and cakes, cooking the chicken and walnut dish he loved so much, and having his head on her lap. She loved the sense of belonging to a greater whole that having him at home gave her. After all, it was because of Doug's birth that Jackie had experienced all the joys of being a mother and a woman.

However, Jackie felt the same loneliness whenever either she or Bill traveled on business. She needed the grounding her family gave her, and she always hurried home after attending conferences. She packed her bags prematurely so she would not miss her flights. When Bill was the one away from the nest, Jackie waited anxiously for him to return. She usually left work early so she could prepare his favorite dishes as his homecoming present. Jackie needed her family in order to feel complete.

That unsatisfied need had been the cause of her sluggishness that morning. Jackie had seen no reason to jump out of bed. She had no breakfasts to fix, no last-minute laundry to do, and no one making welcome demands on her time. Her church offered more than one Sunday Mass; she could go anytime. She could pick up something to eat for breakfast at the fast food place down the street. She had put away all of their clean clothes. Jackie had felt relief when Dee had phoned to invite her out for the day. She would not have to face the loneliness of her house and her life without her husband and son.

Now, as Jackie walked through the dark house illuminated only by the moonlight streaming through the windows, she was alone again. Reaching the library she had commandeered as her office when she wrote her first children's book, she threw her purse onto the desk and fell into the chair. She really should go to bed but that meant climbing the stairs to her empty bedroom.

Looking out the window into the backyard, Jackie saw the tree house that Bill had built for Doug silhouetted in the silvery light. Bill had worked so hard to construct the platform, erect the four-foot sides, and place the handmade ladder at just the right angle. He had felt so proud when Doug and his buddies had climbed up to survey the yard. In their eight-year-old imaginations, the simple tree house had become a fortress and the barking dog had transformed into a mighty dragon.

The tree house sat empty now that Doug had grown up. He had become too big to climb through the trap door. The platform no longer appeared as far from the ground. The dog had become simply his pet. Even the tree that held the house had changed. Its branches had stopped reaching for the sky as it slowly succumbed to old age and blight. One day Bill would take it down and reuse the lumber from the desolate tree house to build Jackie's garden shed.

Rising from her seat, Jackie forced herself to make the climb up the darkened staircase. She could have turned on the lights, but, somehow, the darkness suited her mood. Besides, she knew every cranny of that house. She had walked the floors with a sick child often enough not to need the help of lights to find her way around.

Jackie had tiptoed down the hall to Doug's room so many times that she could no longer count the number. She had peeked in to see him sleeping soundly, with the nightlight providing a soft, comforting glow. His dog had slept at the foot of the bed until Jackie turned out her light, and then the scruffy little animal had left the security of Doug's curled leg and joined her. As soon as Doug's feet hit the floor in the morning, the dog had scampered back to his room as if it had realized that the boy had needed protection.

That night, passing Doug's room, Jackie stopped from habit. She took a deep breath and drew in the memory of his scent before continuing to her own room. Soon the school year would end and once again he would fill the room with energy.

Her room contained the mingled fragrances of her perfume and Bill's after-shave lotion. Instead of making a thundercloud of smell, they united to create a combination that was uniquely their signature aroma. Flipping on the lamp, Jackie changed into her old, faded, comfortable nightgown that Bill and Doug had given her for Mother's Day eight years ago. Slipping her feet into her terrycloth slippers, she padded to the bathroom to scrub off the remaining makeup.

Strangely, although Bill had been away from home for almost a week, Jackie thought she could still smell his cologne in the bathroom. She knew her memory of their smells was particularly active today, but this fragrance was even more vivid than the one she had encountered that morning. It was almost as if Bill had recently been in the room.

The same feeling had swept over her as she passed Doug's room, too. Jackie had almost stopped to pick up the shirt that she did not remember seeing on his bed earlier. She was certain she had put away any of the stray clothes that he had left lying on his bed, but she must have been mistaken.

Jackie adjusted her pillow and climbed into bed. Immediately, she was wide awake. It was not the silence of the empty house that bothered her but a feeling that something was not as she had left it when she went out with Dee. After twisting and turning in the futile effort of falling asleep, Jackie decided to put the nagging thought out of her mind by going downstairs and having a look around the house. She had to satisfy herself that all was as it should be before she could sleep.

This time Jackie flipped on the hall light before descending the stairs. As the light illuminated the risers, she immediately thought about the time Doug had experienced a sleepwalking episode. He had traveled down the stairs, had walked through the kitchen, and had entered the family room door while Jackie and Bill had been watching television. His little footie-clad feet had made hardly any noise as he had approached the door and begun trying to enter the garage. If Jackie had not stopped him, he would have walked out into the night.

Jackie had instantly realized that he had been asleep from the blank stare on his face. She had quietly and gently guided her sleeping son back up the stairs to his bedroom. When he had awakened in the morning, Doug had not remembered anything about the trip. To make sure he never had the opportunity to let himself out of the house again, Bill had moved the key ring beyond the reach of Doug's little fingers.

But Jackie was not sleepwalking as she made her way through the brightly illuminated hall. As she passed each room, she scanned its interior for any signs of open windows or items out of place. Finding nothing, she continued to the kitchen, which was well-lit by the rays of moonlight shining onto the light gray floor.

A stranger would have found nothing out of the ordinary as she surveyed the kitchen. Jackie, however, knew better. She was intimately familiar with every nook and cranny of the room. She had personally placed each print on the wall and hung each artificial flower in the blue lattice that circled the room. She had handed Bill the tiles that he had masterfully applied to the walls behind the countertop. Something was not as she had left it, and Jackie would not sleep until she discovered the source of the problem.

Jackie checked the window and door and found them locked as she turned on the light. She studied the location of every piece of furniture and decorative article on the sideboard and saw nothing out of place. Turning her attention to the counter, Jackie discovered that her white and red teacup still sat on the counter where she had left it that morning before going to church.

Yet, something was different. Running her hands across the counter, Jackie felt a fine grit. Thinking that maybe she had spilled sugar that morning, she reached under the sink for the dish cloth. She moistened it although it was still unexpectedly damp.

Wiping in slow motions, Jackie tried to think back to the morning as she had rushed to get ready for church and her day with Dee. She had drunk a cup of tea while standing at the sink and looking out the window at the finches. Five of the hungry little birds had gathered to feed on the thistle seeds in the feeder. They had twittered happily as they had pecked at the food and had not even noticed she had been watching them.

She had washed out her cup and placed it face down on the counter. Surely, she would have remembered seeing the grit and would have cleaned it up. Yet, Jackie did not remember making the mess.

Returning the cloth to the cabinet, Jackie wandered toward the family room. Along the way, she bumped into a full trash bag sitting by the wall oven. Knowing that she had not moved the trash that morning and that she would never have left the bag in the walkway, Jackie immediately stopped in her tracks and peered into the dark family room.

Seeing nothing out of the ordinary, Jackie reached around the corner and flipped on the light. For a moment, she stood blinded by the light. As her eyes adjusted to the brightness, she gasped in shock. To her surprise, she discovered her husband sleeping in his favorite chair and her son stretched out on the sofa, snoring. Bill was still wearing his suit with the tie pulled loose at the neck, and Doug had slipped out of his uniform and into his favorite sweatsuit.

Both of them were so sound asleep that Jackie hated to awaken them.

Tiptoeing toward them, Jackie smiled as the tears welled in her eyes. A sign that read "Happy Mother's Day, Mommy" lay across Doug's long body. Bill held a half-eaten box of chocolates in his hands as the balloons bobbed overhead.

Opening his eyes and stretching, Doug said accusingly, "What time is it? I thought you'd never come home."

Bill looked out of one eye and added sleepily, "We waited so long we got hungry. Sorry, but this is all that remains of your candy. Where we you all this time? I rushed home to spend the evening with you and you weren't here."

"I spent the day with Dee. She didn't want me to be alone on Mother's Day. Why didn't you guys let me know that you would be coming home. I would have come home sooner" Jackie replied as she kissed Bill on his upturned mouth. Lifting Doug's head into her lap, she took her usual seat on the sofa.

Snuggling against her, Doug answered, "I didn't know that they'd give me leave until after dinner. One of my senior friends who doesn't have an exam tomorrow either drove me home. I have to return by ten tomorrow morning."

"I skipped the closing session and drove like a crazy man to get here. I guess we should have planned ahead. By the way, that's a cute little hat," Bill added with a crooked smile as he rubbed the sleep from his eyes.

"Thank you for noticing, dear. I'm so glad that you guys could make it home. All that matters is that you're here with me for Mother's Day," Jackie replied as she hugged her son and blew a kiss to her husband.

"Hey, that's right. It is still Sunday. Happy Mother's Day, Mommy," Doug said as he smiled into her face.

Jackie had never been happier. Her husband sat safely in his favorite chair, and her son lay within the protection of her arms. Jackie had learned that Mother's Day was more than cards, flowers, and candy. Mother's Day was a time for remembering all the wonderful and heart-wrenching things that made being a mother an enriching experience. Jackie would store the memory of this day in a special compartment in her heart along with all the other treasures that she held dear.

MATERNAL INSTINCTS

Kayla Perrin

In the spirit of Mother's Day
This story is dedicated to my own mother:
Una Perrin.
Your unconditional love and support
mean the world to me.
Thanks for that.
I love you.

One

For the fifth time in as many minutes, Lexy Sinclair glanced at the silver watch gracing her left wrist. Then frowned. Was it possible for time to have actually slowed down? Though it wasn't yet midnight, it seemed like she and her friends had been out for several hours.

"Lexy." Pauline spoke sternly over the pulsating music in the South Beach club as she covered Lexy's watch and pushed her arm down. "Are you gonna keep staring at your watch, or are you gonna finally let loose and enjoy yourself?"

"I've seen more excited expressions on corpses," Lynda chimed with a mock-sour expression as she swayed her hips seductively to the R&B beat. Over Lexy's shoulder, she reached for the frozen daiquiri on the bar behind her. "Drink." She passed the drink to Lexy. "It will loosen you up."

"I'm sorry," Lexy apologized, accepting the drink, though she didn't feel like drinking it. She felt awkward being out, even if she was with her two best friends in the world. "I don't know why I'm so tense."

"Because as long as I've known you, you've never known how to relax. C'mon, shake that booty, girl!" To urge her friend on, Pauline bumped her hip against Lexy's.

Instead of catching the beat, Lexy stumbled and

nearly lost her drink. She recovered her footing before making a total fool of herself.

Lynda and Pauline exchanged concerned stares.

"God, I'm such a klutz!" Lexy exclaimed, turning to place the drink back on the bar.

"I don't know, Pauline," Lynda began. "I'm starting to wonder if we should take this personally."

"Maybe Lexy doesn't want to be out with *us,*" Pauline concluded.

Lynda draped an arm over Lexy's shoulder. "Is that it, hon? You don't want to be out with the girls tonight? Should we hook you up with one of these hot men here?"

"Lynda, please," Lexy retorted. It had been so long since she'd been on a date that she wasn't even sure she'd know how to behave on one. "That's not it and you know it."

"You sure? Because if it's a hot man you want . . ." Lynda's voice trailed off as she watched a tall, very fine brother walk by. "Mmm mmm mmm. Don't even look twice at him, girlfriend, cause that one's mine."

"You can have him," Lexy said, meaning it. If she couldn't be comfortable with her friends, some strange man wasn't going to help ease her tension. "Of course I want to be with my girls." She forced a smile. "It's just that I haven't been out in so long . . ."

"And you're worried about Shauna." Pauline spoke the words as a statement.

She hadn't realized that was the reason for her anxiety until Pauline voiced her subconscious thought. "Yeah, I am," Lexy said slowly. It was the first night in ages she hadn't been around to tuck Shauna into bed. But that's exactly where her daughter was—safe at home, in bed. So why was she worried? "I know it's crazy . . ."

Lynda moved to stand in front of Lexy. "Hey, I hear you, but Shauna is fine. It's not like she's two and can't understand why mommy isn't around. She's ten, girlfriend."

"It's just that I haven't left her with this sitter before."

"But you know her, right?" Lynda asked.

"Oh, yeah. I've known her and her family for years."

"And she's responsible," Lynda added.

Lexy realized where Lynda was going with this line of questioning. "Yes. As far as I know, Rita's very responsible."

"Then why are you worried?" Lynda affectionately rubbed Lexy's arm. "Shauna is fine."

Lynda was right. Lexy should be able to enjoy a night out with her girlfriends and not worry about her daughter. "You're right."

"This has to be a first—you agreeing with me." Lynda grinned. "Now, are you gonna finish that drink so we can hit the dance floor? You might not be interested in finding a man, but I'm still young and I ain't ever been married . . ."

"Okay, okay, okay," Lexy said, holding up a hand. She reached for the daiquiri and took a long sip of the fruity drink just as the opening notes to TLC's latest hit blared across the speakers. "Ooh, I love this song," she said, finally feeling in the mood to dance. "C'mon."

She still had more than half a drink to go, but she could dance and drink. She wasn't *that* much of a klutz. So she stepped before her friends and toward the dance floor, moving her body to the funky beat. It did feel good to let loose.

But while she shook her body, she still couldn't quite shake the nagging feeling that something wasn't right with Shauna.

*   *   *

"Oh, no thanks." Lexy smiled politely. "I don't drink." That wasn't exactly a lie. She didn't drink much, and because she was driving, the daiquiri she'd had was the only alcohol she would consume tonight.

She tried to step around the man, but he blocked her path. "How about a dance, then?"

Now she knew why there was a crowd of men around the women's restroom; they were all waiting to pounce on the single women. "Sorry. My friends are waiting for me at the bar."

"Maybe later then?" the man asked, not willing to give up.

She finally took a good look at him. He was average looking but had a sense of style, judging by the expensive suit he wore. Though Lexy had no idea how he was coping in all those clothes. She was wearing a mini-dress and her sweat glands were working overtime. He was also shorter than her by about an inch—which was a definite no-no. She knew she shouldn't judge a man by his height, but was it wrong to be attracted to taller brothers? Besides, she certainly wasn't looking for a relationship, and Mr. Not-So-Fine struck her as the clingy type. She hated clingy.

"Maybe," she lied, moving past him.

He took her hand before she could get away. Shocked by his boldness, she whirled around. He clearly couldn't understand when a woman wasn't interested, so she would have to give it to him straight.

He smiled. "I'll be waiting."

Forever, Lexy added silently, her choice words for him dying in her throat. She freed her hand. Though a little too aggressive, he seemed nice enough, but she just wasn't interested. She hadn't been interested in anyone since Richard's death. As she made her way through the dense crowd, not daring to look back at him—for she knew he was watching her—she prayed he'd forget about her by the end of the night.

Spotting Lynda and Pauline at the bar, she moved toward them, relieved. She wouldn't leave their sides for the rest of the evening!

Lynda and Pauline were her two dearest friends in the world. They'd met as sophomores in a high school English class and had remained friends ever since. She'd never had a sister, but they more than made up for that.

And even though they didn't see each other all too often—their lives had taken different paths as they'd gotten older—she still hadn't found better friends. She doubted she ever would.

They had stood by her through her darkest hours in high school, when the scandal of being pregnant and seventeen had sent her into a depression. Their support had made the whole situation much easier to bear. And they had been there for her again three years ago when her life had taken another downward spiral. Losing her husband and the father of her daughter had been more difficult than anything she could have imagined, and at times she'd doubted she could effectively parent Shauna alone. Would she have enough money? Would she be strong enough? Through all her doubts, Lynda and Pauline had been there for her, giving her encouragement and support, watching Shauna on the occasions that Lexy just needed peace, and finally, Lexy had moved on. Survived. She had learned that she could be strong for her daughter, which was ultimately the most important thing.

Lynda had never been married, though she'd come close a few times. Pauline had been engaged twice, married once. Lexy had married her first and only boyfriend, and after his death, she hadn't been with anyone else. Though they were all in their late twenties, of the trio, Lexy was the only one who was a mother.

"Remind me not to leave your side again," Lexy announced, making a space for herself at the bar. "I definitely attract all the weird ones."

"Why do you think I've never been married?" Lynda asked, frowning. "It seems they're all weird these days. Of course, all the good ones are taken."

"Your problem is that you ignore the obvious ones," Pauline stated, giving Lynda a pointed look.

"Don't even start."

"It's the truth. Even though you ignore him, Byron is so in love with you."

"He's a good friend," Lynda protested.

"And you don't want to ruin the friendship," Pauline mocked. "Girl, that's how the best relationships start!" Lexy smiled as she listened to her friends banter over the pros and cons of Lynda dating Byron. She had to agree with Pauline on this one. Byron was perfect for Lynda. She hoped Lynda would realize that before it was too late.

Lexy had left her purse with her friends when she'd gone to the restroom, and now she opened it in search of some lipstick. Not that she wanted to impress anyone; her lips were getting a little dry.

She felt something vibrate inside her purse, and for a moment, she was startled. Then she realized that it was her beeper.

Her beeper! Her heart jumped. If she was getting beeped now, it had to be her baby-sitter, Rita.

Shauna.

Instantly her fingers closed around the beeper and she pulled it out of her purse. She checked the number in the dim club lighting. It was her home number.

Oh, God.

"Everything okay?" Pauline asked. She was standing before Lexy, regarding her with concern.

"I don't know." Lexy clutched her purse to her erratically beating heart and pushed her way through the crowd, heading for the club's entrance. The deaf-ening music made the option of using her cell phone in there a non-option.

Still, once outside, she had to hold a hand over one ear as she listened to her home phone ring. Why wasn't Rita answering?

Pauline and Lynda had followed her out, and now they stared at her with a worried expression. But they didn't ask any questions.

Finally, Rita answered the phone. "Hello?"

The anxiety in her baby-sitter's voice didn't escape Lexy, and her heart rate quadrupled. "Rita, what's going on?"

"Oh, Mrs. Sinclair. I'm so sorry!"

Don't panic. "Why, Rita? What's wrong?"

"It's Shauna," Rita replied, and it was clear now that the girl was crying. "She's missing."

"Missing?" The word caused Lexy's head to spin, her world to spin. Dear God in heaven, her baby was missing. It was almost one in the morning, so where on earth could she be?

"I beeped you almost two hours ago."

Lexy had left her beeper in her purse since she'd had no place to put it on her dress. Why hadn't she checked it earlier? Why, oh why had she gone out? "I only got your page a few minutes ago," she replied, trying not to panic. Trying to ignore the guilt eating at her. "Rita, did you call the police?"

Rita sniffed. "Yeah. They're here."

"Okay. I'm on my way." Lexy flipped up the mouth-piece on her phone and hustled down the club's steps.

"What's going on?" Pauline asked, falling into step beside her.

"It's Shauna," Lexy answered, the emotion in her throat almost choking her. "My baby's missing!"

* * *

At first Marcel Kennedy thought he was dreaming. After all, he was flat on his stomach with his face buried in a pillow, and his body felt like a dead weight. For a change, he had actually gone to bed when most of the world did, and he knew the night hadn't drifted away so quickly. So he had to be dreaming, and for that reason, he ignored the phone.

But a couple of moments later, when in his dream the waiter asked, "Aren't you going to answer that?" he was jarred awake with the realization that the phone was actually ringing in the real world. His eyes flew open. Knowing it could be the station, he threw a hand out to retrieve the receiver. It took a bit of fumbling before it reached his ear. "Hello?"

"Marcel, hi. I'm sorry to wake you."

He forced his head up. He hadn't heard his ex-wife's voice in ages, which meant something was definitely wrong. "Pauline?"

"I know it's late, Marcel, and I'm sorry." Her voice held a hint of hysteria. "But we have an emergency and I . . ."

"What's the matter?"

"Lexy's daughter is missing!"

Though it was late and he'd hoped for nothing more than to catch up on some much-needed sleep, Pauline's news awoke him as surely as if he'd been doused with cold water. A missing child was every cop's worst nightmare. He sat up. "Shauna?"

"Uh-huh."

"How long has she been missing?"

"We're not sure, but at least a few hours."

A few hours—that definitely wasn't good. "Did you call the police?"

"The baby-sitter did."

"Where are you now?" There was an echo on the line and Marcel wondered if Pauline was on her cell phone. "Are you driving?"

"We were out when Lexy got the news, so we're heading to her place now. Look, Marcel, I know it's late, but if you could meet us—"

"Say no more. I'll meet you there." He was out of bed and reaching for his jeans the next instant. "Now it's been a while since I've been to her place, so you'll have to tell me how to get there."

Pauline gave him the address and brief directions, then hung up.

Two minutes later, Marcel was dressed and in his car.

It seemed like hours before Lexy pulled her car into the driveway of the small home she rented in Fort Lauderdale, but it was really less than forty minutes. Seeing the police cruisers on the street made the whole thing real, and panic unlike anything she'd ever known gripped her heart. This was worse than when she'd heard about Richard, and that had been absolutely horrifying. Worse because Shauna was her baby.

Her baby. *God, please let her be all right,* she prayed silently, tears already streaming down her face as she dashed from the car.

Because Lynda and Pauline had been drinking, Lexy had driven home. Her nerves were a jumbled mess but she'd made it home safely because she'd had to, because she had to be there for her daughter.

But now that she was home, she felt like she would crumble into a ball on the pavement.

She felt two sets of arms around her as emotion caused her to sway. Lynda and Pauline, always there.

"Come on," Lynda said as they both helped her walk toward the house.

Lexy inhaled a deep breath, drawing strength from her friends. She had to be strong for Shauna.

Pauline had called Marcel Kennedy, her ex-husband and a Miami police officer, en route to Lexy's house. He'd gone to high school with them all, so Lexy knew him too, though she hadn't seen him in years. He had promised to meet them at the house, and Lexy was grateful for that. Seeing a friendly face among the police officers would help ease her stress.

If anything could.

Rita appeared in the doorway, and seeing them, she leaped from the porch and down the steps. "I'm so sorry, Mrs. Sinclair. I-I don't know what happened. She left with her friend Neringa and was supposed to come back, but then she didn't and Neringa said she hasn't seen her since nine o' clock!"

"Nine o'clock?" Somehow, Lexy kept her voice level.

"Mmm hmm." Softly, Rita started crying.

Lexy wanted to tell Rita that it was all right, that she didn't blame her, but all she could think of was the fact that her baby had been missing for more than four hours. Oh, God.

The police officer, an older white man, approached her and introduced himself as a sergeant. "You're Shauna's mother?"

Lexy could only nod.

"So it's true," Lynda said, tightening her arm around her friend. "Shauna's missing?"

He nodded. "I'm afraid so. But we're doing everything to find her. We've set up a command post a few blocks over, which is where her friend Neringa lives, since she was last seen in that area. We also have a couple cruisers searching the streets for her. And a few officers are questioning your neighbors as we speak." He paused, and the expression on his face chilled Lexy to the bone. "And while we don't think this is likely, we can't rule out the possibility that she may be at the beach. With it being so close," he added at Lexy's gasp. "So I've got officers combing that area as well."

The beach. God, no. If her baby was at the beach, out there in the dark, anything could have happened. Could happen.

"We have to find her," Lexy said urgently. She gripped the sergeant's forearm. "You will find her, right?"

"I'd love to promise you that, Mrs. Sinclair. But I can't."

Hearing those words, Lexy couldn't help herself; she burst into tears.

"But we're doing all we can, I promise you that much. Now, Mrs. Sinclair, if you'll come inside, you may be able to give us some clues as to where she might be."

Wiping her tears, Lexy looked up at him, not sure what he meant.

"Favorite places, friends Rita might not know about," he added in response to her unspoken question. "Anything you can tell us might aid in our investigation."

She brushed away her tears, telling herself once again to be strong. "Of course."

"C'mon," Lynda urged.

"I'll wait here for Marcel," Pauline announced.

Lexy felt numb, which she supposed was better than feeling pain. She had to fight the pain now, had to be strong. She let Lynda and the sergeant lead her into the house.

Pauline ran to the red Mustang as soon as it pulled up to the curb alongside Lexy's house. Marcel was out of the car almost before it came to a complete stop.

"Have they found her?" he asked, rounding the

car and hustling to Pauline. His heart paused momentarily as he awaited the answer, but he could see it in her eyes. Shauna hadn't been found.

His heart sank to his stomach. The longer a child was missing, the less likely it was that he or she would be found—alive. He prayed that wherever Shauna was, she was okay.

"God, Marcel. I've never been so scared."

Scared enough to call a cop, even if that cop was her ex-husband. He gave her a reassuring hug. "Everyone's in the house?"

"Yeah. Some sergeant is in there asking Lexy questions."

"Okay. I'll go see what I can do."

He stepped past Pauline and hopped the steps three at a time. Inside he saw a teenage girl, no doubt the baby-sitter, sitting on the armchair, her eyes swollen from crying. Lexy and Lynda sat at the small dining-room table with the sergeant.

He hadn't seen Lexy in how long—three years?—and seeing her like this nearly broke his heart. God, she looked so fragile. He remembered her after Richard's death, how she'd looked like a flower that had literally withered. She'd gone on then, but what would happen to her now if something unthinkable happened to Shauna? He prayed once again that the child would be found unharmed.

"Marcel is here," Pauline announced from behind him.

Lexy, Lynda, the baby-sitter and the sergeant immediately looked to him. A flicker of something—relief, maybe—flashed in Lexy's eyes, a look that so many people gave him when they saw him arrive in his cruiser, as though he was going to make everything all right. It was a level of trust, of confidence, that was hard to live up to, but for Lexy's sake, he hoped this time he could. If nothing else, he would do whatever it took to find her daughter.

He moved through the living room to the dining room table, nodding to the baby-sitter, then saying hello to Lexy and Lynda, and introducing himself to the sergeant.

Lexy stood, greeting him with a hug. "Marcel, I appreciate you coming."

She held him tightly, her full breasts and soft body molding to his. There was a faint smell of cigarette smoke in her hair, but more so, the delicate scent of her perfume floated into his nose. The light fragrance lingered there even after she pulled away from him. It was crazy, he knew, to notice something like her soft body and delicate perfume when the woman's daughter was missing, but he had. He'd also noticed an urge he hadn't felt in a long time—the urge to simply hold and comfort a woman, to protect her.

The last time he'd had that urge was also with Lexy, when he'd seen her at Richard's funeral. He'd held back then, merely giving her a chaste kiss and quick hug. Given the history of the situation and his friendship with Richard, it hadn't seemed appropriate to do more.

But now . . .

"I'm Sergeant Ellis." Marcel turned away from Lexy, greeting the tall officer with a handshake. "Why don't we talk over here?" Leading him to the front door, the sergeant gave Marcel a brief rundown of the situation, which didn't give him many answers. It was a few minutes to two A.M., and there was still no sign of Shauna, which meant she had been missing for close to five hours.

Not good.

Fort Lauderdale wasn't his jurisdiction, and he certainly hadn't appeared on the scene in an official capacity. But he was willing to help out in any way he could, and his knowledge as a nine-year veteran of the Miami Police Department could certainly be helpful.

"Have you gotten the media involved?" Marcel asked.

"Not yet. Not until we have to. But we have alerted all area police departments."

Marcel nodded. Since it was late, notifying the media at this stage wouldn't be that effective. But in the morning, if she was still missing . . .

"My men have gone down this entire block asking neighbors if they've seen the girl, but no luck."

Marcel swallowed, hoping to assuage his anxiety. "How can I help?"

Sergeant Ellis didn't hesitate. "We can always use another man on the streets. It doesn't hurt to retrace our steps. That little girl could be anywhere."

"All right. I'll drive around, see what I can find."

"I'm going to stay here. Wait for word."

"All right. I'll check back every half hour or so."

"Every half hour," Lexy said softly, then moaned.

Marcel was surprised to find Lexy standing behind the sergeant. He hadn't even heard her approach them.

"If we don't find her before that," Marcel told her, realizing he had alarmed her.

She gave him a tight nod, then her eyes held his, voicing a silent plea he understood only too well. *Please find my daughter.*

Turning, Marcel left the small house, determined to do just that.

Two

Whether by fate or sheer luck, the search didn't take long. As Marcel hopped down the front steps of the house toward his car, he heard the sound of screeching tires. Immediately, his head bolted in the direction of the sound, which was only a few feet to the left. A souped-up black Honda halted long enough for a door to open, then a girl stumbled out. She hit the pavement with a loud cry as the car sped off.

Shauna!

Marcel didn't have time to pay attention to the car as it disappeared into the night. His only concern was Shauna, and he sprinted toward her. He met her in the road as she climbed to her feet.

"Shauna," he said gingerly, helping her up. He wasn't sure she remembered him and didn't want to alarm her. "Remember me? I'm your mother's friend, Marcel."

She was sobbing softly, but gave him a weak nod.

"Are you okay? Are you hurt?"

"Not . . . really."

As soon as she opened her mouth, he could smell the alcohol on her breath. Great, she'd been drinking.

He held his comments inside, instead saying, "Come on." He wrapped an arm around her and led her toward the sidewalk. "We've all been so worried about you!"

"I'm sorry." Even her speech was slurred.

"No need to be sorry," he said, giving her shoulder a gentle squeeze. "Come on. Let me get you inside."

She moved with him slowly, but he suspected that was more from being shaken up emotionally and a little tipsy than from being physically injured. Still, if she had been out drinking with teenage boys, who knew what might be possible?

But he would let her mother and the Fort Lauderdale police question her. Right now, he just wanted to see the look on Lexy's face when he brought Shauna inside.

Moments later, Lexy, who was sitting with her legs curled under her on the sofa, her face resting wearily on one hand, jumped to her feet when Marcel opened the door and said, "Guess who I found?"

"Shauna!" Lexy exclaimed. She was at her daughter's side in a second, enveloping her in a bear hug. Happy tears glistened in her eyes. "Oh, Shauna! Where have you been?" She looked heavenward. "Thank you, Jesus!"

Lynda, Pauline, Rita and Sergeant Ellis all crowded Lexy and Shauna, smiles of joy and relief on their faces. Marcel grinned at the sight, his heart filled with warmth. Not every missing child case was resolved this way. Sometimes missing children didn't come home unhurt. Sometimes they didn't come home at all. Breaking bad news to parents was one of the worst parts of his job.

Lexy released her tight hold on Shauna, but let her hands linger on her arms. She crouched until she was eye level with her daughter, looking her over for visible signs of injury. "What happened?"

"I . . . I . . ." Shauna's eyes fell to the floor.

"You've been drinking," Lexy said, instantly smelling the sour scent of beer. Fear seized her heart. "Who were you with? Shauna, who were you drinking with?"

"Julie's brother and his friends."

"Oh my God," Lexy said. "Did they hurt you?" Gripping Shauna's arms, Lexy was well aware of the note of hysteria that had crept into her voice, but she couldn't control it. The first night she'd ever gotten drunk, she'd ended up in Richard Sinclair's bed. Shauna had been the result of that night. "Please, Shauna. You have to tell me."

"N-no," Shauna said finally. "They just made me drink alcohol. But I swear I didn't want to, Mama. They forced me to and they wouldn't let me go home until I did."

Relieved, Lexy stood and wrapped her daughter in her arms. She was thankful that her baby was unhurt. God, her baby had gotten drunk! She sighed softly as she realized that Shauna was growing up way too quickly in a world that didn't want to let children be children.

"I'm sorry, Mama." Shauna's voice was a mere croak.

"It's okay, honey. I'm not mad." Later, she'd give her daughter a good talking-to, but not now.

"I didn't mean it. When I was leaving Neringa's, Julie's older brother was driving by and said he'd take me home. I thought he would, but he went to some friend's place first, and he told me to come inside with him. I didn't like it, 'cause they were all so much older and they were drinking and they kept telling me to relax, that after I had a drink they would take me home. So I drank some beer, but I didn't want to, and then my head started feeling funny, and—"

"This was Julie's brother?"

Shauna nodded. "Dwayne. And some of his friends. I guess they thought they were being cool, showing me what older kids can do, but I didn't like it, Mama. The beer tasted awful, but they'd taken me so far from home that I couldn't walk, and then I was scared to call 'cause I didn't want you to get mad!"

"Shh," Lexy cooed, once again wrapping her daughter in her arms. "Baby, I'm not mad at you. Julie's brother, on the other hand . . ." Lexy cupped Shauna's chin. "You're sure they didn't lay a hand on you?"

"They didn't, Mama. I think they just wanted to have fun, get me drunk . . ." She groaned. "I have a headache. If this is what drinking alcohol is all about, I don't ever want to do it again!"

There were soft chuckles from the adults in the room, and over Shauna's head, Lexy looked from Lynda to Pauline to Rita to Sergeant Ellis, then finally to Marcel.

Finally, she chuckled too, more from nervous energy than anything else.

All was well.

Thank the Lord.

"Thanks so much," Lexy called to Lynda and Pauline, who were walking down the steps toward Marcel's car. Marcel lingered on the porch, and Lexy could only assume that he wanted to say a few words to her privately. She faced him. "And thanks so much, Marcel. You were outside at the right time . . ."

"Don't mention it. I was happy to be here."

Silence fell between them, then she said, "I know this question is a little overdue, but how have you been?"

"I've been busy. Work never ends in Miami. But days like this make it all worth it."

"I heard your mother passed away."

"Yeah. Last year. From cancer."

"I'm sorry." Lexy had neglected to send a card, and now she felt bad for that.

"So am I. But the disease was eating her alive, and it's better this way. She's at peace now."

Lexy nodded, not knowing what else to say. She felt a little out of place with Marcel standing opposite her, his hands planted on his hips, the corners of his mouth curved in a small smile. Though neither said anything, he made no effort to leave, like there was something else he wanted to say.

And suddenly she remembered a time in high school when they'd stood almost exactly as they were now, neither saying anything though she'd known Marcel had had something else on his mind. It had been right after he'd learned she was pregnant, and though he hadn't said it, she'd sensed he was disappointed in her.

The memory of that day and all that followed made her sigh. How silly of her to remember that now, when so much time had passed.

"Sorry. I know it's late," Marcel said, misinterpreting her sigh. "I just wanted to say that it was nice seeing you again, even under these circumstances."

Lexy nodded. "Again, thanks for coming. And I appreciate you offering to give Lynda and Pauline a ride home. There's no way I can drive right now."

"No problem." He paused. "Listen, if you like, I can talk to Julie's brother tomorrow. Maybe if a cop talks to him, he'll realize that what he did wasn't funny, that it had a lot of people worried, not to mention caused several cops to be out canvassing the area."

"You don't have to do that."

"I want to."

His eyes held hers for a long moment, and she looked away, uncomfortable. She was getting a weird vibe from him, but exactly what that vibe was, she couldn't be sure.

"Well, it's been a long night, so I'll call Shauna tomorrow," he said, interrupting her thoughts. "I'll get the information about Julie's brother from her then."

"Okay."

Marcel blew out a breath, knowing he should go, and wondering why he wasn't budging an inch. "All right. You are all right, aren't you? You're not still freaked out?"

"To tell the truth, I'm very freaked out. My stomach is so queasy, and my hands—" she extended them, "—they're shaking."

They were. "Look, if you want me to ask Lynda or Pauline to stay the night . . ."

"I'll be fine. A cup of chamomile tea should help me relax."

"You sure?"

"Mmm hmm." She sighed again. "But thanks for caring."

"Hey, we go way back. Of course I care."

"Of course."

He watched her round hips sway slowly as she turned and walked into the house. "I'll call you tomorrow, then?"

"Please," she replied, facing him once more.

He gave her a small smile, thinking once again how happy he was for her that all had ended well. "Good night."

She returned his smile. "Good night."

It was no laughing matter.

And by the time Marcel was through with Julie's sixteen-year-old brother, Dwayne, and his friends, they understood exactly how serious their actions had been. At least Marcel hoped they did, because stupid pranks like the one on the previous night could get them into major trouble later in life.

As it was, they were lucky that the police hadn't charged them with kidnapping. A good talking-to, some parental discipline, and hopefully these kids would smarten up.

It was early, just after ten o'clock on Sunday morning, but Marcel hadn't been able to sleep so he'd gotten in his car and driven back to Fort Lauderdale more than an hour ago. Once in the area, he'd called Shauna to find out where Dwayne lived. Now, minutes after leaving Dwayne's house, he found himself on Lexy's doorstep. She'd gone to bed late, and he knew he should let her rest, but he didn't want to head back to Miami without seeing her. He rang the doorbell.

Seconds later, the door swung open. "Marcel . . ." Lexy's eyes widened as she spoke, clearly startled to see him standing on her porch.

At least she hadn't been sleeping. "Morning, Lexy."

"I thought you were going to call."

"I did," Marcel replied, "I spoke to Shauna. She didn't tell you?"

"No."

He watched her mouth as it formed a perfect "O" thinking that she had very pretty lips. Then, wondering why he'd suddenly started thinking of her lips, he cleared his throat. "I'm just coming from Julie's house."

Her eyebrows rose. "How did that go?"

"Well. I spoke to Dwayne and his friends—and their parents—and they swear they'll never do anything like this again. He promised to come by some time today and apologize."

"You didn't have to drive here so early to do that."

He shrugged. "I didn't want to wait."

"Well, thank you. I appreciate this." Wearing a black T-shirt and a pair of faded jeans, Marcel's incredible physique was clearly visible. His neatly trimmed mustache and beard framed full, sexy lips. She'd almost forgotten how handsome he was. How long had it been since she'd thought of him in that way? Since the day Richard had asked her to marry him for the sake of their unborn baby. For the sake of their marriage and their child, she'd had to put thoughts of Marcel out of her mind. That had become easier to do once Marcel had gotten engaged to Pauline.

"No problem."

His voice brought Lexy back to the present. "My goodness, where are my manners?" Stepping backward, she held the door open. "Please, come in."

"Thanks."

"You hungry?"

"That depends."

"On what?"

"On what you're offering."

Lexy felt the oddest sensation, a sensation she hadn't felt in years. Was Marcel flirting with her?

Naw. It was her silly memories of high school that had her mind playing tricks on her.

"I've got some grits on the stove, and I can fry up some eggs."

"Mmm. Fried eggs and grits. I can't pass that up."

"All right, then. Follow me."

Lexy led the way to the kitchen, and Marcel followed her. "Can I help with anything?"

"Don't trust me?" she said playfully, glancing at him over her shoulder. It was weird just how comfortable she felt with him, given the fact that she hadn't seen him in years. Not that he should be surprised. They'd been good friends in high school.

"Just doing what my mama taught me to do . . . be helpful. I hear women love helpful men."

That comment stopped Lexy cold. What did *that* mean? Her back faced him as her hand stilled on the carton of eggs, and she was almost afraid to turn around. Had her initial instincts been right? Was Marcel actually flirting with her?

She was saved from having to think about that when Shauna came charging into the kitchen, a bundle of energy. One would never know she'd spent five hours yesterday being held against her will.

Children were nothing if not resilient.

"Morning, Mama. Hey, Marcel."

"Mr. Kennedy," Lexy chastised. Shauna didn't know Marcel well, didn't know whether or not he preferred to be addressed formally. And her daughter was only ten. She tried to instill in her good manners.

"Sorry. Good morning, Mr. Kennedy."

"You can call me Marcel," he said. "Mr. Kennedy makes me feel old."

Shauna gave her mother a victorious smile.

"You still shouldn't address people by 'hey.' That might be all right with your friends, but you know I raised you better than that."

"Sorry."

Lexy placed the eggs on the counter, then approached her daughter. She wrapped her in a warm hug. This was something she'd never gotten from her own parents—positive affirmation after discipline. "You know I love you, sweetheart."

Shauna smiled up at her mother. "I love you, too."

"How you feelin' this morning?"

"Fine," Shauna replied cheerfully. "Can I go out for a while?"

"Out?" It was a simple question, and Shauna had

certainly gone outside many a morning while Lexy prepared breakfast. But after last night . . . "Where?"

"I want to see if Maxine is home."

"Maxine lives two blocks away."

"I know."

"No," Lexy said. At the disappointed look on Shauna's face, she added, "You haven't eaten."

"I'll be back in time for breakfast."

"I said no, Shauna." She felt a nagging sense of guilt at not letting her daughter leave the house, but she wasn't ready to let her out of her sight yet. "I saw your room yesterday. It's a pigsty. Go clean it until I call you for breakfast."

"Yes, Mama," Shauna replied, but the disappointment in her voice was clearly audible.

When she disappeared down the hallway and up the stairs, Lexy's shoulders sagged. Then she nearly jumped out of her skin, startled, when she felt two strong hands on her shoulders.

She'd practically forgotten Marcel was there, and now she whirled around. "You scared me!"

"Sorry."

"No, don't be." She moaned. "I'm just . . . tense."

"That's understandable. Especially after last night."

"I know Shauna's not happy that I didn't let her go out, but . . ." Her voice trailed off as Marcel kept his hands on her shoulders and began rubbing them.

"Turn around."

She did as instructed.

"Wow, you are tense. Take a deep breath, Lexy. Try to relax."

She drew in a deep breath and let it out slowly, trying to loosen up. "Here I am, still shaken up, while Shauna's the one who went through that awful experience—and she seems perfectly fine."

"That's the amazing thing about children. They get over things so quickly."

"Ain't that the truth."

"Now," Marcel whispered, making her nape tingle, "what can I do to make her mother relax?"

"This is good," she replied softly.

His thumbs went lower, to her shoulder blades, pressing firmly. It had been ages since she'd had a massage, and his hands felt wonderful on her shoulders, her neck, deftly massaging away the tension. She wanted to simply stand there and let him work his magic forever. But maybe because it had been so long since she'd been that close to a man, she suddenly felt uncomfortable. She stepped away.

"Uh, breakfast," she said, the words escaping on a shaky breath.

"Hmm." She was spooked, Marcel knew, and perhaps he was a little spooked, too. He couldn't remember the last time he'd given a woman a spontaneous massage, and truth be told, he wasn't exactly sure what had possessed him to give one to Lexy.

"You know what?" He glanced at his watch. "I really should head out of here."

"I thought you were hungry."

Was that disappointment or relief he detected in her eyes? He let his gaze fall from her face, downward past her large bosom hidden beneath her crossed arms, to her hips, then to her legs. She was slightly larger than she'd been a few years before, but the extra weight had simply rounded out her figure. She looked good.

"Marcel?"

Remembering her question, he threw his eyes to hers. "Uh, I am hungry, but I've got a lot to do. Rain check?"

"Sure."

When he turned and started for the door, Lexy

closed her eyes, then slowly opened them. Goodness, Marcel had just been checking her out! More surprising, she'd enjoyed every moment of it.

What was going on? Surely Marcel couldn't be attracted to her. Or could he?

Lexy didn't want to think about it. Instead, she pushed the question out of her mind and followed him to the door.

His hand was on the doorknob when he abruptly turned. He stared at her with intense yet tentative eyes, and Lexy wondered exactly what that look meant.

He glanced away, then back at her. "Lexy, I want to ask you something."

"Sure."

"This is going to sound weird," he began as he walked back toward her, "but are you seeing anyone?"

"Me?" she asked, as though there were someone else in the room.

"Yeah. You." He smiled.

He did have a sweet smile. If things hadn't turned out the way they had that night with Richard . . . She stopped that thought, partly because she didn't regret having Shauna and partly because she knew that no matter how hard one wished for it, no one could turn back the hands of time and erase the past . . . "N-no. I'm not seeing anyone."

He took another step toward her, and Lexy's heart stopped. "Then would it be forward of me to ask if we could . . . go out sometime?"

Good Lord, he was asking her out! Marcel Kennedy, the one man she'd always found irresistible in high school, but who hadn't given her the time of day. The man who had married her best friend. And divorced her best friend. "Like a date?" she asked, then felt stupid.

"Yeah."

"Why?"

"Why not?" he countered.

She shrugged. This was all so unexpected, so unreal. "I don't know. I mean, you're Pauline's ex. I'm her best friend."

"And you think she'll have a problem with us going out?"

"Don't you?"

He shook his head. "Not really. Pauline has been engaged since our divorce."

"But not to your best friend."

"No, but our marriage ended seven years ago. She's over me. I'm over her. Besides, I'm just asking for a date—not your hand in marriage."

His comment was all too true, making Lexy wonder why she couldn't just say yes. Still, she didn't back down. "It's not only Pauline. I . . . I wouldn't feel comfortable leaving Shauna alone."

"Oh."

He was disappointed. She could hear it in his voice, see it in his eyes. "You know . . . after last night . . ."

"Mmm."

"Maybe in the future . . ."

Marcel wished he could take the question back. Clearly, asking Lexy out had been a bad idea. She was coming up with all sorts of excuses to avoid going out with him. Though he shouldn't be surprised. He'd been interested in her in high school, but she'd always been interested in Richard, his best friend and star athlete. Compared to Richard, Marcel hadn't had a chance.

Lexy said, "It's not personal."

He forced a smile. "Hey, don't worry about it."

"You should go, Mama."

Both Marcel and Lexy turned to see Shauna standing behind them.

"Shauna," Lexy began, "how many times have I told you it's not polite to eavesdrop?"

"I wasn't. I just couldn't help overhearing."

Marcel chuckled softly, and Lexy turned back to him. "I'm sorry. I know you have to go. Why don't I call you sometime—"

"Mama, you've only been on one date since Daddy died and Marcel is *much* nicer than that other guy."

"Shauna!" Lexy exclaimed, her face erupting in flames. She didn't need Marcel knowing a history of her nonexistent love life.

"Well, he is."

"Of course Marcel is nice."

"Then why not go out with him?"

"Shauna," Lexy said, exasperated.

Marcel cleared his throat. "It's okay, Shauna. Maybe another time."

Lexy turned to him. "I am so sorry. She's not usually like this."

"Hey, I know," Shauna said in a sing-song voice. "We can all go out together. That way, Mama doesn't have to worry about me. She always worries about leaving me."

Was Lexy really that overprotective? But looking at her now, he knew she was. Last night, she'd seemed not only distraught at Shauna being missing, but guilty for having gone out.

Marcel said, "That's an idea."

Lexy met his eyes. "I . . . I guess we could do that."

"Great!" Shauna exclaimed. "Maybe we can go swimming at the beach!"

"I don't think so." Lexy didn't like the beach. The waves were too unpredictable. Besides, there was no way Lexy would be caught dead in a bathing suit around Marcel. She didn't have the trim, size ten body she'd once had.

"I was thinking more along the lines of dinner,"

Marcel said. "But," he added after some thought, "there are restaurants along the beach strip. That way, we could go for a walk on the beach afterwards."

"Okay," Shauna said.

Lexy said, "Shauna, will you please excuse me and Marcel?"

"Bye, Marcel," Shauna said. She gave him a warm smile.

"See you soon," he replied, returning her smile.

Marcel waited until he heard Shauna's feet hit the top of the stairs before speaking. "So, are we on?"

"Well, Shauna's all excited."

Marcel wanted to ask how she felt, but didn't. "That's a yes?"

"Yes."

"Great. How about Saturday?"

"Saturday!" Lexy repeated, then was embarrassed by the sound of panic in her voice.

"If that's a bad time—"

"No."

The more he stood opposite Lexy, the more he knew he wanted to spend time with her. But she didn't at all seem like she wanted to spend time with him. So he said, "Why don't we do this. You call me, let me know when you're free."

He turned to the door.

"Wait," Lexy said.

He faced her again.

An old friend was asking her for a date. What was the big deal? Lexy realized she was being really stupid. "Saturday will be fine."

"Around three?"

"Okay."

He flashed her a smile. "I'll see you then." Turning toward the door, he opened it, then stepped onto the porch.

He was at the foot of the steps when he looked

back. Lexy was still standing in the doorway, watching him. She waved.

He waved back, then watched as she closed the door and disappeared.

Three

She had no clue what to wear. Most of the fancy clothes in her closet didn't fit her anymore, thanks to the stubborn bulges around her waist. Marcel had called the day before and told her it would be a casual date, meaning she didn't have to wear anything special, but since this was her first date in years, she wanted to look good.

Even if she wasn't interested in pursuing anything serious with him.

Yes, there was a time she'd really liked Marcel. There was a time she'd even fantasized that they'd get together. But she'd gotten involved with Richard, he with Pauline, and their lives had gone in different directions.

"Why don't you wear that blue dress with all the flowers?" Shauna asked.

Startled at the sound of her daughter's voice, Lexy turned around. Shauna sported her new denim dress with a pink T-shirt beneath; both had been gifts from Pauline for her recent birthday. Her long hair was combed in two ponytails, each with a pink ribbon at the end.

"Wow," Lexy began, approaching her. "Aren't you looking all spiffy."

She smiled brightly. "Thanks. Now, I think you

should wear that blue dress. It's really pretty and makes you look really pretty, Mama."

Lexy strolled back to her closet. Searching through its contents, she found the dress in question and withdrew it. A smile touched her lips as she realized Shauna was right. The dress was beautiful, delicate, and definitely flattered her figure.

When she'd put the dress on, Shauna said, "Wow, Mama. You look great. Marcel won't be able to resist you."

Lexy placed both hands firmly on her hips. "Excuse me?"

"He won't. You look great."

"And just what would you know about a man not being able to resist a woman?"

"I'm not a baby, Mama."

Rendered speechless, all Lexy could do was stare at her daughter. God, Shauna really wasn't a baby anymore. Where had the years gone?

"I like Marcel," Shauna continued, dropping herself onto the queen-sized bed. "I think he'd be a good boyfriend."

Lexy's mouth literally dropped to the floor. "This is a friendly date, Shauna. Nothing more."

"I think he likes you," Shauna said.

Lexy couldn't believe she was having this conversation with her ten-year-old daughter. Maybe it was time she had a conversation with Shauna about the facts of life.

Hell, she probably already knew all there was to know.

That thought made her shudder, but looking at the mischievous smile on Shauna's face, Lexy couldn't help chuckling.

Silently, she prayed Shauna's teenage years would take an eternity to arrive.

* * *

As far as dates went, it was wonderful.

Marcel had treated Lexy to a lovely seafood dinner at a Fort Lauderdale restaurant along the beach. Not only did it serve an outstanding variety of fish, it had a children's menu that consisted of burgers, fries, and other popular items for kids who weren't impressed by salmon steak. Clearly, Marcel had thought of Shauna when making the dinner arrangements, and Lexy appreciated that.

And it was obvious that Marcel was truly interested in Shauna for Shauna, and not simply because he was interested in Lexy. In fact, as they'd sat at an outside table, Lexy practically hadn't noticed the rhythmic sound of the waves lapping at the shore and the soft romantic sounds of salsa music coming from the live band. Instead, she'd been absorbed in watching Marcel with her daughter. The two had talked and laughed almost from the moment he'd picked them up. About school. About her friends. About things she liked and didn't like. Lexy had never seen her daughter so instantly comfortable with a man other than her father.

And while she was glad to see that Shauna and Marcel had formed an instant rapport, that reality also scared her. Lexy didn't want Shauna to start missing her father again. For the first year after his death, she had constantly asked for a new daddy, and Lexy realized that Richard's death had taken a major toll on Shauna as well. But she'd eventually gotten used to the fact that it was just the two of them.

But now, if she liked Marcel—and it was clear she did—she might start looking to him as a father figure.

"You seem a million miles away," Marcel said.

"Oh," Lexy replied, startled out of her thoughts.

She was almost surprised to find they were walking barefoot in the sand. "I'm sorry."

"Penny for your thoughts."

She giggled nervously. "They're hardly worth that much."

He raised a curious eyebrow. "Humor me."

"You really want to know?"

He stopped walking and took her hand. "I want to know everything about you."

Lexy wasn't sure what to say. If she told him what was really on her mind, he'd no doubt think she was crazy for jumping the gun. A simple date didn't mean marriage or even a serious relationship. But maybe if she *did* tell him what was on her mind, he'd understand that she didn't want to pursue anything serious.

"Mama! Marcel!" Shauna called, running toward them. She had been walking ahead of them, playing at the edge of the water and searching for shells in the sand. "I am finding some awesome shells!"

Shauna held up a handful of shells for their inspection. "Yes, those are nice," Lexy replied, though she hardly noticed them.

Shauna ran ahead of them once more, heading for the water where some other children played.

"Shauna," Lexy said. "Don't go too far in the water."

"I won't," Shauna responded, not bothering to turn around as she spoke.

"That child," Lexy said. "I swear she's gonna send me to an early grave."

Marcel chuckled. "She's a good kid."

Facing him, Lexy grinned. "I know. Thanks."

"You really worry about her, don't you?"

"She's my whole world, Marcel. I don't know what I'd do if anything happened to her."

"She's young, she's tough."

"But it seems so many bad things happen to children these days. When I was young abductions weren't common at all. Now—"

"Mama!" Shauna called as she ran toward them at full speed. "Wow! Look at this one!"

Her eyes dancing with excitement, Shauna held up a large, colorful shell.

"It's beautiful," Lexy told her. Shauna was gone almost before the words left Lexy's mouth.

Marcel laughed, and looking at him, Lexy couldn't help laughing, too.

But as his eyes met and held hers, he stopped laughing, then stopped walking. Lexy stopped, too. "What?" she asked.

Marcel reached into his pocket and withdrew a penny. "You were about to tell me what you were thinking."

"Oh," Lexy said, glancing down at the sand. "It's not important."

With a finger, he gently lifted her chin, forcing her to look into his eyes. "You want to know what I'm thinking?"

"What?" She sounded breathless, all because he was touching her. Goodness, she'd forgotten the right man's touch could make her head spin.

"I'm thinking that you're very beautiful," he replied softly.

Lexy waved off his compliment. "Oh, come on."

"What?" he asked, puzzled.

"You don't have to say that."

The wind blew her black tresses around her face and Marcel reached for the stray strands, smoothing them behind her ear. "I wouldn't say it if it wasn't true."

His fingers barely skimmed her flesh, yet her skin tingled at his touch. There was no mistaking it— somehow the attraction she'd felt for Marcel all those years ago had returned. She would almost think he was feeling something for her too, if the idea wern't completely ridiculous.

Or was it?

"You must know I've always thought you were beautiful."

"Marcel," Lexy said quickly, moving away from him.

He followed her, stepping back into her space. "It's true."

All right. So he thought she was beautiful. That didn't mean anything.

"Isn't it amazing how time flies? Standing here with you, it's like high school was only yesterday. Yet it also seems like a lifetime ago, so much has happened."

So much *had* happened. Like Lexy marrying Richard. Like Marcel marrying Pauline.

"Which makes me think there's so much we don't know about each other now." He ran a finger along the length of her jaw. "And I'd like to find out everything there is to know about you."

She eyed him curiously. "Why?"

He smiled. "Isn't that obvious?"

Her chest rose and fell with each deep breath she took in. "I don't think anything's obvious."

"All right. Let me make it perfectly clear what I'm thinking." He wrapped his arms around her waist and pulled her to him. Then, before she could protest, he placed his lips over hers and gently kissed her.

Part of her told her she should pull away, that she didn't want Shauna to see her like this. But another part of her, the part that hadn't been held or kissed by a man in years, didn't let her, so she stayed in his arms and closed her eyes as his lips moved over hers in the sweetest of kisses.

"Mama, come look at this."

Lexy leaped out of Marcel's arms, instantly covering her lips with a hand. Looking to her left, she saw Shauna crouching in the sand, her back to them. Thank God she hadn't seen her kissing Marcel.

Lexy hurried toward her daughter, a ton of different emotions swirling inside her. God, Marcel had kissed her! And she'd loved every second of it.

But this was Marcel Kennedy, her best friend's ex. And worse than the fact that he was Pauline's ex-husband, he was a cop. Of all the jobs he could have, he had one that put him in mortal danger every day. There was no way she could get involved with him.

Yet that fact didn't stop her from remembering the way his full lips had felt on hers only moments before, didn't stop her from wishing he would kiss her again. She needed to think, and as she neared Shauna, she was thankful for the cool breeze on her face. But even the breeze didn't help, because Marcel placed a hand across her shoulders, making her effort to think clearly practically impossible.

"Look what I found in the sand," Shauna said, producing a small, gold-colored heart charm as she looked up at them. "I think it's real gold."

"Let me see that," Lexy said, moving to stand on the opposite side of Shauna, across from Marcel. She was thankful that he didn't follow her. Still, as she glanced down at the small locket in her palm, she didn't really see it.

"You can even put a picture inside," Shauna said, excited. "Can I keep it? Please, Mama?"

"What does the officer think?" Lexy asked, finally looking at Marcel. Though she'd just addressed him, she was surprised to find that he was staring at her—and not as though he was at all interested in the locket.

Shauna looked at him. "It was just in the sand. There's no way to know whose it is."

"You're right," Marcel said, but his eyes still held

Lexy's. After a moment, he looked down at Shauna. "Can I see it?" She passed it to him. "Well, it's real gold. And it looks like it's yours now."

"All right!" Shauna exclaimed. "I'm gonna find a picture to put inside here." Lexy watched her run off again.

"Lexy," Marcel began. She felt his presence as he moved behind her.

She turned and held up a hand to quiet him. "Marcel, before you say anything, I have something to say."

"What?" Closing the distance between them, he placed his arms around her again.

Lord help her, the words literally died in her throat.

He nuzzled her nose with his. "Hmm?"

"I . . ."

He pulled back and looked at her with a charming smile that melted her resistance. Maybe if she hadn't been so crazy in love with him back in the day . . .

"I think I know what you're going to say," he announced.

"You do?"

"Yeah," he said, nodding. "You're going to tell me that this is wrong. You and me."

Her mouth opened to say something, anything, but she couldn't refute his words.

He trailed his fingers up and down her arms, causing goosebumps to pop out over her skin. She liked the way he was making her feel, but this was . . . wrong.

She stepped out of his embrace. "Yes, this is wrong, Marcel."

"I want to see you again."

Clearly, he hadn't heard a word she'd said. "Marcel . . ."

"Why not?" he asked. "I'm single. You're single."

"I have a daughter."

"Yeah, you have a daughter."

"Which means I'm a mother. I have to *be* a mother. I can't just go gallivanting all over the place."

"Gallivanting? I'm only asking for another date. I'd like to get to know you." His mustache lifted as he smiled. "Again."

Lexy sighed, though she enjoyed the attention. God, it had been so long. "Why?"

"Why?" He looked at her as if she were crazy. But it was a teasing look, and she wasn't offended. "You've got to know that I'm attracted to you."

"That's exactly what I'm talking about," Lexy said. "Why now? I mean, it's not like we were attracted to each other in high school." Knowing that wasn't exactly true, for she had been attracted to him, she turned away from him, lifting her dress and heading for the water. She didn't want him to see the lie in her eyes.

But in the next instant, he was behind her, brushing her hair to one side and resting his face against hers. "That's where you're wrong," he said softly into her ear, and she shuddered. "I was always attracted to you then. But you were in love with Richard, so I stayed away."

Her heart pounded so hard in her chest, Lexy was sure Marcel would hear it. Certainly she had heard him wrong. "What did you say?"

"You heard me."

She did turn then, searching his face for the truth. "Marcel, you can't be serious."

"I am. And there was a time I thought that maybe you were interested in me, but then you got pregnant . . ."

God, was he telling her the truth? Had he really been interested in her?

"I . . ."

"I know." Sensing that his news was too much for

her, he stepped backward and placed his hands in his pants pockets. "Look, what happened or didn't happen in high school is over, and a lot has changed. I don't know how you felt about me then, but I know that there's nothing standing between us now." He shrugged. "Why now? I don't know. I only know that when I saw you again, it's like the feelings I had for you all came back."

Marcel waited, letting her digest his words. If he'd made a mistake in telling how he felt, so be it. Life was too short not to take chances.

"You want to know something?" she finally asked.

"What?"

"I . . ." She paused and ran a hand through her long hair. "I always had a crush on you in high school."

Now he was surprised. "Yeah, right."

"I did. That night of the party, the night I got pregnant, I'd only gone to that party because I thought you'd be there. Then, I started drinking and didn't know a thing about alcohol." She glanced at Shauna. Seeing her talking to a few other children, she faced Marcel once more. "I ended up in bed with Richard, and to this day, I can't tell you how that happened."

"But you married him."

"I was carrying his child. My parents would have it no other way."

"Wow," Marcel said softly, digesting what she'd told him. So, she hadn't been head-over-heels in love with Richard?

"I grew to love him," she added in response to his unspoken question. "And I don't regret Shauna at all."

Marcel smiled as he looked at Shauna. She and the other children were laughing about something. "No doubt. She's great."

Silence fell between them, and Marcel turned, staring out at the dark water as dusk descended over them. Finally, he faced Lexy. "So."

"So," she repeated.

"So, what now?"

"It's getting dark," she replied. "I think we should get Shauna." She didn't wait for his reply before walking off in the sand toward her daughter.

Marcel watched her for a long moment before heading toward them. His heart was pounding overtime, a feeling he was only used to when his adrenaline pumped in the line of duty. Even with Pauline, he hadn't felt this crazy, indescribable fluttering of his heart and butterflies in his stomach.

Lexy had just told him that she'd liked him back in the day. But then she'd walked away from him without taking the conversation further. He didn't know what to make of that. Was she interested? Wasn't she?

"Ready?" Lexy asked him as he reached her and Shauna.

"I guess so."

Lexy avoided Marcel's eyes and instead faced her daughter. "Sweetheart, let's go wash our feet off." Shauna's hands were full of shells, so Lexy placed a hand on her back and led her toward the shower area.

She was well aware that Marcel was watching her, but she didn't want to glance back at him. If she did, she'd give him the wrong idea, and she didn't want to do that.

She may have been interested in him in high school, and maybe he had been interested in her. But that was a lifetime ago. Everything had changed, and as much as she wished she were single and free to pursue a relationship with him, she simply wasn't.

She was a mother, and Shauna had to be her top priority.

Four

"All our books about nutrition and health are in the second aisle on your right" Lexy said to the middle-aged man, pointing in that direction.

"Thanks," he said.

"No problem."

As the man walked away, Lexy took a moment to lean a hip against the edge of the counter. With Mother's Day approaching in a little more than a week, the bookstore was busier than usual. It hadn't helped that two people had called in sick, leaving her to fill in at the cash register, deal with customer inquiries and generally oversee the operation of the store. It had been one of those days, but she didn't have the luxury of complaining. She was the manager and ultimately responsible for the store.

She doubted she'd even get out of there by seven like she'd promised Pauline. Goodness, what would she do next week when the last-minute Mother's Day shoppers swarmed the store?

She didn't want to think about that. Right now, she was simply relieved to have a moment to relax. She slipped out of her shoes and wiggled her toes.

"Lexy Sinclair, line three."

Brother, Lexy thought, knowing she shouldn't have dared to hope. She walked the few steps to the phone and answered line three.

"Lexy speaking. May I help you?"

"Hey, girl. What's up?"

"Hey yourself," Lexy replied, her lips widening in a grin. "How are you?"

"I'm cool. Though traffic on the I-95 is a nightmare."

"You think you'll make it to my house by five-thirty?" Lexy glanced at the clock above her and saw that it was nine minutes after five. "Shauna's always home by five-thirty after her gymnastics class."

"Yeah, I'll be there."

"If not, I can call Rita and see if she can watch her. Or even Mrs. Jessop."

"I'm two exits away," Pauline told her.

"All right," Lexy said, relaxing.

"Hey, buddy," Pauline shouted, clearly addressing another motorist. "Move it, will ya?"

"Okay, Pauline. I'm gonna go. Call me when you get there."

"No problem."

"See ya."

"Wait."

"What?"

"I heard something very interesting today."

"Oh," Lexy said, her curiosity piqued.

"Mmm hmm. I spoke to Marcel this morning. He told me that you two went out on a date."

"He said that?"

"Yes," Pauline continued. "Though what I want to know is why *you* didn't tell me."

Lexy groaned. She wished Marcel hadn't spoken to Pauline without consulting her. "I'm sorry, Pauline. I meant to tell you earlier. It's just that it was no big deal."

"That's not what Marcel said."

Oh, God. "What did he say?"

"That he really likes you."

"God, Pauline. I don't know what he's thinking, but—"

"I think you'd be great together."

Not sure she had heard her friend correctly, Lexy pulled the receiver in front of her face, stared at it, then returned it to her ear. "Come again?"

"Marcel told me you might be worried about what I'll think, so if you are, don't. Marcel and I never should have gotten married. We were never truly in love. You know that."

"Well . . ." That much was true. Lexy had always known that Pauline and Marcel had been infatuated with each other, but she'd doubted from the start if their marriage would last. In the end, it hadn't, but they'd remained good friends.

"Besides," Pauline continued, "he was always crazy about you."

"Gimme a break."

"Girlfriend, I was there."

"Why didn't anyone tell me?" Lexy asked softly, though she didn't really expect an answer.

"Because of Richard. Anyway, I just want you to know that if you and Marcel were to get together, I'd be okay with that."

"Excuse me," someone said, and Lexy's eyes flew to the elderly woman opposite the counter.

Lexy held up a finger to the woman, then said to Pauline, "I've gotta go. We'll talk later."

"All right," Pauline said, chuckling.

Lexy held the receiver to her ear for a good five seconds after Pauline had hung up, considering what her friend had said.

So dating Marcel wouldn't offend Pauline. In a way, Lexy was relieved to hear that. Though why she was relieved, she wasn't sure. Whether or not Pauline was cool with her dating Marcel was not the bigger issue. The bottom line was, Lexy was a working mother who hardly had time to spend with her daughter, let alone to date. And if and when the time came, she wanted to give Shauna a stable family life, and that included having a father whom she could trust to be around. Given Marcel's job, he was hardly an ideal candidate to be the new daddy in Shauna's life.

There she went again, jumping the gun.

"Miss?" the elderly woman said.

Lexy promptly hung up the phone, then stepped forward to help her new customer.

Patience had never been one of Marcel's best qualities.

So when Lexy told him she couldn't see him all week because she was working at the bookstore, he decided that the mountain would go to Mohammed.

It was a free country, Marcel told himself as he strolled into the large bookstore. He could shop where he wanted.

Even if that meant traveling an hour away from his home in rush-hour traffic.

The bookstore was huge and crowded, but, thankfully, to the immediate right was an information desk. Unlike a lot of men, Marcel believed in asking questions.

"I'm looking for the manager, Lexy Sinclair," Marcel told the young man behind the desk.

"Is there something I can help you with?" the man asked.

"No," Marcel replied, a grin spreading on his face as an illicit thought flashed through his mind. This clerk definitely couldn't help him with *that.* "I need to speak with Lexy."

The man told Marcel to wait, then paged her.

Moments later, Marcel heard her before he saw her. "What is it, Frank?" Lexy was saying as she rounded the end of an aisle toward the information desk. "I'm doing inventory in the—" She stopped dead in her tracks. "Marcel."

Marcel smiled at the surprise that flashed over her face when she saw him. "Hey, Lexy."

She was silent for a moment as she regarded him with an expression that said she couldn't believe he was actually there. "What are you doing here?"

"You know what they say. If Mohammed won't go to the mountain . . ."

"You didn't."

He nodded. "I did."

"You are crazy."

Maybe he was. He'd taken a chance going there, not knowing if she would have any time to spend with him. The idea had come to him when he'd spoken with Pauline that morning and learned that Lexy would be working late. And while it was crazy, the trip had been worth it. Just seeing her beautiful face again made his day.

"You have a minute or two for a crazy old friend?"

Shaking her head, Lexy said, "Come on. I think I'm due for a break."

He followed her as she walked to the cafeteria area. She looked around and frowned. "You're not hungry, are you?"

She asked the question as though she hoped he'd say no. So he did.

"Good. Then let's go outside. I don't want my staff getting into my business."

Marcel knew he shouldn't be disappointed, but he was. He doubted her staff would make anything of her having a drink or a sandwich with a friend; he doubted they would care. True, he hadn't told her he was coming, but surely she could sit down and spend a few minutes with him without worrying what people would think.

But he followed her outside without comment. She rounded the side of the building toward a bench, then sat.

Marcel sat beside her and took her hand in his. "I missed you."

"I don't believe you."

"What?"

"You're really serious about dating me, aren't you?"

He met her eyes head-on. "Yeah."

A car drove by and Lexy's gaze followed it. After a moment, she turned back to him. "I don't know about this."

"What's not to know?"

"This is all happening too fast. One minute, you're at my house helping me look for Shauna, the next you're talking about dating me."

"I've always been attracted to you," he said. "I told you that."

"I know, but—"

Reaching for her face, Marcel ran a thumb over her bottom lip. Lexy closed her eyes and moaned softly.

"You see that?" he asked. "You're attracted to me, too."

"I never said I didn't like you."

"Then what's the problem?"

"It's just that . . ." She paused. Shrugged. "I've finally gotten into a rhythm. My life is going exactly how I'd planned—"

"What sign are you?" Marcel asked, cutting her off.

She eyed him quizzically. "What does that have to do with anything?"

"What sign?" he repeated.

"Aries."

"Ah," he said, nodding slowly. "Figures."

Lexy flashed him a wry smile. "Why does that figure?"

"Because Aries always have to be in control. You never let loose and go with the flow, so to speak."

"That's not true."

"Really?" he challenged. "When was the last time you did something spontaneously, just because you wanted to?"

"That's not fair," Lexy protested. "I have a job. I have a daughter. And I'm taking a night school course."

"In other words, you can't remember when."

"Okay, fine," she gave in, holding up both hands in surrender. "I don't have time for spontaneous. So sue me."

"I'd like to do something else to you."

"Marcel!" she exclaimed, but she was giggling.

It was good to see her laughing, to see her blush. "You are so sexy when your eyes bug out like that."

She buried her face in her hands. "I do not believe this."

"Okay," Marcel said. "Back to you being an Aries. I bet you have a detailed five-year plan for your life— at home and in the office, right?"

God, how did he know? "For your information, I have only one five-year plan. And it's on my bedroom wall—not in the office."

"What did I say?" He smiled victoriously.

"But before you get too cocky," she added, playfully punching him on the arm, "I've only been doing a five-year plan for the past two years now. So there."

"Was I right, or was I right?"

Looking at the silly smirk on Marcel's face, Lexy couldn't help laughing. "You think you know me so well."

"I know you well enough to know that you probably haven't laughed like this in the longest time."

Again, he was right. "I guess that makes you Mr. Know-It-All." But she was still laughing.

Marcel took her hand again, his smile fading as he gave her a serious look. "Not really. I don't know how you feel about spending time with me."

"Marcel," Lexy began. "I've already told you."

"Uh-uh," he said. "I won't let you use the excuse that you're too busy, or that I'm not in your five-year plan." She giggled, and he brought her hand to his lips. Her laughter faded. "All right. Here's the test. I'm going to kiss you—"

"Marcel—"

"Let me finish." He edged closer to her and snaked his free hand around her waist. "I'm going to kiss you, and if you sigh or moan or see stars, you have to agree to date me so we can see where this relationship can go. But if you feel nothing, I'll walk away and we remain friends."

"What if I don't want to risk our friendship?"

"Sweetheart, you have to know that if we give it a shot and it doesn't work, I'll always be your friend."

She did know that, deep in her heart. "You are crazy."

"So they tell me." He moved his face closer to hers, his eyes dancing with excitement. "Ready?"

"Mar—"

He silenced her protest with a kiss, stealing her breath as his lips moved skillfully over hers. Not tentative and shy, but hot and demanding.

And damn if she didn't sigh, moan, *and* see the brightest stars she'd seen in a long, long while.

Five

She'd accused Marcel of being crazy, but maybe she was the one who'd lost her mind.

Lexy Sinclair simply wasn't herself. In the days since their impromptu date outside her bookstore, she had become a different person.

This Lexy literally couldn't stop smiling. Never in her life had she smiled so much. Now, the corners of her lips seemed permanently curled upward.

This Lexy was less stressed. Though she still ran around the store all day like a chicken with its head cut off, she didn't worry as much about what had gone wrong or could go wrong.

Because the moment she started worrying, she saw Marcel's silly smirk as he told her he knew she had a five-year plan. Or she heard his voice when he called the store to make sure she was okay, that she'd taken a break from being so serious.

She'd always been too serious. At least her friends had always told her she'd been too serious. But now, after one silly date with Marcel, she actually found she could laugh about things that would have irked her before.

She hadn't completely lost her mind. When the shipment of books hadn't arrived for an author who was signing at her store, she did go berserk. But not for long, because her mind kept drifting back to Marcel's kiss and the fact that he'd actually made her see stars.

Damn the man, she could hardly think of anything but him!

Now, sitting outside on the same bench she'd shared with Marcel just days before, she blushed as she remembered that kiss, remembered how good it had felt to be in his arms and know that he wanted her. Yes, it had felt good. And it had been too long.

She couldn't believe she was sitting outside blushing over something that had happened days before! Who was this Lexy Sinclair?

Tilting her head upward, Lexy let the sun beam down on her face. Closing her eyes, she listened to the sound of birds singing in the various trees. Being outside like this was extremely relaxing; she loved it. Before the break she'd taken with Marcel just days before, she couldn't remember the last time she'd taken her break outside as opposed to inside the stuffy, cramped back office of the bookstore.

Lexy sighed wistfully. She still had no clue what she was getting herself into. But she did know that she believed Marcel when he said that no matter what happened, he'd always be her friend.

It seemed like a win-win situation. So, why not take a chance?

"Not even tomorrow?" Marcel asked.

"I've got two romance authors doing signings at my store tomorrow," Lexy said. "This is the beginning of Mother's Day madness."

Lying on the bed with the phone perched on his ear, Marcel frowned as he stared into the darkened room. This was the fifth day he'd spoken with Lexy, asking for another date. This was the fifth day she'd told him she couldn't see him.

"And as much as I'd like to see you, if you come to the store, I won't have any time to spend with you."

"Hmm."

"I dunno. Maybe next week?"

"Next week?" That seemed like a lifetime away.

"I'm sorry, Marcel. I won't have any time before then."

And he thought *he* had a crazy schedule with regular duty and off-duty assignments. "What are you doing for Mother's Day?"

"Mother's Day?"

As a cop he knew that repeating the question was always a bad sign. "Yeah, Mother's Day. Are you working?"

"No. I'm off."

"Any special plans?"

"I always spend Mother's Day with Shauna."

The way she said that left no room for misunderstandings; she wasn't willing to fit him into her Mother's Day plans.

"All right," he said, trying to be understanding, though he knew he sounded exasperated.

"I didn't think I'd have to say this, but maybe I do. Marcel, whatever happens between us, Shauna has to be my number one priority."

"Of course." Though he didn't understand why Lexy found it so hard to be a mother and seriously date him. "I guess it'll have to be some time after Mother's Day."

"I guess so."

That would mean more than a week without seeing her. "I hope I can last that long without seeing you."

"Dream of me every night," she whispered in a seductive voice, then giggled.

Her laughter eased the tension. "I will."

And he meant it.

* * *

When the phone rang a second time, Marcel hung up. He had planned to leave Lexy a message, but at the last second decided against it. Leaving her a message wouldn't change the facts: she had no time for him this week.

He stood and stretched, then strolled to the window. It was a gorgeous May day, with a vibrant sun in a clear blue sky. It was just the kind of day he'd love to spend with Lexy, but no such luck.

He was en route to the bathroom when the phone rang. Hurrying to his night table, he glanced at the caller ID. His pulse accelerated at the sight of Lexy's number. Wondering if she no longer had to work this Sunday, Marcel quickly answered the phone. "Hey, sexy."

"Hello?"

"Hello?" Marcel responded cautiously.

"Marcel?"

"Shauna?"

"Yeah." Giggle.

Oops. "Hi, Shauna."

"Hi, Marcel."

Hearing the smile in her voice, he realized that he missed not only Lexy, but Shauna, too. "How are you?"

"I'm fine." She paused quickly, then asked, "Did you just call here and hang up?"

He could picture her, one hand on her hip, a smirk on her face, as she asked the question. "You can't hide anything with caller ID, can you?"

"Nope."

"Yeah, I called. I was hoping to reach your mom, then I remembered she's working, so I hung up."

"Okay. That makes sense."

"You sure?"

Shauna giggled. "Yeah. Actually, I'm glad you called and hung up."

"Why's that?" Marcel asked, raising an eyebrow.

"Because now I have your phone number and I want to ask you something."

"Uh-oh. You didn't get yourself arrested, did you?" Marcel joked.

"No."

"Then what can I help you with?"

"Are you in love with my mother?"

Marcel nearly choked on his saliva. "What?"

"I know you've been talking a lot and you make her laugh, so I was just wondering if you're in love with her."

"Uh," he began, trying to think of how to answer her. "Well, I like her a lot."

"Cool! I think she likes you, too."

Now, Marcel was intrigued. "Really?"

"Uh huh. You're the first guy she's talked to this much since my daddy died."

Well, that was good to know—though Marcel could picture Lexy's horrified expression if she could hear her daughter now. "Would you mind if I dated your mother?" Marcel asked cautiously.

"That would be great! She could use a man like you."

Marcel couldn't help chuckling. "Could she, now?"

"Mmm hmm. But my mother's always too busy, either at the bookstore or with me. She rarely goes out. I know she loves me a lot and wants to be with me, but I want to see her go out more and be happy."

Marcel couldn't believe his ears. Shauna had summed up the situation as effectively as any adult. "I agree."

"Good. 'Cause I have a favor to ask you."

He was still trying to accept the fact that Shauna

had given him the okay to date her mother. That meant a lot to him. If he was to pursue anything serious with Lexy, he wanted her daughter to like him. "What can I do for you?"

"Help me plan a treat for my mother. Mother's Day is a week from today."

"True."

"A friend in my class said she's giving her mother a day at the spa and I'd like to do that too, but I don't know where one is."

"I can check that out for you."

"Great." Pause. "And I was thinking that I could surprise her with a dinner—for the two of you."

"Oh," was all Marcel could say. "For me and your mother?"

"Yeah. Like a date. But without me, so you two can be alone."

Was Shauna actually only ten years old? She sounded wise beyond her years. "I see."

"Will you?"

Even if he hadn't been interested for himself, Marcel wouldn't have been able to deny Shauna. "Sure." Maybe spending time with Shauna and Lexy would help assuage the sadness he knew would come with missing his own mother on Mother's Day. "I don't have any other plans."

"Great!" she exclaimed. "This has to be a secret, so don't tell her anything."

"I won't."

"All right. I'll call you on Friday to find out about the spa, okay?"

"Right." That gave him five days. Plenty of time.

"And don't worry. I've got money to pay for it."

"Is that so?" A smile lifted his lips.

"Uh huh."

Shauna was clearly a child very much in control. It

was no wonder, considering Lexy was her mother. Like her mother, Shauna was definitely special.

He said, "If you're going to pay for the spa, then it's only fair I pay for the dinner. Sound good?"

"Sounds good to me," she replied, then giggled. "Mama is gonna be so surprised!"

"Yes," Marcel answered softly, envisioning the bright smile on Shauna's face and hoping he'd see a similar smile on Lexy's face on Sunday. "She most definitely will be."

"Bye, Marcel."

"Wait."

"Yes?"

"Thanks," he said. "For including me."

"No problem," Shauna replied. "In case you haven't figured it out, *I* like you, too."

As Marcel hung up, he couldn't help smiling. He could definitely get used to having Lexy and Shauna in his life.

On Friday, Marcel called Shauna to tell her that he'd found the perfect spa in Palm Aire where Lexy could have a massage and generally be pampered for a few hours. It was going to be costly, but he'd pay for the lion's share of the bill. He didn't have a woman to spend money on these days, and spending some on Lexy would be well worth it.

When he was married to Pauline, she always worked and paid for her own manicures, pedicures and days at the hair salon. He'd always wanted to treat her, but she'd made a point of treating herself. It was like she hadn't needed him.

Which, in fact, was exactly the way things had been.

Marcel was the type of man who liked to splurge on a woman. If he could make a woman happy, then he was happy. Whether it was genetic or learned behavior, Marcel was like his father. His father had always doted on his mother, and Marcel had never seen his mother without a smile. Not even when she had cancer. It had been a long time since Marcel had had the opportunity to pamper a woman.

And if anyone deserved some pampering, it was Lexy. She rarely stopped to take a break. Her whole world literally revolved around Shauna and work. Though they'd made headway when he'd seen her at her store and the times they'd talked on the phone, she still hadn't been able to fit him into her schedule. She was a devoted mother and he admired that quality in her, but even devoted mothers needed a break every so often.

Well, she'd get pampering on Sunday. And plenty of it.

Marcel glanced at his bedroom phone, but decided not to call Lexy at the bookstore. He knew what she would say. That she was busy and couldn't talk. He believed she was busy and not deliberately avoiding him, but even if she was avoiding him, in a way, he would understand. This was too new even to him, and the fact that they possibly had a real chance to go for what they never had as teenagers was scary. But even if Lexy was cautious, Marcel was willing to take that chance. You didn't gain anything without taking risks.

He missed her. Missed the feel of her soft body pressed to his, the scent of her perfume in his nose, her supple lips beneath his. He couldn't explain the attraction, for he didn't understand it himself, but it was there, real and strong.

God, he hoped she felt the same way about him.

Well, in two days, he'd see her again. And in two days, he'd get his answer.

Six

Lexy had been awake for a good half hour, ever since the scent of bacon wafting up from the kitchen first hit her, though she still lay in bed. It was Mother's Day, and like her daughter had done in past years, she was preparing her breakfast. Last year was the first time she'd attempted anything other than cold cereal, having prepared scrambled eggs— though Lexy had suspected she'd meant to fry them. Now, Shauna was getting braver, making bacon as well.

Lexy hoped she didn't burn the house down. But with that thought came an ear-to-ear smile. Shauna was so precious, Lexy couldn't imagine a world without her.

She'd lost a child just over three years ago, and at the time she'd been devastated. Then, she'd felt something was missing from her life and from her marriage, and she'd wanted that baby so badly. But only months afterward, Richard had been killed in a tragic motorcycle accident. Ultimately, having another baby without a husband would have been a huge burden, so while it was hard to fathom, she'd lost the baby because it simply hadn't been the right time for her to have another child. Like her own mother had always told her, God did know what was best.

Lexy thought of the little angel downstairs preparing a Mother's Day breakfast for her; the disturbing memory of her lost husband and baby made her appreciate Shauna even more.

Hearing her daughter's footsteps as she climbed the oak staircase, Lexy lay down, closed her eyes, and snuggled beneath the covers. As the door creaked open, she could barely keep the snicker from her lips.

"Time to get up, Mama," Shauna said.

Lexy stirred, pretending to wake up. Sitting up, she opened her eyes, then made a grand show of yawning. "Hey, sweetheart."

A bright smile danced on Shauna's face as she walked to the bed, proudly holding a tray of food. "Happy Mother's Day."

"Oh, sweetheart. You didn't have to do this."

"I know. I wanted to."

"Thank you," Lexy said, her eyes misting. She extended her arms, and Shauna placed the tray on the nearby night table, then slipped into her mother's embrace. Lexy pulled her onto her lap, smothering her face with kisses.

"You're welcome." Shauna planted a kiss on her forehead, then stood. Reaching for the tray, she lifted and placed it on Lexy's lap. "Eat it while it's hot."

Lexy looked down at the three pieces of crispy bacon and two fried eggs. Once again, she realized that Shauna was truly growing up. The breakfast was a definite improvement over last year's.

"It looks delicious," Lexy said, meaning every word.

Standing before her mother, Shauna placed both hands on her hips. "Eat every bite. And after you finish your breakfast, you have one hour to get ready."

"Ready for what?"

"If I told you, it wouldn't be a surprise."

A surprise? Lexy's heart filled with warmth. Her daughter had planned a surprise for her.

Shauna headed to the bedroom door, then turned before she stepped out of the room. "One hour," she stated sternly.

"Yes, ma'am," Lexy replied, then giggled as Shauna disappeared.

Lexy was slipping simple hoops into her ears when she heard the distinctly masculine voice downstairs. Her hands stilled as she strained to listen.

That couldn't be . . ."

"Mama, are you ready?" Shauna called.

Lexy finished with the earrings, then made her way downstairs. Her heart skipped a beat at the sight of Marcel standing in her foyer.

"Marcel, what are you doing here?"

"Happy Mother's Day," he said, as she stepped onto the landing.

"Thank you."

"These are for you." He produced a bouquet of yellow roses from behind his back.

"Marcel," Lexy crooned, pleasantly surprised. "You didn't have to."

"I wanted to." He passed them to her, and she accepted them.

"They're beautiful." She stuck her nose in the bouquet and inhaled the sweet scent.

"Let me smell," Shauna said. Lexy lowered the bouquet for her.

"Sweetheart, can you put these in a vase for me?"

"Sure." Shauna took the bouquet and disappeared.

"That's a pretty color on you," Marcel said, his eyes roaming over her dress.

"Oh," Lexy replied, glancing down at her simple mauve-colored dress. "Thanks."

Leaning forward, Marcel surprised her with a soft kiss on the lips. "Boy, you are one hard lady to schedule a date with."

She shrugged. "You know how it is. Busy busy busy."

"All work and no play. Not good."

Lexy crossed her arms over her breasts. "So, what brings you by?"

"Uh," he hedged.

His eyes darted past her, and Lexy looked around. Shauna stood behind her.

"Marcel is helping me with your surprise," Shauna announced.

"Oh?" Lexy asked curiously.

"Uh huh. He's gonna drive us there."

Lexy looked from her daughter to Marcel. "Really?"

Marcel merely nodded.

"When did you two plan this?"

"You ask too many questions, Mama," Shauna said.

Marcel smiled. He was thinking the same thing.

"So, what now?" Marcel asked, as he and Shauna sat on a bench outside the Palm Aire Spa. They'd just left an excited Lexy for a day of pampering, which would include a massage, manicure and pedicure.

"Aunt Lynda said she'll take care of me this afternoon," Shauna answered. "Even longer, if you stay out late. So all you have to do is take me to her place, then come back here and get my mom."

It was hard to believe, but this little girl had everything planned out. She was exactly the type of girl any man would be proud to call his own.

With that thought, bitterness washed over him, and

he looked away. He'd always wanted children while married to Pauline, but she hadn't, and it had been a major area of conflict in their marriage. Closing his eyes, he shook his head, hoping to shake off the memory. He and Pauline had divorced seven years ago, and there was no point in dwelling on past pains.

"What are you thinking?" Shauna asked.

Marcel faced her. "I'm thinking that your mother's very lucky to have such a beautiful, smart daughter like you."

Shauna blushed. "Thanks."

"Now," Marcel began, then rose, "you ready?"

"Uh huh." She stood and they began walking, but she stopped suddenly and looked up at him.

"What?"

"You'd be a cool dad."

Marcel wasn't sure what had possessed Shauna to tell him that, nor what it meant. "You think so?"

"I know so."

Rubbing her head, he flashed her a warm smile. Her faith in him meant the world.

She smiled back, then reached for his hand.

They walked hand-in-hand back to his car, and for that moment in time, Marcel pretended she was his.

When Lexy saw Marcel sitting in the lounge area of the spa without Shauna, fear wrapped around her heart like a snake coiling around its prey, squeezing, smothering, reducing her breath to mere gasps. Gathering her purse over her shoulder, she scurried to him, trying not to attract the attention of the others in the large, sun-filled foyer. But it was clear to all that she was troubled, and as she reached Marcel, she was aware that people stared at her.

"Where's Shauna?" she asked in a hushed but anxious voice.

Marcel stood to meet her, his expression conveying his bewilderment over her demeanor. "She's fine."

"Where is she?" Lexy repeated, glancing behind him through the large glass windows, then back at him. She hated that she sounded so scared, but after the incident a few weeks before, she couldn't help worrying.

Marcel met her eyes with a level gaze. "She's with Lynda."

Her shoulders sagging, Lexy blew out a relieved breath. Marcel watched as her eyes fluttered shut, as her chest rose and fell quickly, not sure what to make of her fear. It was obvious she was truly worried, but that made him wonder—didn't she trust him? "You have to know I wouldn't let anything happen to her."

"I'm sorry. It's just that I—"

"Worry too much," Marcel finished. Shaking his head, he gave her a rueful smile. She was an enigma he could try to solve all day, but he gave her the benefit of the doubt in terms of not trusting him, deciding she simply wasn't used to not being in control of any given situation. Besides, Shauna had gone to a lot of effort to set up this date for them, and he didn't want to ruin the mood. So, he injected a happy note to his voice and asked, "How was the massage?"

"Fine."

Disappointment caused his stomach to flutter. "That's all? Just fine?"

Lexy ignored him. "Why is Shauna with Lynda?"

He gave her a long, pointed look, wondering why she wasn't satisfied knowing Shauna was safe. "This was part of her surprise," he finally explained. "She wanted to give us time alone so I could treat you to a Mother's Day dinner."

"What?" Lexy asked, as though he'd just told her they would be dining on the moon. Sighing, she bit down hard on her bottom lip, glanced away, then back at him. Doubt was written all over her face. "Are you sure this was Shauna's idea, or your own?"

"Excuse me?" Marcel's brow furrowed as he stared at her. Her eyes were steady on his, telling him she meant every word she'd just said. Instantly, anger swept over him. The one thing he despised was being accused of lying, whether indirectly or not.

"You've been asking me out for the past two weeks, Marcel. Maybe since you weren't having any luck, you went through my daughter to get to me."

"Let's get one thing straight right now." Marcel was aware that his raised voice had garnered curious stares, but he didn't care. "I would never consider using Shauna to get to you. And no, this wasn't my idea. It was Shauna's. But I can see it was a bad one so I'll just take you home."

Turning, Marcel stalked out the front door. Lexy watched him go, the rippling muscles beneath his shirt contracting and releasing with each powerful stride. He was angry, no doubt about it, and realizing that she'd offended him made her understand how lame she had sounded. Feeling a modicum of embarrassment that there had been witnesses to this public spectacle, she glanced sheepishly at the patrons around her, then started after him.

"Wait," she called as she stepped outside.

Marcel had reached the top of the steps, but hearing her voice, he stopped and slowly turned. A sour expression marred his handsome features.

God, what she'd do to take her words back. "I'm sorry," she said, regret washing over her. The last thing she wanted was to upset him when he'd been nothing but good to her. When she reached his side, she apologized again.

But Marcel ignored her, turning and descending the few steps. Lexy's stomach lurched, panic of a different kind enveloping her. She didn't know why, but it was suddenly very important that Marcel understand she hadn't meant to hurt him.

"Marcel . . ."

Still, he ignored her, instead strolling to the large Banyan tree. A lump forming in her throat, Lexy watched as he leaned a forearm on the tree, then wearily rested his forehead on that arm.

Her heart suddenly felt like a balloon that had been jabbed with a pin—deflated. Was this it? Had she so offended him that he was no longer interested in a relationship with her? And if that were the case, why did that very thought send her stomach spinning in a nosedive?

Tentatively, she made her way down the steps, approaching him, determined not to let him shut her out. As she stepped behind him, she knew he must have heard her, yet he didn't turn around. Slowly, she extended a hand and placed it on his shoulder. "Marcel, please forgive me."

He blew out a breath filled with frustration, then faced her.

"I really didn't mean that. I . . . I shouldn't have . . ."

He inhaled deeply, exhaled slowly. "It's all right."

She couldn't tell if his words were sincere. "You have to understand," she continued. "When you love someone as much as I love Shauna, emotion sometimes takes control of you. Maybe that doesn't make sense to you . . ."

His dark eyes narrowed, disappointment flashing in their depths. "Lexy, I may not be a parent, but I'm a son and a brother. I love my family members as much as you love Shauna."

She was saying all the wrong things. "I'm sorry. I didn't mean to imply—"

"Do me a favor," he said, cutting her off. "Stop apologizing."

"I'm so—" She realized what she'd been about to say and stopped herself short. And when she saw that Marcel's expression had softened, his frown replaced by a lopsided grin, she giggled.

"That's better," he told her. As he stared at her, his eyes darkened, intense with an emotion that scared her: passion. "I want to see you smiling." Reaching for her face, he traced the outline of her lips. "Happy."

Immediately, desire drowned out the guilt Lexy had felt only a moment before. Why was it that her body came alive when he touched her? "It's not always easy," she confessed softly.

"I want to make you happy."

Her breath snagged in her throat, but not out of fear or worry. Instead, she could hardly draw breath because she heard a second meaning behind Marcel's words, saw it in his eyes. He wanted to make love with her.

The very thought made her flush as sexual longing heated every part of her body. Lord help her, she wanted him just as badly as he wanted her.

"Will you let me?" he asked, snaking his fingers through her hair, tilting her face upward. "Will you let me make you happy?"

"I want to," she admitted, surprising herself.

"Shauna told me we could take as long as we wanted," he said, emphasizing the word *long*.

"She did?" Lexy tried to sound shocked, but she managed only a raspy whisper that betrayed how much she wanted him.

"Mmm hmm." He drew her face nearer to his. "I don't think we should disappoint her."

The heat consuming her body had parched her throat, and Lexy swallowed. "Y-you don't?"

"Uh-uh." Softly, he suckled one corner of her

mouth. "She might not think we had a good time if we pick her up too early."

"Oh," Lexy moaned.

He trailed his lips along her cheek to her ear, nibbling her lobe. "What do you think?"

She was thinking that she couldn't think! Inside her body it was the Fourth of July, a dozen sensations she hadn't experienced in ages exploding inside her like fireworks. Right now, she'd agree to anything Marcel said, just to savor this sweet feeling.

"Hmm?"

When he flicked his tongue inside her ear, Lexy thought she would die from the pleasure. She gripped his shoulders for balance, her eyes fluttering shut. She could barely manage to speak between ragged breaths. "Are you saying . . . do you mean . . ."

"You bet."

Her eyes flew to his.

"Does that surprise you?" When she didn't answer, he continued. "You're beautiful, Lexy. No man in his right mind wouldn't want to make love to you."

But he wasn't any man. He was Marcel Kennedy.

God, this wasn't real.

"It is real."

Lexy didn't realize she'd spoken aloud until she heard Marcel's reply. "It is, isn't it?"

He answered her by pressing his full, warm lips over hers, telling her in no uncertain terms that he wanted her. His tongue delved into her mouth, hot, sweet and demanding.

When he broke the kiss, they were both breathless. Marcel nuzzled his nose with hers. "Well?"

"Let's get out of here," she whispered, thinking with her heart for once, not her head. "And don't you ever say that I'm not spontaneous."

"Never." He flashed her a devilish grin.

Lexy took his hand. "Come on," she said, chuckling. The thought of making love with Marcel suddenly had her very excited—and very impatient. "Let's go."

So much for a Mother's Day dinner.

But as Lexy and Marcel lay spoon-fashion in his bed, his arms securely wrapped around her waist, the last thing on her mind was food.

Instead, she couldn't stop thinking about how Marcel had feasted on her body and how she had feasted on his, as if they were all the nourishment either needed.

While she told herself that she should feel embarrassment or shame—she and Marcel had been totally uninhibited between the sheets—all she could feel was happiness way down in her soul.

She glanced out the window, noting that dusk had settled like a maroon-colored quilt over the sky. Making love with Marcel had been unlike anything she'd ever experienced. He was an intense and passionate lover, seeming to know instinctively how to please her. With Richard, it had taken time to figure out a rhythm they both liked, and once they did, Richard never strayed from it. Their lovemaking had been satisfying, but nothing nearly as powerful as what she and Marcel had just shared.

With that thought came a tiny measure of guilt. Richard had been gone for years; it wasn't like Lexy was betraying him. But somehow it seemed wrong to enjoy sex with Marcel more than she had with her husband.

Maybe it had just been too long since she'd shared a man's bed and she'd forgotten how wonderful it could be.

Sighing, she ran her fingers over Marcel's hand, softly stroking his flesh. The truth was, she and Marcel had clicked in a way she hadn't with any other man. She'd thought she would be uncomfortable showing him her less-than-perfect body, but when he'd taken her in his arms and kissed her, then slowly begun to disrobe her, her extra pounds hadn't been an issue at all. She'd felt totally comfortable with him, totally sexy, totally cherished. Which made her wonder what might have been if she hadn't gotten pregnant all those years ago. Would she and Marcel ultimately have ended up married?

Stirring, Marcel tightened his arms around her, and Lexy's body flooded with warmth. The warmth chased away the melancholy and guilt. She couldn't turn back the clock. She couldn't change what had happened in her past.

"Hey, sweetheart."

It was hard to believe, but the mere sound of his voice turned her on. Shifting in his arms, she repositioned her body so that she faced him. "Hey, yourself."

"Penny for your thoughts."

She wanted to tell him that they'd just gone too far too quickly, but the truth was, she didn't believe that. Their attraction for each other went way back; maybe they hadn't gotten together before because it hadn't been the right time.

"Hmm?"

"I'm thinking," she responded slowly, "that I could get used to this."

"Good," Marcel said, planting a soft kiss on her nose. "Because if I have my way, I won't ever let you go."

Seven

"This is a bad week," Lexy said, facing Marcel as she sat opposite him in his Mustang. "It's almost the end of the school year and I promised Shauna I'd help her class with their year-end production. I'll be busy sewing outfits, making decorations." She groaned. "*Maybe* I could make some time on Wednesday, but that's only if I finish my exam early. I dunno."

"You never did tell me what you're studying."

"Oh," Lexy said. "I'm taking a course in social work. I took one last semester, too. The plan is to eventually get my degree."

Marcel was intrigued. "Really?"

"Mmm hmm. I'd love to work with troubled teens."

From what he remembered, Lexy had always been good at counseling others. That would be a good line of work for her. "I'm proud of you."

Her soft smile illuminated the dark car. "Thanks."

"When does your class normally finish?"

"Nine. But the exam starts at six, so if I finish it in a couple hours, I could spend *some* time with you. If I'm there longer than a couple hours . . ." She shrugged. "The sitter never stays later than ten."

"Hmm." Marcel was about to suggest that he could come over to her place after her class, but something held him back. "I'm supposed to work an off-duty job Wednesday evening, anyway," he finally told her.

"So Wednesday won't work," she said flatly.

"Well," Marcel began, thinking. "If you knew you'd finish early, I could find someone to take my place. But I'd have to know by tomorrow."

Lexy waved off the idea. "I don't want you going to that much trouble over me."

In the darkness of the car, Marcel's eyes met and held hers. He wanted to tell her she'd be worth it, but didn't. He'd just spent the most incredible hours of his life with her, but now he didn't know what to think. He wanted her, he'd made that clear, but if she wanted him even half as much, wouldn't she make more of an effort to be with him?

"The weekend?" he asked.

"Can't. I'll be swamped."

"Can't fit me into your schedule?" he asked in a teasing voice, though he meant every word.

"I'll see what I can do," she said. She glanced at the car's digital clock, then back at him. "Look, I'd better go get Shauna. It's late." She yawned, as if on cue. "As it is, Lynda is going to grill me to death."

"She's already staring out the window."

"What?" Lexy asked, horrified.

"Up there," Marcel replied, pointing to the upstairs window where it was clear the curtain was being held apart.

"That nosy—" Shaking her head, Lexy waved. The curtain promptly fell back into place.

"So you'll let me know," he said when she turned her attention back to him.

"Sure."

She placed one hand on the door handle, but Marcel placed a hand on hers, and she paused. He didn't want her to get Shauna just yet.

"What is it?"

"Any regrets?"

She paused. Sighed. "You want the truth?"

Marcel's heart fluttered, but he nodded. Lies would do him no good.

"Do I regret being with you? No. That was . . . incredible."

"But?" he asked, knowing there was one.

"But do I have questions? Yes."

"Like what?"

"Like, what am I getting myself into. I hadn't planned on a relationship at this time in my life."

"You don't plan relationships, Lexy."

"I know," she said, but she didn't sound convinced. "But if I *were* to plan one, this wouldn't be the time. I'm swamped with work, I'm planning on finally going to college full time in the fall. And above all else, I have my daughter to take care of."

With every word she said, Marcel saw his hopes for something permanent dying. And he couldn't help feeling some regrets of his own. Like Pauline, Lexy was a strong woman. She had to be to raise a daughter on her own, but it was her very strength and independence that made him wonder if she needed him. Yes, he wanted a strong woman, but he didn't want one so strong that she didn't believe a man would enhance her life. He believed in two-parent families, in a husband and wife working as a team for a common goal. He enjoyed the companionship of being married and wanted to grow old with one person, the way his parents had with each other. Pauline hadn't shared his outlook on life, and after his experience with her, Marcel had vowed to stay away from that type of woman. Now, he had to wonder if Lexy was more like Pauline than he knew.

If she was, she may very well break his heart.

He said, "You do have regrets."

"I'm not saying that."

"Then what are you saying?"

"That maybe . . . maybe I didn't give this enough thought."

He couldn't believe this was happening. Not after what they'd shared only hours before.

But then she did something that left him speechless. She leaned forward and kissed him, a long, slow, sensual kiss that made him want to get naked with her right there in his car, in the driveway of her best friend's home.

"Anyone ever tell you you worry too much?" she asked when she finally pulled away.

He looked at her cautiously, not sure what to think.

"This may not be what I planned, Marcel. But I sure am enjoying it. I'm trying to go with the flow, as someone once told me." She winked. "Just be patient with me. Okay?"

Finally, a smile crept onto his face. "Okay."

"Now," she said, gripping the door handle. "I have to get Shauna—before I get real spontaneous and act on the feelings I'm having right now."

She kept her eyes on him as she opened the car door and stepped outside. Then, before she closed the door, she blew him a kiss.

Marcel caught the kiss with his hand, then held it to his heart.

Lexy had escaped Lynda's questions partly because Shauna had been in the room and partly because Marcel had been waiting in the car. But now that she opened the door to her home and turned to wave to Marcel as he drove away, the mischievous gleam in Shauna's eyes made it clear she would not escape her daughter's inquisition.

Before Lexy turned the lock on the door, Shauna

started. "How was the date? Did you have fun? Did he *kiss* you?"

"Shauna," Lexy said sternly, though she was smiling. "I can only answer one question at a time."

"He *did* kiss you." Shauna squealed with delight. "You're blushing, Mama!"

Was she? Lexy brought a hand to her face. She did feel warm. Lord knew, she'd probably feel warm all week.

Lexy flashed her manicured nails before her daughter's face. "Don't you want to know about the manicure? My massage?"

"No," Shauna replied succinctly. "I wanna know about Marcel!"

"You wanna know what we ate?" she asked, teasing her daughter. Lexy slipped out of her shoes and strolled to the kitchen.

"No," Shauna whined, following her mother. "Come on, Mama. Did he kiss you?"

"All right," Lexy told her daughter, since she knew she wouldn't rest until she'd heard the truth from her. She flicked on the light switch, then leaned a hip against the counter. "Yes, he did kiss me."

Shauna's eyes lit up. "Did you like it?"

"Shauna!" Lexy protested.

"Did you?"

Shauna's excitement was contagious, and Lexy giggled. If her daughter only knew. "Yes, I did like it. He's a good kisser."

Dancing on the tips of her toes, Shauna released another squeal. "Oh, that is *so* cool, Mama! He likes you, and you like him. So maybe he can be my new daddy."

Shauna's words caused Lexy's silly grin to fade. This was exactly what she was afraid of, her daughter looking to Marcel as a father figure when she had no clue how far their relationship would go.

Lexy knelt before Shauna. "Sweetheart, just because we like each other doesn't mean he'll be your new father."

"Why not?"

At times, Shauna seemed so much like an adult; now, her simplicity of thought made Lexy remember that she was very much a child. Which made her happy in a way, because she wanted Shauna to enjoy her childhood years as much as possible.

"Because," Lexy began, "life doesn't work that way. We have to date for a while, see how we get along. See if our feelings for each other grow."

"I think he's perfect for you," Shauna said, not willing to hear anything else.

"We don't know that yet, sweetheart. And until we do, I don't want you getting your hopes up by thinking he's gonna be your new daddy, because I can't promise you that."

"He will," Shauna said, then kissed her mother on the forehead. "I know it."

Lexy savored the kiss, not knowing what else to say. Clearly, Shauna had made up her mind. Lexy could only hope this was a passing phase.

"Did you have a nice Mother's Day?" Shauna asked, changing the subject.

Lexy pulled her into her arms. "Yes, sweetheart. The best."

"Good," Shauna announced. "Cause you're the best mother in the world."

Lexy's eyes misted. "Oh, sweetheart. You're the best daughter in the world."

Shauna pulled back and stared into her mother's eyes. "We're just the best."

Giggling, Lexy squeezed her daughter's nose between two fingers. "I love you, you know that?"

"I know. And I love you, too."

* * *

Shauna couldn't sleep. She was too excited. Her mother might not know it yet, but Marcel *would* be her new daddy. She was sure of it.

Sometimes, her mother missed the obvious. This was one of those times.

Marcel was nice, funny, reliable. He was perfect.

But Shauna wasn't sure her mother would figure that out any time soon, so she decided to pray about it. Lying on her stomach, she closed her eyes and folded her hands on the pillow.

"Dear God," she whispered. "Please let my mama see that Marcel is the man for her. Please let him be my new daddy. Amen."

Satisfied, Shauna rolled onto her back and snuggled up beneath the covers.

It was like someone had put a hex on her.

She couldn't stop thinking about him.

She couldn't stop thinking about the incredible evening she'd spent with him on Mother's Day.

It was like her body had finally received rain after a very long drought—and she didn't even known she needed rain. Now, she wanted more.

Maybe that was why she found herself doing something she never would have imagined this Wednesday evening. Lexy Sinclair, who never missed a class, called her professor and told him she was sick.

She was going to miss her exam and write it next week, all so that she could see Marcel.

If that wasn't crazy, she didn't know what was. Yet as she dabbed perfume behind her ears in her small bathroom, she couldn't lose the silly smile on her face.

Marcel had told her the supermarket where he

worked off-duty on Wednesday evenings, and tonight she would surprise him. She wanted to see the look on his face when he saw her and realized that she'd been spontaneous . . . again.

He was bringing out a whole new side to her. A side she was starting to like.

She brushed out her long hair, then stood a moment gazing at her reflection. Satisfied, she flicked off the lights and made her way downstairs.

As soon as she slipped one smooth, caramel-colored leg out of the car and onto the pavement, Marcel noticed.

Noticed that at the bottom of that smooth leg was a simple gold anklet and a high-heeled black pump.

Noticed that above her knee, a shiny black raincoat covered her thigh.

Noticed that her face . . . She looked like . . .

Marcel swallowed. No. It couldn't be Lexy.

He shook his head, closing his eyes. First of all, she was writing an exam. Second, raincoats and pumps weren't her style.

But when he opened his eyes, he saw her strutting purposefully toward him. Maybe he was dreaming, he decided, for the woman he saw *did* look exactly like Lexy, but she was still wearing that coat and those shoes.

And with every step she took, the caramel-colored skin of a thigh peered through the opening in her coat.

He pinched himself. He wasn't dreaming.

Her mouth curled in a smile as she neared him, her eyes never leaving his. Marcel's heart was beating so fast, he was sure it would explode inside his chest.

"Lexy?" he asked in disbelief as she stopped in front of him.

"Hi, Marcel." She even sounded sexier, her voice low and raspy.

He swallowed. "W-what are you doing here?"

"Being spontaneous."

His eyes roamed from the top of her body to the bottom. Her makeup was darker, more dramatic. She looked like Lexy, but bolder, more brazen. And her outfit . . . There had been no rain that day and it wasn't supposed to rain that evening. So what was she doing wearing a raincoat buttoned up past her breasts?

As his gaze lingered over her body, he felt a weird and sudden twinge at his nape.

No.

She didn't.

But as he eyed her ample cleavage, not seeing any sign of fabric beneath, he had to wonder if she did.

Marcel suddenly remembered where they were—a *very* public place. Quickly, he grabbed her arm and led her around the side of the grocery store.

Lexy chuckled.

When he had her safely out of view, he asked, "Tell me you didn't."

A coy smile played on her lips. "Didn't what?"

He glanced around, then back at her. "Didn't wear anything under that . . . coat."

"All right. I didn't."

"You *didn't?* You mean, you're . . . *naked* under there?"

"My, my, my. It almost seems like the guy who told me I needed to be more spontaneous—"

"My God," he gasped, but at the mere thought of her soft, naked body beneath the coat, he hardened. "You are."

"Not quite," Lexy told him. "I'm wearing this anklet." She raised a foot to show him. His eyes nearly popped out of his head. "And . . ." She shrugged.

"I'm wearing underwear. My mama always said you should never leave home without underwear."

Marcel released a nervous chuckle. "I thought you were writing an exam."

"I wanted to see you."

"Damn, you wanted to torture me." Once again, he glanced around, and seeing no one in the immediate area, he stroked her breast.

"Mmm." Arching her neck, Lexy moaned. She hadn't planned this, and to tell the truth, she'd been so nervous driving along the I-95, she was certain that everyone passing her knew she was practically naked beneath her coat. But being with Marcel now, seeing his reaction to her body, she felt more alive than she'd felt all her life.

And she felt so incredibly sexy.

He blew out a hot, frustrated breath against her face, then immediately stepped backward at the sound of footsteps. A young couple walked toward them.

"Excuse me, officer," the man said. "Can you tell me how to get to Michigan Avenue?"

Lexy gripped the top of her coat, trying to suppress the laughter bubbling from her throat as she listened to Marcel give the couple directions. He was totally flustered, all because of her.

And it felt great.

As the couple walked off hand in hand, Marcel made his way back to her. "I don't believe you."

She reached for the top button on her coat. "Not spontaneous enough?"

Quickly, he took her hands in his. "As much as I'd love for you to get crazier—and believe me, this is pretty crazy right now—I'm working, baby." He groaned his frustration. "Man."

"Kiss me."

"I . . ." He looked around for spectators. Surely

people would start wondering what a uniformed cop was doing at the side of a grocery store with a not-so-clad sexy woman.

"I didn't come all this way to leave without even a kiss," she told him, pouting.

Man, she was irresistible. Truthfully, he didn't want to resist her. So he dipped his head and captured her lips with his.

Then pulled away a mere second later.

"Marcel," she protested.

"That's the best I can do." He linked his fingers with hers. "But if we hook up later—"

The air around them exploded with the unmistakable sound of gunshots. Instantly, Marcel took Lexy in his arms, forcing her to the ground.

"Get down!"

For a moment, Lexy didn't understand what was happening. But when screams erupted all around her and people scrambled for cover, she realized the gravity of the situation.

Someone was shooting!

Oh, God!

"Stay here," Marcel told her, rising off her body and reaching for his gun.

"Marcel!" Lexy cried. She was terrified. "Don't leave me."

But he was already running toward the street, his gun in hand, ready to fire.

Eight

All night, she tossed and turned, sleep eluding her.

It didn't matter that Marcel had called her only hours after the shooting to say that he'd arrested the culprit. It didn't matter that the man who'd been shot had survived. It didn't matter that Marcel had assured her he was okay, that he'd taken down bad guys before. None of that mattered, because it didn't assuage Lexy's frame of mind.

She was still so frightened over what had happened that she trembled beneath the covers. Not even the extra comforter she'd put on the bed chased away the chill.

Staring into the darkened room, Lexy drew in several deep breaths, hoping to calm her nerves. But her heart still pounded erratically, and her hands and feet were still cold.

One minute, she'd been absorbed in her role as seductress, enjoying how much she'd turned Marcel on. The next thing she knew, he was pushing her to the ground and running off after a madman.

The room was still and quiet, a stark contrast to the inner turmoil raging inside her.

No matter how hard she tried, she couldn't stop reliving the horror of that moment. Couldn't stop feeling the fear she'd felt when he'd run off to chase a crazed shooter.

He could have been killed.

That thought caused a sharp pain to stab at her heart. Lexy placed a hand on her chest and tightly closed her eyes.

Lynda believed that everything happened for a reason. Maybe she was right. The more Lexy thought about it, the more she had to consider that what had happened tonight must have happened for a reason. She never skipped class, yet she'd not only skipped class but postponed an exam. And Lord knew, she *never* walked around half-naked in a raincoat.

It was like she'd lost her mind over the past month. In a way she had, for she'd fallen for Marcel— again. It hadn't been hard; deep down, she'd probably always loved him. But the truth was, as much as she might love him, he wasn't the right man for her.

Tonight's disaster illustrated that point as nothing else had. It was time she came down from her fantasy world and got back to her normal, sane life.

Without Marcel.

And wasn't it better to figure that out sooner rather than later? If not for her own sake, then for Shauna's?

Sighing, Lexy rolled over, but her new position was no more comfortable than the last. She had too much weighing on her mind, and her heart, to truly relax.

It would never work, she told herself. *It's better this way.*

But while her brain told her that ending her relationship with Marcel was the right thing to do, her heart told her otherwise.

In the end, her brain won the battle. She had to end things with Marcel.

Having made her decision, Lexy figured she owed it to Marcel to tell him as soon as possible. She knew he got up early for work, and as she couldn't sleep, she decided to call him shortly after seven A.M.

"Hey," he said, answering the phone. "How are you?"

Clearly, he knew it was her because of caller ID. "Honestly? I'm still shaking."

He exhaled his frustration. "I'm so sorry you were there. Of all the nights for you to show up . . ."

"Marcel, we need to talk."

Pause. "What is it?"

"Everything. What happened yesterday. The fact that I didn't get any sleep last."

"You're really shaken up."

"I've never been so scared in my life." She paused. Drew in a deep breath. "And it made me realize something, Marcel. You and me . . . it won't work."

He was silent for a minute, and Lexy wondered if he heard her. But finally he said, "I don't understand."

"I gave it a shot, Marcel. But your job . . . I was never comfortable with it, but seeing you in action, knowing that you could have been killed . . ." Her voice trailed off. "I can't live like that. Wondering every day if you'll come home. Putting Shauna through that."

"Everyone faces risks every day, Lexy. When you get behind the wheel, you risk getting into an accident. Goodness, walking down the street isn't even safe. Yeah, I'm a cop, but I'm a trained one. I'm prepared to deal with a ton of different situations."

"But your job puts you at a greater risk than the average person, Marcel. You can't deny that."

"You're really serious, aren't you?"

She could hear the disbelief and disappointment in his voice, and it broke her heart, yet she couldn't back down. "Yes."

"Lexy, I can't talk about this now. But I can come see you later."

No. She couldn't see him. It was easier this way. "No, Marcel. That won't change anything."

"What happened to you?"

"What do you mean?"

"You've changed." When she didn't say anything, he continued. "You used to be so full of life, not afraid of anything."

"That was a long time ago," Lexy replied. "I'm a mother now . . ."

"But you're not dead."

She swallowed, his words hurting her more than she was willing to admit even to herself. "No, but I have someone else to think of now. A person whose life I'm responsible for."

"That's fine. But why does that mean you have to stop living?"

"I haven't . . ."

"Sure, you're still breathing, but what do you do to feel alive? Other than me, you don't date; you rarely go out. You spend all your free time with Shauna, but even that can't protect her from everything that can go wrong.

"Lexy, you and Shauna can stay locked in the house all day, never go outside to avoid danger, and you know what? Your house could still burn down. Sweetheart, the facts of life don't change just because you hide from them."

"Why are you doing this to me?" Lexy asked. Angrily, she brushed away a tear that slowly trickled down her cheek. "You don't know what I've been through. We lost Richard and it was the worst time of my life. Shauna was the only one who kept me from drowning, because I had to be there for her. I'm all she has and I'm not going to let her down.

"I do not want to expose her to boyfriend after

boyfriend and see her disappointed when those relationships don't work out. She's already lost her father and now she deserves some stability."

"So you're going to stop living, all to make sure your daughter doesn't get hurt."

"If that's what I have to do."

What scared Marcel was that Lexy was dead serious. She'd erected a wall between them so high he didn't know if he'd be able to climb over it. "I'm sorry to tell you this, but the reality of life is that there will always be pain. No matter how hard you try to shelter Shauna from that reality, you can't. There are no guarantees in life."

She was silent for a long moment, so Marcel continued. "Sweetheart, if you don't take chances in life, you'll never truly be happy."

"Look where taking chances got Richard." Richard had insisted on gambling with his life over and over with that stupid motorcycle, and in the end he'd lost.

"Is that what you're afraid of?"

"Dying?" she asked. "Partly. But not because I'm afraid to die, but because Shauna needs me; I'm all she has. I told Richard a thousand times that that motorcycle was dangerous, but he wouldn't listen. Now, he's six feet under and I'm left to raise my daughter alone."

"You don't have to raise her alone."

"What does that mean?"

"Only that if you keep your options open, I'm sure you'll find love again."

"With you?"

Pause. "Would that be so bad?"

"I'm sorry, Marcel," she said softly. "I can't. I know this isn't what you want to hear, but you put your life on the line every day, Marcel. Even if I could live with the risk, do you think I could put Shauna through that? She's lost one father already."

Marcel sighed. "Lexy, let's meet. Tonight. Let's talk about this face to face."

"No," Lexy replied quickly. "I've made up my mind."

Then, before Marcel could say anything else, Lexy hung up and burst into tears.

"Mama," Shauna said, approaching her tentatively as she washed lettuce in the kitchen sink. "Marcel's on the phone."

Lexy turned off the tap and reached for a dishcloth to dry her hands. "I don't want to talk to him."

"But why not?"

"I didn't want to talk to him the last time he called and I don't want to talk to him now," Lexy snapped.

Frowning, Shauna ran back into the living room. Lexy heard her say, "Uh, she's in the shower . . . Sure, I'll tell her. Bye."

Lexy closed her eyes and counted to five. Marcel had called several times since their breakup days before, but she hadn't taken his calls. Until now, Shauna hadn't asked any questions, seeming to understand that Lexy needed space. But now, as she walked back into the kitchen, she stared at her mother with a confused expression.

"What happened?" Shauna asked.

"Not now." Lexy turned back to the sink.

"Did you and Marcel break up?"

What point was there in lying? "Yes."

"Why?"

"Sweetheart, I don't need any questions right now, okay?"

"But I don't understand. When he was your boyfriend, you were happy. Now, all you do is frown."

Lexy opened her mouth to say something, but she couldn't form the words. Her daughter was right. She had been in a funk since last week. The fact that she wasn't back to her normal, happy self surprised her. Yes, this was difficult, but she'd dealt with worse in her life and had gone on.

It would be no different with Marcel, she assured herself. It was simply taking longer than she'd expected. "I think you should talk to him, Mama."

Turning from the sink, Lexy walked to the small, round table and sat down. She patted the chair next to her. "Come here."

Shauna did as told, seating herself beside her mother.

"Sweetheart, I know how much you like Marcel, how much you want him to be your new daddy. But . . ." Sighing, she ran a hand over Shauna's face, then cupped her chin. "It wasn't meant to be. We're too different."

"But opposites attract. I even learned that in my science class."

"Yes . . . and no. In this case, there are too many differences, sweetheart. We thought we could make each other happy, but it's obvious now that we can't."

"But why not?"

Lexy wrapped an arm around Shauna. "You're too young to understand. But you will when you're older."

They were silent for a long while, then Shauna spoke. "Marcel told me to ask you something."

Lexy stiffened at the thought that Marcel might try to use Shauna to get to her. "What?"

"He told me to ask if you remembered when he said he'd always be your friend. Then he said for you to call him."

Lexy's whole body sagged, and not wanting Shauna to know his words had affected her, she hugged her tightly to her body. But not even Shauna's warmth chased away the guilt eating at her heart. Marcel had assured her that if they tried a relationship and failed, he would always be her friend. Clearly, despite everything, he was still willing to do that.

Ironically, it was now Lexy who wasn't.

Nine

"Where are you going?" Lexy asked Shauna as she ran down the stairs and toward the front door.

"Neringa invited me over, so we can practice our dance routine for tomorrow."

"Wait a minute. You're supposed to wash the dishes."

"I'll do them later," Shauna said curtly, not even bothering to glance at her mother. "I have to go."

Cocking an eyebrow, Lexy walked from the kitchen to meet Shauna in the doorway. Over the past several days, she'd been acting up. Talking back. Not doing her chores.

Ever since Lexy had told her that she and Marcel didn't have a future.

Shauna gripped the door handle. "I've gotta go."

"Wait," Lexy said sharply. Her daughter may be upset with her decision to stop seeing Marcel, but she had no right to act as if she were twice her age. "Just where do you get off *telling* me what you're doing? You're supposed to *ask* me."

"All right," Shauna said, rolling her eyes as she opened the door. "Can I go?"

Oh no, Lexy thought, unable to believe Shauna's disrespect. "It seems you have a problem hearing."

"I just asked, Mama," Shauna complained.

"If you call that asking—" Lexy drew in a breath to calm herself. "You're not going."

"Mama," Shauna whined, frowning.

"You watch that tone of voice with me."

"But we have to practice before tomorrow."

"You should have thought of that before you decided to act all high and mighty."

"But Mama—"

"You can practice by yourself." Lexy gave her daughter a stern look. "In your room."

Shauna huffed, then charged up the stairs.

"If you keep that up," Lexy called, "you won't be going anywhere tomorrow."

Shauna's bedroom door slammed shut.

Lexy had a mind to go up there and discipline Shauna for slamming the door, but all she could do was grip the handrail for support. Closing her eyes, she fought the urge to cry, because she didn't understand it.

Lord, that child was going to send her to an early grave! But it wasn't simply her clash with Shauna that had her feeling so on edge. It was the fact that she felt she'd lost control.

Of her child. Of her life. Of her happiness.

Yes, that was it, Lexy realized, sinking onto one of the steps. She was unhappy. And her unhappiness seemed to have rubbed off on Shauna, for she too had been sulking around for the past week.

Marcel popped into her mind then, and she had the urge to call him. But she fought it. Calling him wouldn't help the situation; it would make it worse.

All she needed was time. And in time, Shauna would feel better, too.

* * *

Shauna didn't understand it. Ever since her mother and Marcel had broken up, her mother didn't want to let her do *any*thing.

She knew her mother was sad; she even heard her crying in her bedroom that night.

But that didn't give her a right to be so mean. And right now, Shauna was angry. She couldn't believe her mother had said she might not let her go to school tomorrow.

So, when she was sure her mother was sleeping, Shauna took the small bag she'd packed and crept down the stairs. Then she slipped outside into the night.

When the first rays of sunlight spilled through the blinds and onto the bed, Lexy didn't bother pulling the comforter over her face. Instead, she sat up.

During the night, she'd had a lot of time to think. Shauna was acting up, but Lexy had come to accept that she was doing that because she missed Marcel. The bottom line was Shauna was still a child, a child who couldn't understand the complexities of relationships.

It would take time for her to understand, but one day she would. Until then, Lexy needed to exercise patience.

Hadn't Shauna exhibited a similar feistiness after Richard's death? While her breakup with Marcel was hardly of a similar serious nature, Shauna was still going through a period of adjustment because she'd gotten her hopes up, only to learn her dream wasn't going to come true.

And despite her own desire to be strong, Lexy had to admit that life without Marcel required an adjustment on her part. She'd fallen for him, but she couldn't have him, and she was in pain.

Lynda and Pauline were like Shauna: they didn't understand her decision to end things with Marcel. Maybe she was the only one who could fathom the reality that she had to do this for Shauna's best interests.

Groaning, Lexy stood and stretched. She didn't want to think about Marcel right then. For her sanity, she had to put him out of her mind.

Instead, she slipped on a robe and slippers and went down the hall to Shauna's bedroom. She was vaguely aware that the house was too quiet; normally, it was alive with the sounds of Shauna getting ready for school. A wave of guilt washed over her. Shauna had probably been so upset last night that she didn't sleep well. The poor thing was no doubt still resting.

"Shauna," Lexy called softly, opening the door.

Instantly, her blood turned to ice.

Shauna wasn't in the room.

The bed was neatly made.

"Shauna!" Whirling around, Lexy ran to the bathroom and threw open the door. But her daughter wasn't there either.

Her heart rate accelerated as she practically flew down the stairs to the main level. Shauna wasn't in the living room. Nor the kitchen.

God, where could she be?

Finally, Lexy ran to the front door. Opening it, she jumped onto the porch, but the street was quiet. Almost ominously quiet.

Of course. It was too early for Shauna to have left for school.

Her head spun and Lexy gripped the door for support. *Be strong*, she told herself. Drawing in a deep breath, she ran back into the house and to the phone.

* * *

Marcel hadn't heard from her in several days, so when he saw her number on his phone as he woke up in the morning, he quickly snatched it up.

Before he could say a greeting, he heard Lexy's frantic voice, but he couldn't make out a word she said.

"Lexy," Marcel stated firmly. "Calm down. I can't understand you."

"Sh-Shauna . . ."

"Something's happened to Shauna?" he asked, his stomach lurching. If anyone had hurt that girl, he didn't know what he'd do.

"She's not here," Lexy cried. "Oh, Marcel, I don't know what to do . . ."

"I'm on my way."

First, Marcel called work to let them know he'd be late, then drove like a man possessed from his home in Miami Lakes to Fort Lauderdale.

As he pulled up to the curb in front of Lexy's house, he had an eerie feeling of déjà vu. The last time, all had ended well. He prayed this time would be no different.

Lexy rushed onto the porch and down the steps when she heard him arrive. She wore a silk robe and slippers and seemed oblivious to the fact that she wasn't properly dressed.

He jumped out of the car and ran to her. "What happened?"

"I don't know," she cried. "Last night, she went to bed. This morning, I went to her room . . . and she wasn't . . . she wasn't there!"

Marcel gripped her shoulders and stared into her eyes. "Did you call the police?"

She shook her head. "I . . . I called you first."

"Okay." Adrenaline coursed through his veins. "Tell me everything that happened."

"I don't know," Lexy wailed.

"You have to think," Marcel told her. But all she did was cry. He wrapped an arm over her shoulder and pulled her to him, offering comfort while crazed emotions whirled inside him. It felt good to hold her, comfort her, feel her body pressed to his. But the more he held her, the more his heart ached, because he remembered that she didn't want him.

He nudged her shoulder. "Let's go inside."

Inside, he sat her at the table in the kitchen. She'd stopped crying and now brushed away her tears. He asked, "Did you check the house for any signs of forced entry?"

Lexy looked at him as if he spoke Chinese.

"Were any windows or doors forced open?"

"I . . . I don't think so." She whimpered. "I don't know."

"All right. Let me check, okay."

Lexy nodded, and Marcel stood. But both turned their attention to the door when they heard it open.

Shauna stepped into the house.

Lexy leaped to her feet. "Shauna!"

Behind them, Marcel closed his eyes and blew out a relieved breath. Then he slowly made his way to the foyer, where Lexy knelt before her daughter, squeezing the life out of her.

"Where were you?" Lexy asked when she finally released her.

"I . . ." Shauna began. Her bottom lip quivered, and Marcel knew she was going to cry.

Giving her a bright smile, he stooped beside her and ran a hand over her back. "Hi there."

"Hi," she said softly.

"What happened?" Lexy asked again. "Did you go to school early to practice?"

Shauna shook her head.

"Then what?"

"I left last night," Shauna admitted, her voice so low, Lexy wouldn't have heard her if she wasn't kneeling in front of her.

"You *what?*"

"I thought you weren't going to let me go to the recital. And I had to go, Mama."

"You did this deliberately?" The realization that her daughter had scared the life out of her on purpose made her angry. "How could you?"

Instead of answering, Shauna started crying.

Lexy was so tempted to smack Shauna's rump that she stood and stormed up the stairs. She needed to put distance between her and her child.

As Lexy disappeared, Shauna threw her arms around Marcel's neck. Her small body shook as tears poured down her face. He wanted to comfort both the mother and the daughter, but right then, he lifted Shauna into his arms and carried her into the living room.

He said nothing, merely holding her as she cried. Finally, her sobs grew softer. Then she pulled her head back and stared at him.

"I'm sorry," she said softly.

"Shauna, do you know how much your mother loves you?" When she nodded, he continued. "She was very scared. Now, I don't know if you meant to scare her, but I do know that you hurt her."

"She said she wasn't gonna let me go to the recital. And I *had* to go, Marcel. I was gonna come back after school. But I forgot my outfit and that's why I came back now."

"You were gonna let your mother worry about you all day?" He shook his head in disbelief. "Why would you do that?"

"I was mad at her."

He hugged her tighter. "I don't care how mad you are at her, you have to promise me you'll never do that again."

"I won't."

"Where did you stay?"

"At my friend Neringa's house."

Marcel was surprised Neringa's mother hadn't called. But maybe she hadn't known Shauna was even there.

Hearing footsteps, Marcel turned. Lexy strolled toward him.

"It's late," Lexy announced calmly. "You better get your shower, then go to school."

Shauna peered at her mother from behind Marcel's head. "You're gonna let me go?"

Lexy glanced at the floor, then back at her. "Yes, you can go. But after today, you're grounded."

"Yes, Mama."

Marcel released her. Shauna ran from the living room and up the stairs, leaving Marcel and Lexy alone.

They stared at each other for a long moment, but neither said anything.

Finally, Lexy spoke. "Thank you . . . for coming."

Marcel stepped toward her, but she quickly stepped backward, as though she didn't want to be near him.

God, was this what it had come to? Ruefully, Marcel shook his head. "So I could hold you only moments ago, but now you don't want me near you?"

Lexy's gaze fell to the floor.

"You know what doesn't make sense?" he asked. "You hate the fact that I'm a cop, yet I was the first person you called. Guess I'm only good in times of trouble, right?"

"Marcel—" Lexy began.

But he cut her off. "Think about that. Think about how ironic that is."

Then he stalked past her and walked out of the house, leaving her to ponder that thought.

Lexy's body shook as the door closed and Marcel disappeared. It took all the strength she possessed not to crumble onto the floor and cry her eyes out.

Marcel was right, of course. She was a hypocrite.

She hated the idea of his being a cop, yet he was the first one she'd called when she hadn't been able to find Shauna.

She couldn't have it both ways, yet it seemed that's exactly what she wanted.

She wanted guarantees—the guarantee that he would always be there, that he would never leave her, that nothing bad would ever happen. Yet life offered no guarantees.

Moaning, Lexy buried her face in both hands. Right now, she didn't want to think of Marcel. She didn't want to think of the scare Shauna had given her. For once, she wanted to forget that life was a complicated mess she couldn't always control.

With that thought in mind, she headed back upstairs, knowing that the only place she could truly find peace was in dreamless slumber.

"Mama?"

Lexy had been in that haze-like stage between consciousness and sleep, but hearing her daughter's voice fully awoke her. Though she was angry with her for what she'd done, her heart leaped with happiness at the sight of her. Despite everything, she loved Shauna fiercely and hated when there was tension between them.

"Hey, sweetheart."

"Your note said you wanted to talk to me."

Lexy sat up. The edges of Shauna's mouth curled downward in a small frown, marring her pretty face with a sad expression that nearly broke Lexy's heart.

"Yes, sweetheart. I do."

Slowly, Shauna approached the bed, then lowered herself onto its edge. Lexy wanted to extend her arms and wrap her in a hug, but now wasn't the time. Shauna needed to be disciplined first.

Shauna merely looked down at her folded hands, as though being in the same room with her was causing her major grief. The mere thought made Lexy want to break down, but she gathered all the strength she had and spoke. "What you did today—do you know how serious that was? You had me worried half out of my mind. I didn't know what to think. I didn't know what to do. And to know that you *knew* what you were doing when you left this house . . . Shauna, that breaks my heart."

Her bottom lip quivering, Shauna raised her head and met her mother's eyes. "I'm sorry, Mama. I didn't mean it."

"I know you were probably angry with me, but you have to understand that you're only ten years old. I'm your mother. Even if you don't like it when I tell you something, you have to listen to me. Everything I say and do, I'm thinking of what's best for you."

"But that's the problem," Shauna countered softly. Before Lexy could say anything, Shauna continued. "I know you love me, but sometimes, it's like you smother me. You hardly want to let me do anything."

"Shauna, if you're trying to justify sneaking out of the house—"

"I'm not, Mama. I know that was wrong. But you didn't even listen to me when I tried to tell you how important the practice was."

"That doesn't excuse your behavior."

"No, but it's like you don't care how I feel anymore."

Lexy's chest felt like a heavy weight was on it, crushing her, forcing the air from her lungs. "That's not true."

"I really thought you might have made me stay home today, Mama. And that's not like you. That's why I left last night."

"I would have let you go," Lexy said softly, her voice sounding hollow to her own ears.

"But I couldn't be sure. You've changed so much lately."

Lexy shook her head, trying to deny what in her heart she knew was true. "No."

"You have. What's wrong with me going to Maxine's house in the evenings? Or Neringa's? You always used to let me go before."

Lexy's mouth opened, then promptly closed. She didn't know how to answer that without sounding lame. Because the truth was, she knew exactly what "before" referred to. And her daughter was right.

"I know you were scared that night when Dwayne and his friends took me in their car, but Mama, I know better now. I'm not gonna let that happen again."

Lexy's eyes misted. "I just want to keep you safe."

Shauna edged closer to her, placing her small hands on hers. "I know, Mama. But bad things can happen anywhere."

She sounded like Marcel. And for the first time, his comments really hit home. Because she was hearing them from her ten-year-old daughter.

She couldn't protect Shauna from all the negative realities of life. No matter how hard she tried to shelter her, she would never be able to keep her completely safe.

Life had no guarantees.

"I know you worry about me a lot, but Mama, you can't worry about me forever."

"Mothers worry . . ."

"But you worry too much and you don't let me do stuff that other moms let their daughters do. It's like you don't trust me."

"It's not you I don't trust," Lexy said, framing Shauna's face with both hands. She was a good child. Marcel had told her as much. "It's the world."

"I know. A lot of bad things can happen, but you taught me what to do. Mama, you have to let me grow up."

"Oh, sweetheart . . ."

"And you have to start having your own life."

Lexy's eyes widened, and her hands fell to Shauna's shoulders. "I do have a life."

"You hardly do *any*thing. I want you to do stuff and have fun. Not worry so much about me."

Lexy felt a pain in her heart, almost as though she were losing her daughter.

"I'll always be here, Mama," Shauna added, as though she heard her mother's concern. "I'll always love you. And I know you'll always love me. That's why it won't bother me if you get married again and I have a new daddy."

"You mean Marcel."

Shauna's eyes lit up at the mere mention of his name. "He's *so* in love with you. And I think you're in love with him, too. You're just scared."

"Maybe I am."

"Don't be scared, Mama. You have to be strong."

There Shauna went again, sounding as smart as any adult. "You're right, sweetheart."

"I'm only telling you what you taught me," Shauna said, resting her head against Lexy's bosom.

She'd taught her baby well, but had forgotten her own lessons somewhere along the way. Smiling through the tears that now fell onto her cheeks, Lexy wrapped Shauna in a long, hard hug.

The next evening, Lexy decided to take her daughter's advice and go for it. She called Rita to watch Shauna, leaving her strict instructions that Shauna not leave the house—she was still grounded—then she headed to Marcel's home.

God, she certainly *had* become spontaneous. She hadn't even called him, and didn't know if he'd be home. She only knew that when she saw him, she wanted him to be surprised.

As surprised as she was that she was actually doing this.

And he was, judging by his slackened jaw and widened eyes when he opened the door for her.

"Can I come in?" Lexy asked.

"Yeah," he replied, though he seemed unsure. "Sure."

Slowly, she entered his apartment.

"To what do I owe this honor?"

Facing him, Lexy couldn't tell if he was being sincere or sarcastic. Straightening her back, she told herself it didn't matter; by the end of her visit, she hoped to get through to him.

"It seems like my life has turned upside down over the past several weeks," she told him. "First, Shauna was practically kidnapped. Then I met you again, and my world changed. And now over the days since Shauna's stunt, I've had time to think. And I'm sorry."

Marcel looked at her long and hard, wondering if she knew she hadn't made much sense.

"You're confused," she stated, seeing his expression. "God, I don't blame you." She paused. "Marcel, I want you to know that I really appreciated you dropping everything and coming over when I called you a few days ago. I was scared to death and didn't know what to do." Pause. "And I know that after the way I treated you, you didn't owe me anything."

"I promised I'd always be your friend," he reminded her softly. "Even if you weren't ready for that. I never desert my friends."

"No," Lexy said softly, knowing he spoke the truth. "You don't, do you?"

Lexy watched the rise and fall of his Adam's apple. "Is that why you came here? To tell me you're ready to be my friend?"

She shook her head.

"Then why?"

"Because . . . what I was trying to say earlier is that ever since I met you again, my world has turned upside down. But ever since I pushed you away, it's plummeted. I've never been so miserable in my entire life."

A smile slowly spread on his face. "Really?"

"You don't have to be so happy about it," Lexy told him, relief flooding her at the sight of his smile. God, how had she been crazy enough to think she could live without him?

His smile faded. "I'm still a cop."

"And the world is still round, and the sun still rises in the east and sets in the west."

"What are you saying?"

She sighed and took a step toward him. "I'm saying, you were right. Some things in life you can control, most you can't. I can't keep hiding in a shell, thinking that's gonna protect me from the things I can't control. The best I can do is pray about it and leave it in God's hands."

"Where does this leave me?" He swallowed. "Us?"

She took a couple more steps, closing the distance

between them. "I want to take a risk, Marcel. For happiness."

"With me?"

"With you."

He raised a tentative eyebrow. "Even though I'm a cop?"

"Because I'd never forgive myself if I let my fears get the better of me. You're the best thing that's ever happened to me, and I don't want to lose you."

Releasing a loud howl, Marcel threw his arms around her and lifted her off her feet, whirling her around and around until she was dizzy. Screaming happily, she clung to him for dear life.

Finally, he set her down. "You're sure?"

"I'm sure," she replied, her lips curling in a grin. "Besides, Shauna is so smitten with you that I don't think she'd forgive me for not marrying you."

"Marrying?" he asked, clearly surprised.

"Oh," Lexy said, realizing her faux pas. "I didn't mean . . ."

He tilted his head. "So you don't want to marry me?"

"Well," she hedged. "We haven't talked about it. You haven't asked."

Taking both of her hands in his, Marcel dropped to one knee.

"Oh, God," Lexy gasped.

"Spontaneity is a good thing, right?" He winked.

"As long as you're not crazy."

"I'm not the one who showed up half-naked at *your* workplace."

Lexy threw a hand to her face. "God, don't remind me."

"So what do you say?" He brought the hand he still held to his mouth and gently kissed it. "Will you marry me?"

This may not have been part of her five-year plan,

but to heck with long-range goals and well-plotted calendars and neatly planned schedules. Life had a funny way of sending you in a new direction when you least expected it.

"Yes!" Lexy exclaimed.

"Oh, sweetheart." Rising, Marcel drew her into his arms and hugged her as if he were trying to merge their bodies. He rained kisses over her face and neck.

Lexy never knew that it could make her so happy just knowing she'd made Marcel happy. But as she clung to him now, she knew she'd spend a lifetime trying to make him happy, because his happiness alone would be her reward.

His and Shauna's.

"Shauna," they both said in unison, then giggled as they scrambled to the phone.

Epilogue

Lexy didn't normally cry at weddings, but this time, she couldn't help it. Because in a symbolic gesture of their new family union, both she and Shauna walked down the aisle together.

Marcel had tears in his eyes as they met him, and Lexy thanked God for the thousandth time that they'd found each other. Shauna had been right; Marcel *was* the perfect man for her.

As they settled at the front of the church opposite Marcel, Lexy looked around. The crowd was small, only close family and friends, and everyone dabbed at their eyes with Kleenex, handkerchiefs or their fingers.

Even Shauna had two tears streaming down her cheeks.

It was a simple but poignant ceremony. Shauna stood beside her the entire time.

When the minister told them they could exchange rings, Marcel spoke. "There's something I want to do first."

Puzzled, Lexy looked at him.

He reached into his jacket pocket and withdrew a small jewelry box. Then he stepped toward Shauna.

Given the shocked expression on Shauna's face, she had no idea what he was doing either.

He knelt before her. "Shauna," he said. "Today,

I'm not only marrying your mother. I'm marrying you. I promise that I'll always be there for you as a father, that I'll always love you."

He opened the small velvet box. Inside was a gold necklace with a heart-shaped locket.

"This is like the one you found on the beach that day several months ago," he told her as he lifted it from the box. "But inside, there's a picture. It's a picture of you, me and your mom. Our new family."

Lexy's heart swelled with joy as she watched Marcel place the necklace around Shauna's neck. Overwhelmed, Shauna threw her arms around him and sobbed happily.

"I love you," he said, pulling back to look at her.

"I love you, too, Daddy," Shauna said.

Marcel stood to meet Lexy once more, a love like nothing she'd ever known glowing on his face. Smiling at each other, they reached for each other's faces and wiped the tears from their cheeks.

When the minister said Marcel could kiss his bride, and as their lips met for a soft, sweet kiss, Lexy knew that finally her life was complete.